DARK DUTY

A DETECTIVE MARCY KENDRICK THRILLER

THEO BAXTER

INKUBATOR
BOOKS

Published by Inkubator Books
www.inkubatorbooks.com

ISBN (eBook): 978-1-83756-342-5
ISBN (Paperback): 978-1-83756-343-2
ISBN (Hardback): 978-1-83756-344-9

1

IT SHOULD NEVER HAVE COME TO THIS

It wasn't that I wanted to do this. No. I took no pleasure in what I was about to do. But it was necessary. Rumors were circulating—Selene had seen to that—Grant had been arrested, and a price needed to be paid. In blood. And I was the only one willing to make sure that price was paid by everyone involved.

It was nearly two in the morning, and the bar would be closing soon. I had sat parked in a stolen delivery van near Elixir for hours, watching various patrons enter and exit until I saw Sam go in at around eleven. Then I'd repositioned the van, pulling it in to the delivery area. Elixir wasn't the most ideal for what I had planned, but it was where Sam liked to drink and pick up women, so I didn't have much choice.

I supposed I could have done this when he was still at home, but there was some satisfaction in knowing his dick would be his downfall. I had gotten lucky—perhaps that was the wrong term... luck had nothing to do with finding my like-minded and eager partner for this endeavor. Carrie had firsthand experience in what men like Sam were like. And tonight, everything hinged on her doing her part.

I was about to give up hope that she'd be successful, when I saw Elixir's side door open, and she stumbled out with Sam. I felt a sick sort of happiness that he'd taken the bait. Carrie looked different from the last time I'd seen her. She had dark-brown hair, which she wore in a pixie cut, but now she was wearing a blonde wig that fell just past her shoulders. I imagined she'd put in colored contacts as well, changing her normally brown eyes to blue. At least that was the plan. And I had planned this out down to the very last detail, instructing her in all of it.

I'd been over the scenario of what would happen in my head so many times. I'd seen how I wanted it to play out and I'd tried to plan for every way in which it could go wrong. For now, everything seemed to be going as I had intended.

She laughed and the sound carried on the breeze through the open window of the van. It sounded like fairies ringing little bells, and completely fake. Sam seemed not to notice though. He was all in on what he thought was about to go down.

My gloved fingers tightened on the steering wheel as I watched him push her up against the brick wall of the building between the bar and the fish market. They were in a small delivery parking lot that was nearly dark. No building lights operated there.

I could tell that Sam was starting to get rough with her, and I wondered how long I should let this go on. I wanted to make sure he was good and distracted so he wouldn't notice me. It would be best if he didn't see me. Not at this point, at any rate.

Carrie rolled her head against the brick wall and stared

in my direction. I knew she couldn't see me sitting here in the van, but her eyes seemed to be begging me to hurry up. Then Sam moved his hand to her throat. It was time to get busy.

I opened the door to the van and slid out. After pulling my ski mask down over my face, I strapped the GoPro camera to my forehead, then turned it on. I grabbed the towel I had drenched in chloroform from the plastic bag on the passenger seat. It was an overwhelming smell and I had to keep it well away from my face or I'd get dizzy, and I couldn't have that. I needed to be on my A game. I couldn't let Sam get the drop on me, and he would if I was woozy from the chloroform too.

From the glovebox, I pulled out the ketamine syringe I'd picked up from a back-alley deal. I had a contingency plan if either the ketamine or the chloroform didn't work. On my hip I wore a taser, and in my pocket was a tactical folding knife. It was a multipurpose tool, and it would be used well tonight.

This was it. Time to dance with the reaper.

I moved silently toward my partner and Sam. Coming up behind him, I used both hands to bring the towel down over his face and pulled backwards, catching him off guard. I knew he was going to struggle, but I hadn't expected him to be so quick. He grunted and cussed beneath the towel. His hands wrapped my wrists, trying to get me to loosen my grip.

I was stronger than Sam, and he was drunk and uncoordinated. I maneuvered my wrists, twisting them about until he lost his hold, then stomped on his foot to distract him more. I gripped both sides of the towel with one hand and pulled the needle with the ketamine from my pocket. I flicked the plastic protective tip off, and injected the needle into his neck.

I knew the chloroform would knock him out, but I also knew that unlike in the movies, that shit took at least five minutes to fully work. That was why I added the ketamine. While chloroform would keep him knocked out for half an hour at max, ketamine would last longer. I needed that extra time to get him where I needed him to be. It wouldn't be ideal for him to wake up before I was ready.

"It's about damn time you joined us," Carrie said, yanking her skirt down as I caught Sam's weight and lowered him down to the ground. "I'm going to have bruises everywhere tomorrow."

I rolled my eyes. It wasn't as though she wasn't used to men like Sam. "Look at it this way, with what I'm paying you for your cooperation with these things, you won't have to deal with any fuckers like this ever again."

She sighed as she pulled a pair of clear plastic gloves from her purse, put them on, then reached for Sam's dick. She slid the condom off him, tucked his dick back in his jeans, and zipped him up. Pulling the gloves off, she wrapped them around the condom and then pulled a small bag from her purse as well and dropped the gloves with the condom in it.

I hefted Sam beneath his arms. He was dead weight at the moment. "Help me get him into the van."

She grabbed his feet with the bag hanging from her wrist. Together we carted him over to the side of the van. I slid the door open, and we tossed him inside. I kept my camera turned away from the image I'd put on the side of the van. I'd found a place that made decals, and used it to create a fake liquor delivery logo. Even though it was fake, I didn't want it traced back to me.

Once Sam was snoozing on the van floor, I tossed the towel over his face, figuring he might as well keep breathing it in, while my partner tossed in the glove-and-condom-filled bag. I reached in my inside jacket pocket and pulled out a stack of money. Turning to her, I said, "Twenty thousand, just like we discussed."

Her lips curved up in a smile. She took it and shoved it in her purse, then glanced at Sam. "What are you gonna do with the sick fuck?"

"You'll be seeing all of this online tomorrow." I pointed to the camera attached to my forehead.

Her eyes widened. "You didn't say anything about me being on camera. I didn't agree—"

I shook my head. "Don't worry. I'll blur your features and distort your voice just as I'll be doing to mine. Nobody will know it's you. Nothing will trace back to either of us."

"It damn well better not. I don't plan to spend the rest of my life in jail for this asshole."

"Once we're done, and you've got your payments, you can disappear, and nobody will ever know your part in this unless you tell them. You've got my word."

"I hope your word is as good as you say. Otherwise, we're both screwed." Her lips twisted cynically.

"Trust me. I've got us covered."

"Good." She backed away from the van and started moving toward the front of the building. "Let me know when you need me again."

"I'll be in touch."

I watched as she disappeared around the corner, then I

turned back to the van. I looked in on Sam, thinking about what needed to be done with him before sliding the door closed. Everything was in motion now. There was no turning back. I was resigned to do this. It was my duty to see it through.

I hurried around to the driver side door, climbed in, and drove to my secondary location. It was basically just down the street at an abandoned shop. There were quite a few of them in this neighborhood. It had been going downhill for some time. Crime had been skyrocketing over the last few years here and nothing was being done about it. That worked in my favor now. I pulled out of the delivery parking area and onto the street.

From this point on, it would all be on me.

I thought back over everything that had brought me to this moment in time. What had happened should never have happened, but now that it had, I was going to finish it in the only way I knew how.

People had to atone, and Sam was going to be the first.

2

A FEW BAD APPLES
MARCY

S tress was killing me. We were all feeling it right now, the whole of the LAPD, all because of a few possible bad apples. I didn't want to believe it, but it was starting to look like it was all true. And what was worse, the public believed it, not just of the one officer who'd been arrested, but of the rest of us as well.

It was hard doing this job when the public trusted you, but doing it when there was blatant mistrust was ten times as hard and stressful. You never knew in a given day if it would be your last. That was exhausting. I was in serious need of a vacation. Wine and bubble baths were no longer cutting it. I needed some other form of stress relief, and soon.

I was part of the Homicide Special Section Unit, so I tended to be sent after serial killers, the real sociopaths and psychopaths, and I was good at it. But when we didn't have any active serial killers in the greater LA area, I was back to doing regular detective work. That was the case at the moment. No serial killers for me to chase. That was a good thing for Los Angeles, of course. It meant the people were somewhat safer in their day-to-day lives. I was always okay with that.

Today was full of assholes with guns, knives, one had a hammer, and another a nail gun... that had been interesting. A nail gun to the face was not a pretty sight. Think Pinhead from the Hellraiser horror movies. He and the guy with the hammer had been arrested after a trip to the ER to remove the twenty nails in the guy's face, and to stitch him up. I was now off-duty, finally, and heading to meet my brother for dinner at our favorite Mexican restaurant.

These days I drove myself to and from work because Angel was fully back to good physical health and was no longer dependent on me to drive him around, not that I'd minded in the least. He was a good guy, a great friend and partner, but some days it was just nice to grab my shit and go home or wherever. I was sure that Angel felt the same. I knew he hated being dependent on me or others to get him around.

Pulled into the parking lot, I parked in the open space next to Stephen's truck. I grabbed my purse from the passenger seat and headed in. I knew Stephen would be sitting in the bar. There was always seating available, and it was seat yourself in there. As I'd expected, he had a table for us, and he was already eating chips and salsa. I gave him a tired smile and slid into the booth across from him.

"Hey, sis. You look... like crap. What's up?" he said, frowning at me.

I gave a sarcastic chuckle, and replied, "That's a Pandora's box you may not want to open."

His frown deepened and he waved the waitress over. "Penny, can you bring my sister a watermelon margarita?"

"Of course," Penny replied.

"And can we get some of the queso blanco to go with these chips?" I asked.

"Sure, I'll be right back out with those. And I'll bring you a menu too." She hurried off.

"Okay, spill it. What's going on?" Stephen said.

"I don't even know where to start. There's the overall general shitshow going on at the LAPD right now with Selene Webb's accusations coming to light, and there's Detective Grant Weaver's arrest. Plus, Jordan's put me on call all week."

Stephen dipped a chip in his salsa and bit into it, munching as his brow furrowed. "That sucks. Weaver's not in your division though, right?"

I sighed. "No, he's Gang and Narcotic Division. He's the one who went undercover and took down the Serpents Motorcycle Club a few years back. In fact, that's where he apparently came across Selene Webb. She's the daughter of one of the members."

"So the rumors are true?" he asked.

"Here you go," Penny murmured as she set the margarita down along with the white cheese sauce I'd asked for. "And here's the menu. I'll give you a few minutes to decide."

"Thanks." I smiled and took the offered menu.

Once she was gone, I opened the menu. I didn't want to have to build my meal, so fajitas were out. I glanced up to see Stephen looking at me expectantly. "What?"

"The rumors are true?"

"Oh, that. Yeah, it's looking that way. They've arrested Weaver, and the judge is holding him without bail until the trial. I think they're looking to make an example of him."

"So he really got that girl hooked on heroin and prostituted her to some of his cop buddies?"

"I can't say that he did—I wasn't involved, and I haven't seen the evidence—but that is what he's being charged with, along with rape, child molestation, and a slew of other charges, considering she was only sixteen at the time it all started."

"If he did it to one, you know he probably did it to more." Stephen's voice was full of disgust.

"You're not wrong. Apparently, she wasn't the only one, but whoever the other girls are, they've not been found yet, if they even exist. It's a bad look for the LAPD. He's a decorated hero who we celebrated, and now..." I shook my head and went back to the menu.

Penny returned a few minutes later. "What did you decide?"

"I'll go with the number three platter, but with steak, not chicken." I pointed to the menu. "Can you add some of the queso blanco to the enchilada and burrito? And I'd like extra guac and sour cream, please."

"Of course, and for you?" She looked over at Stephen.

"Actually, that sounds good. I'll have the same."

"I'll get that right in for you." Penny headed for the kitchen.

"So how are things going for you other than all that crap with Weaver?" he asked, mixing his salsa with some of the queso.

I mixed up my own bowl of the salsa and queso before answering. "Jordan's been on a rampage since news broke, and I'm always first on his hit list."

Jordan Brasswell was my ex-husband, and he'd gotten promoted to lieutenant over me. I'd probably been more qualified, but I was under IA investigation, thanks to him pitching a fit at the fact I'd killed a serial killer. I'd been cleared of any wrongdoing but by the time the investigation had finished, the brass had made their choice, and I wasn't it.

"What did you ever see in that asshole?" Stephen asked.

"I was young and stupid, apparently."

I'd been in love with Jordan, and I'd thought he was in love with me. Turned out he'd just wanted someone to control. He quickly learned I was uncontrollable. Still, we'd muddled along for a while. I'd put up with a lot of crap from him just because I valued our marriage and I'd taken my vows seriously, but then I discovered he'd been cheating on me and that was it.

"You've never been stupid. He just hid his assholish ways well."

Penny returned with our food, and we began eating. The food was so good that it was all I could focus on until I got about halfway in. I lifted my margarita and took a sip. This was just what I needed. Not the conversation about work, but a dinner out with my brother, just relaxing.

"So, how was your appointment?" I asked, glancing up at him.

Stephen had been out of Shine View, a mental health facility, for a few weeks now, but he'd still been seeing Dr. Faulkner a couple of times a week so he could maintain his forward progress. I sometimes went with him, sitting in when he asked me to, just so he could ask questions of things he misremembered. It had been enlightening. Therapy had really been helping him to heal and I realized that my group therapy sessions with Dr. Fellows helped me as well. I still managed to get in a session about once a week, even looked forward to them.

"It was good. We talked more about when we were kids. Do you remember a guy Mom brought home, Rick?"

I looked at him, bewildered. "No."

"Sure you do. Remember, the guy who took us to Disneyland? He was maybe five foot ten, had really blond hair and brown eyes?"

I laughed. "Stephen, I have a vague memory of Disneyland, but I don't remember the guy who took us. I was only three."

Sighing, he twisted his fork between his fingers.

"What about this man did you remember?" I asked.

He glanced back up at me and a small smile touched his lips. "I remember really liking him. I thought he was going to marry Mom and we'd be a family. He said he wanted to get Mom sober and that he'd be around to take care of us. He used to take me with him to the grocery store and let me pick out my own cereal and stuff."

"What happened to him?" I asked.

"I don't know. When he stopped coming around, I asked Mom about it, and she got angry. She slapped me and told me never to mention his name again."

"I'm sorry." I reached across the table and gripped his hand.

I had once thought my mother was an imperfect but perfect woman. I'd put her on a pedestal, defended her to anyone and everyone. But I'd learned that my mother was not the woman I'd thought she was. She'd treated me like a princess, but she'd abused Stephen in every possible way. My mother had been a pedophile. She may not have deserved to die the way she did, murdered by a serial killer in front of me and Stephen, but I no longer regretted not saving her. What she'd done was vile.

"You have nothing to be sorry about. You didn't do it." Stephen quirked a smile at me. "Anyway, after talking to Dr. Faulkner, she's encouraged me to search out Rick. It might be a good project for me, you know?"

"I think it's a good idea. It will keep you busy and not put too much stress on you."

His smile grew. He took a drink of his water and then grabbed the last chip from the basket. "That's the idea."

My phone beeped, and I glanced at it.

"Work?"

I shook my head. "It's Angel. He's noticed an issue with his new car and wants me to pick him up tomorrow." I sent a text back telling him I would be there first thing.

"What's up with it?"

"No idea. He didn't say." I yawned.

"You should head home and get some sleep. I got this." Stephen indicated our meal.

"You sure?"

"Go on. I'll see you later."

Giving him a hug, I headed home. Halfway there, my phone buzzed, and I had to pull over to answer it. "Kendrick."

"Detective, this is dispatch. Sorry to be calling you when you're supposed to be off-duty—"

"I'm on call, so it's fine." I sighed. "What do you need?"

"There's been a homicide on East 6th and Maple Avenue, your GPS shows you in the vicinity, and Lieutenant Brasswell said to send you."

I gritted my teeth. Of course he did. "I'm on my way." After hanging up, I tossed my siren on my dash, pulled back onto the street, and turned my car around, heading to the scene.

3

LOVE IS HARD
ANGEL

I'd been out on a date last night when the engine light came on in my new car. I didn't want to drive it if there was a problem, so I'd texted Marcy to see if I could get a ride into the precinct with her early this morning. I even promised to buy her coffee. She'd said yes, of course, because that was the kind of partner she was. It was one of the things I loved about her. Her willingness to bend over backwards for the people she loved.

I was lucky to be counted among the handful she cared for. That didn't mean she was in love with me. And even though I was half in love with her, I recognized that it would be detrimental to our partnership if we were to be together. At least that's what I told myself. So I'd joined a dating app and I'd been on a few dates with various women. They were nice, but until last night I hadn't met anyone I'd want to see again.

Marcy pulled in and parked in my driveway, then honked the horn. I was already pulling the door open before she got a second honk in. I hurried to the car with a grin.

"Good morning," I said as I climbed in and put on my seat belt.

Her gaze slid to me, and her brow arched. "You're pretty chipper this morning. Something you want to tell me?"

I chuckled. She knew I'd started dating again. "Can't I just be in a good mood?"

She gave me a suspicious look and pursed her lips. "No." Then she laughed. "Good date last night?"

"It really was," I answered.

She pulled the car out of the drive and onto the street. "Who is she, did you sleep with her, and are you seeing her again?"

I only hesitated for a moment before telling her. Marcy was probably my best friend; she always had my back, and she was happy for me. "Calista Sawyer. She goes by Callie. No, I didn't sleep with her. It was our first date. And yes, I want to see her again. I think she wants to see me again too."

"Calista... sounds fancy..." Marcy grinned as she teased me. "Callie sounds a little more down to earth though. What does she do?"

"She's a hairstylist, and she owns her own salon," I shared. I'd been impressed that she had worked hard and achieved that dream.

"Does she have crazy hair?"

I laughed. "No, it's normal. Pretty, dark blonde with copper-looking highlights. And long." Even though she'd worn her hair braided over her shoulder, I knew when it was loose it fell almost to her waist. She'd shown me pictures.

"I'd forgotten you had a thing for long hair." She laughed.

I shrugged. I did like a woman with long hair, but it was her choice. It wasn't like I'd be pissed off if she cut it. Marcy didn't wear her hair long and I thought she was very attractive. It was really more about the person than the hair, but it was a nice bonus. I also liked Callie's smile and her laugh. It was sweet and melodic. Plus, she was just the right height for me. She could wear four-inch heels and I could still comfortably drape my arm around her shoulders. We fit nicely together.

I looked over at Marcy again. She and Callie were probably similar in height. Marcy might be a half an inch taller. And they both had similar body shapes with curves in all the right places. I shook my head, realizing where my brain was going. I didn't want to compare them in that way. It wasn't fair to either of them.

As that thought crossed my mind, I realized I'd need to make sure Callie wasn't the jealous type. I wasn't going to give up my friendship or partnership with Marcy. She'd have to be okay with her. I really hoped they could become friends too. It would be nice to maybe hang out with them both occasionally. Then again, maybe I was getting ahead of myself. After all, we'd only been on one date so far.

A moment later, Marcy asked, "She knows you're a cop?"

"Yeah. She seemed to be okay with it."

I had told Callie that I was a homicide detective with the HSS unit. She hadn't known what that was, so I gave her a minimal explanation. I hadn't wanted to go into detail about me and Marcy chasing down serial killers. In my head I thought that could only go one of two ways. Either she was a true crime junkie and she'd want to hear about the gory details, or she'd be repulsed by it and wonder why I would want to do a job like that. That would probably lead to her thinking I was sick in the head because I really loved my job. And that was just a lot to uncover on a first date.

"Make sure she really knows what she's getting into before you two take it beyond casual, yeah?" Marcy suggested.

I knew what she was getting at. The job could take a toll on a relationship. Cheating was rampant, because officers worked such long hours. We tended not to share much about our days because of what we dealt with. So we were emotionally unavailable a lot of the time, and many of us knew how to shut our emotions down so we'd be numb to what we saw at work. Then there was always the chance that we'd never walk through the door again because our jobs could be deadly. On top of all that, there was the current political climate where some people hated cops just on principle. This whole issue with Selene Webb didn't help. It just painted us all in a bad light when it was a handful of dirty cops who were to blame among the thousands who worked the job.

"Angel?" Marcy broke me from my thoughts as she pulled into the coffee shop and parked.

"Sorry, yeah. I'll make sure to talk to her about it." I smiled at her as I clicked my seat belt, and put my hand on the door handle.

"So what did you do last night?" she asked as she pushed her door open.

"I—" I started to say, but my phone rang. Sighing, I said, "Hang on, it's Jordan." I still hadn't gotten used to calling him Lieutenant, and honestly, I didn't think he actually deserved the title, but I definitely wasn't using it when it was just me and Marcy. "Reyes," I answered, holding the phone to my ear.

"Don't bother coming in to the precinct. We've got a body on Towne Ave. Need you to get over there ASAP. I don't want the press getting wind of this before you get there. Patrol is on their way to keep the civilians away and hold the scene. I'll call Marcy—"

"No need. We're together," I replied.

"You're what?" Jordan sounded as though he was about to go ballistic.

I hadn't said it to screw with him, but since he took it that way, I slid my gaze to Marcy as I said, "She stayed over last night. We'll head out now. Just text me the address." I hung up with a smirk.

Marcy laughed so hard her eyes watered. "I can just picture his face." She scooted back into the car and closed the door.

"He's a dumbass."

My phone beeped with a text from Jordan.

> You fucker! She's my wife! Keep your dick out of her. 1234 Towne Ave.

I grinned. "Well, that's a keeper." I sent him a text back.

> She divorced you, so…

"Where are we headed?" She turned the car on and pulled back out of the parking space.

I tossed the siren up on the dash and turned it on as I gave her the address. It sucked that we were leaving without stopping for our coffee, but when the job called, we didn't have much choice.

She wove through traffic, getting us there within eight minutes. I was suddenly glad I hadn't had a coffee; it would have spilled everywhere with the way she swerved between cars. It didn't really bother me; I drove the same way when we were headed to a scene. Neither of us was reckless, but if you weren't used to it, you might lose your lunch.

Marcy slammed on the brakes and pulled in behind a patrol car. I looked before opening my door. The last thing I needed was to be hit while getting out after I'd just spent forever healing from my own car accident. I was still seeing a physical therapist once a week because of it.

Once the street was clear, I was out of the car. I glanced up at the building. The sign read: Let Them Eat Cake, but there was a 'for sale' sign in the window. That seemed to be par for the course around Skid Row. A lot of the buildings were abandoned or for sale, so it didn't surprise me a body had been left here.

I pulled my badge from my pocket. It was time to get to work.

4

WINDOW DRESSING
MARCY

"Jordan's going to be pissed," I muttered, looking around and seeing four news vans parked on the street.

Angel followed my gaze. "Hell. What do you want to do?"

I glanced at the patrol officer standing in front of the large display window. There was another pair of officers inside with their backs to us. "Lopez, what have we got?" I asked as I flashed my badge. He knew who I was, but it was procedure to show my badge.

Lopez tilted his head to the side and back toward the window. "Body in the window. You're not going to like it."

"Probably not, especially if those news crews get a good shot of the scene. Anyone called crime scene?"

"Curtis did, ma'am," he replied. "He and Garcia are doing their best to block the body from view. We've got more officers on their way to deal with this." He gestured toward the crowd gathering on the sidewalk trying to get a peek in the window.

Before I could tell him to do his best, I heard my name being shouted.

"Detective Kendrick! Can you tell us what you know?" one of the reporters asked; she was holding a mike for Channel 4 news.

"I just got here," I replied.

"Is it a serial killer?" the news reporter from Channel 5 interjected.

"No comment."

"Should the city be worried?" the news reporter from Channel 4 interjected.

I was losing my patience. I needed to get inside and see what we were dealing with.

"What can you tell us about Grant Weaver's arrest?" a reporter from the *LA Times* asked.

I gritted my teeth. "No comment."

"The people deserve to know how many of you bastards are corrupt!" someone else shouted from among the crowd of what I thought were civilians.

I spun, looking for the jerk who'd said it. I was full of rage and my fingers clenched into a fist.

Angel grabbed hold of my jacket sleeve, cautioning me.

"All you pigs are fucking corrupt!" the same voice shouted.

This time I saw the man. He was a skinny, hipster-looking twenty-something-year-old. He pointed the latest iPhone at us. I strode toward him, and got in his face. I knew better than to touch him, because I didn't want to be caught on camera doing something I'd later regret. It was one thing for me to shoot a pedophile or a gangbanger, or even a serial killer, but a civilian? That was just asking for an abuse of power lawsuit.

"If you don't walk away right now, I will have you arrested for tampering with a crime scene and disturbing the peace." My eyes flashed to the rest of the crowd around him. "That goes for all of you."

"You can't do that," one of the hipster's buddies said.

"Try me." I gave him a hard look, staring right into his face until he backed down and dropped his gaze to his feet.

He gripped his hipster friend by the sleeve and took a step backward. "Let's go. Ain't nothing here worth getting stitched up over."

I turned back around to see Angel had followed me, backing me up. I gave him a tight smile, took a breath, and started back toward Lopez.

I could hear sirens blaring and a moment later, several more officers were there, setting up a barrier with yellow crime scene tape to keep everyone at bay.

"When the coroner and crime scene gets here, send them in," I said to Lopez.

"Yes, ma'am, I will."

"Let's go see what we've got," I muttered to Angel.

We entered the shop, which was rather dim. "No lights?" I questioned.

"No, ma'am. We've put a call in to get the electric turned on for us, but at the moment all we have is what little sunlight can get past us," Garcia answered.

"Great. Guess that means we can't block the window either until we have electric." I sighed as I moved toward them. I stepped up onto the wide window display next to the two officers and turned to view the body.

The naked and eviscerated body of a man who'd been stabbed multiple times.

"Hell."

"Yes, ma'am," Curtis said under his breath, his eyes on the corpse.

"Any idea who he is?"

"Hard to say, ma'am. His face is... well..." Garcia gestured to the body. "As far as we can tell, there's no clothing or wallet anywhere around to tell us. But for all we know it could be stashed somewhere in here."

"Right. Without lights it's hard to say."

Angel put his foot on the display, and I held a hand out to steady him as he hopped up next to me. He was still working on returning the strength that he'd had before to his leg. He turned his gaze to the body and his brow furrowed.

"What is it?" I asked him.

"Not sure. Something familiar about that tattoo, but I don't know why." Angel pointed to a black dragon on the victim's right shoulder, or at least, what was left of it.

"Criminal you arrested?" I asked, looking from it to Angel.

He shook his head slowly. "I don't think so—"

The lights came on and we got a clearer picture of the victim.

"What's that?" Curtis said, pointing to something under the chair the victim was tied to.

I squatted down to get a better look and sucked in a breath. "It's a broken fucking LAPD badge."

"Son of a bitch, I know where I've seen that tattoo," Angel gasped.

I glanced over my shoulder and up at him, afraid of his answer. "Who?"

"Sam Finlay. Gang and Narco Division."

A wrapped a hand over my mouth. We weren't dealing

with just another victim. This was a cop. "Get this window covered now." My voice brooked no argument.

"Yes, ma'am." Curtis partially turned and tapped the glass.

He connected his gaze to Lopez's outside and held up three fingers. Lopez nodded. A moment later we heard Lopez's voice on the radio, asking three officers to join us inside. The door opened, and several officers appeared.

I glanced at them and said, "Find something to block this view. Angel, help them, please?"

He nodded and they searched the front of the shop, but there really wasn't anything there. "We'll check the back."

I stayed where I was studying the body, but it didn't take too long for them to reappear with a large sheet. "Where did you get that?" I asked, glancing up as they came toward us.

"It was covering a bunch of equipment. Not sure how we're going to hang it though," Angel replied.

Officer Allen came running forward shaking a container. "I found push pins in the office."

They worked quickly and got the window nearly all blocked as Lindsey Stone, head of crime scene investigations, and a few of her techs came into the shop, followed by Dr. Damien Black, our coroner.

I stood up and joined them before they reached the body. "I think we've got a dead cop—Sam Finlay," I said, keeping my voice low.

Damien whistled.

"Shit," Lindsey swore as she stared past me toward the body.

Damien moved toward the body. "Everyone out unless you're a crime scene tech or a detective," he announced.

"I don't want this getting out, so keep your mouths shut,"

I said before any of them could move. "No talking to the press. Don't even talk to the other officers out there. I don't want anyone overheard. There will be disciplinary action if I hear even one peep about this before I get back to the precinct, clear?"

"Yes, ma'am," several officers responded before leaving.

"Curtis, one moment," I said, moving toward him before he could leave.

"Ma'am? Did you need something else from me?"

"Yes. Who called this in?"

Curtis pulled his notebook from his pocket and opened it. "Mr. Jackson and his girlfriend, Miss Santiago. They were out jogging around sunrise and happened past. I've got their information."

"Great. Did they stay on the scene?"

"I'm not sure, ma'am. Once I verified who they were and took their information, I told them they could leave."

"That's fine. Let's go see if they're still here. If not, I'll track them down." I followed him out of the shop. "Do you see them?"

He scanned the crowd gathered behind the crime scene tape. "Yes, ma'am, just over there."

I looked around, wondering where I could speak to them without being overheard.

"Why don't I bring them around to the back of the shop, ma'am?"

It wasn't ideal—there could be evidence back there—but then again, I didn't have much of a choice considering the absolute circus this was turning into, I thought as I looked around and noticed more media showing up. "Fine. See if you can get them back there without being noticed, okay?"

"I've got an idea, ma'am," Curtis replied. "Go in and open the back door. I'll have them there shortly."

I watched him pull out his personal phone and it dawned on me that he was going to call them. "Good thinking, Curtis." I turned on my heel and headed back into the shop. "Angel, with me," I called as I strode to the back room.

Angel jogged over. "What's up?"

"Curtis is having our witnesses meet us back here."

"Good idea," he murmured as we stepped into the back of the shop.

There was an industrial kitchen back here, a walk-in freezer, and lots of storage and shelving. We headed to the doorway, and I opened the door.

Officer Curtis arrived a moment later. "They should be here in just a moment, ma'am."

We didn't have to wait long. A woman with long dark hair and a man with blond hair and blue eyes behind a pair of square-framed glasses appeared around the corner.

I kept an eye on the mouth of the alley to make sure they weren't followed. Thankfully, they weren't. "Mr. Jackson? Miss Santiago?"

"Yes, that's us," the man answered for them both.

"I'm Detective Kendrick and this is my partner, Detective Reyes. You know Officer Curtis. Thank you for accommodating us. We'd like to keep this off the news as much as possible for the time being."

"So you don't want us talking to the reporters?" the woman asked, giving me a suspicious look. "Isn't that against our First Amendment rights?"

I bit the inside of my cheek. "I am asking that you kindly not speak to them until we have a chance to make a proper identification, inform the family, and attempt to catch the killer. With the way the killer posed the body in front of the window, we are aware that they were seeking massive attention. It would be best not to give it to them."

The man gave his girlfriend a hard look. "We won't speak to them, Detective."

"Thank you. Now, can you tell me what you were doing in the area and what drew your attention to the body in the window?"

"We walk this route early every morning," Mr. Jackson said. "It's part of our daily exercise regime. We come down this block and turn at the corner. The sun was barely up, but the sun's rays hit the window and drew my attention. That's when I saw the man. I took a closer look and... well." He looked a little pale. "So we called it in and waited for Officer Curtis to arrive."

"You didn't try to go into the shop?"

"No way," Miss Santiago said, shaking her head almost violently. "I didn't even want to stick around. I mean, what if the killer was still here?"

"I'd have protected you," Mr. Jackson said. "Besides, that looked personal, not random."

I arched a brow. "What do you mean?"

"I'm a psychologist. The man in the chair... he had his—" he gestured to his nether region, "stabbed multiple times. To me that says the guy was probably a pedophile or something along those lines. Probably put on display as a warning to others."

I had a feeling he probably wasn't too far off the mark. The problem with that was that if it was true, we could have a vigilante on our hands. Someone who was seeking justice where they believed they weren't getting it. If that was the case, it could be possible we'd see more killings like this.

"Thank you for your insight, Mr. Jackson. Can you tell me if you noticed anyone hanging around when you came across the body?"

"No, there wasn't anyone out and about from what I could tell. There weren't even too many cars that passed by, and none of them went by slowly or anything."

I nodded. "Alright, thanks. Officer Curtis has your information in case we need to speak to you again, correct?"

"Yes," he answered.

"We'll let you go now. Thank you for cooperating."

Mr. Jackson wrapped his arm around his girlfriend and led her down the alley in the opposite direction from where they'd entered.

I turned to Angel and Officer Curtis.

"I'll get my report to you as soon as possible, ma'am."

"Thanks, Curtis."

He left me and Angel alone in the back room.

"What do you think?" I asked Angel.

"I know it's just one death, but I think we might have a serial killer."

5

GROW THE HELL UP
MARCY

I pulled into the precinct and felt my anxiety kick up. I loved my job, but there were aspects of it that I currently hated. Dealing with Jordan was one of them. And of course, I couldn't avoid having to interact with him. He was the lieutenant, my literal boss. Sometimes I could bypass him and go straight to Captain Robinson, but lately Robinson had been under a lot of stress from home. He and his wife were splitting up and it made him a little bit on edge. So I was left with going to Jordan for damn near everything. And didn't he make that difficult every single time. Still, I was determined to be professional and adult about it all.

We headed into the building and to our desks in the detective pool. I had hoped to have a moment to breathe and put my purse away before Jordan accosted us, but no such luck. He was waiting for us when we entered the room.

"It's fine," Angel murmured. "He just wants an update."

"Right." I gave him a slight nod and walked further into the room, my head held high.

"What have we got?" Jordan demanded. "Do you know who the vic is? Do you have a lead on the perp?"

I slid my gaze to the detectives nearby, who seemed to be invested in our conversation. "Maybe we should take this to your office—"

"Spit it out, Kendrick," Jordan interrupted. "I don't have time to mollycoddle you today. We've got fucking work to do."

"We don't have a confirmation on the victim's ID, but we are fairly certain that it's Sam Finlay." I tried to keep my voice down, but I could see several heads swivel in our direction.

"That's impossible. You've fucked up somewhere," Jordan said, berating me. "There is no way he would be murdered like that."

I arched a brow. "You don't even know how he was killed." I stared at him, my eyes narrowed on his face.

Jordan got huffy and crossed his arms over his chest. "How? Tell me how someone got the drop on a guy like Finlay. A decorated, seasoned detective who deals with gangs and narcotics on the daily."

"Look, I don't know anything yet. All I know is what I saw at the scene. Damien and Lindsey will have their report to us soon and we'll know more. What I can tell you is he was tied to a chair and looked as though he had been stabbed numerous times, probably tortured, and then was left to bleed out in the window of an abandoned bake shop. Maybe it had something to do with the job, or maybe it didn't, but we will figure it out."

Hummel glanced over at us and said, "Maybe it's got something to do with that Selene woman."

"The biker's daughter who's accused Grant of pimping her out?" I questioned.

"Yeah, maybe Finlay was one of the cops using her," Hummel suggested.

"Maybe, but we have no proof of that, nor do we have any proof that his death is related to her accusations, not yet anyway."

"Then find out," Jordan said. "I want to know exactly what happened to Finlay and how this occurred. Get busy." He started to turn away then looked back at me. "Kendrick, I want that report on last night's homicide on my desk within the hour," he said before taking off for his office.

"Last night's homicide?" Angel questioned.

"I was called in on a homicide of a homeless man on East 6th and Maple last night after I left dinner with Stephen. Shot in the head, but we caught everything on surveillance. I recognized the perp. It was Maurice Lawerence, better known as DJ LAW. I sent Officers Kim and Desmond to arrest him. He's confessed and is already in lock-up. It's a clear open-and-shut case."

"Why'd he kill the homeless man?" Angel asked.

"Apparently the homeless man stole some equipment from him. CSI is still working on ID for him. It won't take me a minute to write that up, which is why I didn't bother coming back here last night to do it," I said as we went back to our desks. Angel took his seat at his as well. "You want to look at Sam's back cases while I get this done real quick?" I suggested.

Angel nodded. "Sure thing."

"When I'm done, I'll start looking into Sam's life, social media, friends, family. Once we have a positive ID, we'll have to go inform the family."

Angel agreed and we both got to work.

Two hours later, Ken, one of Lindsey's techs, stepped into the office and handed me a file folder. "Lindsey sent me up with this. She had me grab the coroner's initial report as well." He held it out to me.

Opening the file, I could see they'd run a fingerprint and had a positive ID. "So it was Sam Finlay."

"Yeah." He shuffled from one foot to the other, waiting, I supposed, to be dismissed.

I glanced at him and then back to the folder. There was a stack of crime scene photos as well as notes on several of them. The most important note I saw proved my guess correct. Finlay had bled out from the numerous stab wounds. "Was there anything else?"

"Yes, ma'am. The coroner is rushing the autopsy and will be conducting it in thirty minutes. He said he knew you'd want to meet him afterwards and to give him an hour."

"Thanks."

Ken gave me a tight smile and then turned and left the room, his sneakers squeaking on the hallway floor as he hurried back to his lab.

I stood holding the folder and flipped through the images. I met Angel's gaze and tilted my head to one of the empty incident rooms. I had a feeling we were going to need the space to set things up and go over it all.

Angel pushed away from his desk and followed me into the room.

I shut the door behind us and set the folder on the table.

"Hang these?" he said, tapping the images spilling out of the folder.

"Yeah. I'll set up the board."

At the top of the board I wrote Sam's name, age, rank,

and manner of death. After going through his social media, I noticed he had numerous pictures with various women, as well as several other cops, including Grant. I wrote Grant's name on the board with a question mark. I wondered if he had anything to do with what happened to Sam.

Once everything was set up, we headed for the coroner's office to see Damien about the initial autopsy. It wasn't a long walk as it was in the same huge building, just on a different floor. We found Damien in his office, typing up notes.

"Hey, so what can you tell us?" I said, after knocking on his open office door.

Damien looked at us and held up a finger, finished typing and then stood up. "Come with me."

We followed him into the lab and to a body on the table covered with a sheet. The room had a wall of cold storage slabs where numerous bodies were kept until Damien, or his team were finished with them and they were claimed or sent to the funeral home. The work area had three tables, but the one we were standing at was the only one with a body.

"What are we looking at?" I asked, unsure why he couldn't just tell us without the visual aid.

"I wanted you to see these..." He lifted Sam's lifeless arm and turned it over. "See this?" He pointed at a couple of small, barely there cuts. "These are hesitation cuts. See how shallow they are? I think this was our killer's first kill, at least with this method. I can't say one hundred percent that our killer hasn't taken a life before, but it could be that it's the first time they've taken a life up close and personal."

I considered it and nodded. "It also looked to me like he was tortured, like there were cuts in places that would hurt and bleed a lot, but not allow him to die quickly."

"Yes, it does look that way. I've sent samples to toxicology. I'll know if he was conscious or not soon, hopefully, if the labs aren't too backed up."

"Torture wouldn't have worked if Sam was unconscious though, right?" Angel asked.

"True. If that turns out to be the case, then it could be the killer just wanted him to bleed out slowly. However, there would have been no guarantee he wouldn't have survived. Someone could have found him, especially with the way he was left in that window."

That made me pause for a moment. "Wait, if he was killed there, where was all the blood?"

"Ah, good catch," Damien said. "He wasn't killed in that spot, not exactly. We found pools of blood in the walk-in freezer. It wasn't on, since there was no electricity to the shop, but once the team went over the shop, they found it." He frowned. "It should have been in the report. Was it not?"

"I admit I was focused more on the photos than on the report. I'll go read it more thoroughly," I replied. "Anything else?"

"Just this," he answered, pointing at some burn marks. "A taser was used on him. He's got several of these marks on his body."

I really hoped he wasn't awake for all that was done to him. "Okay. Is that all?"

"It is for right now. I'll let you know when I have more."

"Thanks, Damien."

We headed back out of his lab and toward the bank of elevators.

"Lunch?" I asked, looking over at Angel as we pulled open the door to the detective pool.

"Sure. Wanna hit one of the food trucks?"

"Who's here today?" I grabbed my purse from my desk drawer.

"The Tropic Truck and Guerrilla Tacos."

"I'm not in the mood for Caribbean, so let's try Guerrilla," I suggested.

Outside, we found the truck and, after studying the menu, put in our orders.

"You'll have to let me try a bite of that pocho one," Angel said as we waited.

"No way. If you want to try wild boar, you'll have to get your own," I teased. I'd also ordered one of the lomo saltados, which was steak, just in case I didn't like the wild boar. Either way, I figured I would share it with Angel.

Our number was called, and we grabbed our food, then went to sit at one of the outdoor tables with benches.

I unwrapped the wild boar first. It came with an avocado salsa and tasted really good. After my second bite though, I handed it over to Angel. "Here, you can have it. I think you'll like it."

He had his mouth full, but took it with glee in his eyes as he set his own taco down. A moment later, he had devoured the entire thing, moaning in pleasure as he ate each bite. "So good," he murmured.

We finished up and went back in. I didn't even make it to my desk before Jordan was in my face.

"What did you do?" he demanded, his hands on his hips.

"Nothing. We just got lunch." I pursed my lips. "What has you all..." I waved my hand up and down, "like this?"

"IA wants to see you. Immediately." He had a smug look on his face, as though he was happy I was being called in front of internal affairs.

I rolled my eyes. "Grow the hell up, Jordan. I'm sure it's to do with Sam Finlay and this case, not me."

"Watch it, Kendrick. I could have you written up for insubordination and whatever else I want," he threatened.

I could feel my nerves going on edge. "Take your complaints to the captain, because I don't have to put up with your harassment." I glared at him.

Jordan didn't say anything else, just turned and left us to go about our business.

"Well, that was fun," Angel muttered.

Sighing, I set my purse back in my desk drawer. "Look, why don't you go back to the incident room and grab the report. You can go over it while I go see what IA wants with me."

He nodded. "I'm sure it's nothing. Don't worry about it."

My lips quirked up. "I'm not." I straightened my shoulders and left the office.

I had lied. I was extremely nervous. Despite my assurance that it had to be the Finlay case, I had to wonder... *What if it's not?*

6

ONE OF THE ACCUSED

MARCY

I knocked on Lieutenant II Zachery Hartley's door and waited.

The door swung open, and Detective III Sabrina Mills stood there. She had a sour look on her face, but that wasn't unexpected. She always looked that way. Like she was always sucking on a lemon. She wasn't a fan of mine.

I gave her a tight smile. "I understand you wanted to see me?"

"Come in, Detective Kendrick." She stepped out of the way, and pulled the door further open.

I stepped across the threshold, and she shut the door behind me. I almost felt trapped, but I knew I wasn't in trouble this time. I'd met with them on several occasions previously, usually because I'd shot a suspect. "How can I help you today?" I asked.

"Please, have a seat," Lieutenant Hartley replied, gesturing to the seats in front of his desk. He was the officer in charge, so I was fairly certain he was the one who had asked me here.

I took a seat and Detective Mills took the other.

"I understand you're in charge of the Finlay killing," Hartley said. It wasn't really a question; more of a statement.

Still, I answered, "I am."

"What can you tell us about that?" Mills put in.

I turned to look at her. "It's still early. I don't know what I can tell you, other than he was definitely murdered. We think he was possibly tortured, but we're waiting on toxicology to finish the labs. He was stabbed multiple times and left to bleed out, naked and tied to a chair. He was moved in front of a window after death."

Hartley nodded. "So he was put on display."

"It looks that way. Why?" I frowned. Something wasn't adding up. "What's your interest in Sam Finlay?"

The two shared a look and then Hartley said, "Finlay was under investigation. You are aware of the accusations made by Selene Webb?"

"The biker's daughter? Yes. I know you've already arrested Grant Weaver and he's being held at the detention center without bond. I know Sam has a number of pictures on his social media of himself and Grant. I haven't gotten a chance to look further into the connection."

"Finlay was specifically named by Ms. Webb as not only a participant in her prostitution, but a major player. He was the one who trafficked her between LA and Santa Monica, bringing her to flop houses where she was forced to engage in sexual activities with various police personnel."

I sucked in a breath but didn't ask the questions I really wanted to know the answers to. Instead, I kept my focus on Sam Finlay. "So, you think there may be a connection between your investigation and Sam's murder?"

Mills' eyes narrowed slightly, and her lip twitched. "We do."

"I suppose it's possible. Though if he was killed for being part of Ms. Webb's abuse, then either she's a suspect..."

"Or we have a leak," Hartley said, his voice soft.

I didn't know if what he was saying was true. "That wasn't what I was going to say. My thought was that either Selene Webb or someone close to her is a suspect or one of the others involved is nervous about being identified and took out Finlay before he could talk."

Hartley ran a hand across his jaw as he thought about my reply. "Yes, that could be a better explanation. I'd hate to think we have a leak in the IA. It's not a good look. We need you to keep us looped in on your investigation. Anything crosses your desk that ties into our investigation, we want to see it. Hell, even if it doesn't, we want to see it."

"Okay. Can you tell me more about what your investigation entails? What has she accused these cops of? I've heard the rumors and I've seen some of the news accounts, but the reports are all very speculative."

"We're trying to keep things as under wraps as possible. What I can tell you is Ms. Webb has proof of these officers who call themselves the Circle of Justice dealing heroin, keeping her and numerous other women hooked on the drug and captive so they could prostitute them to various other men."

"She's claiming they got her hooked on the drug?" I asked skeptically. "Wasn't her father the head of the Serpents MC?"

Hartley nodded. "Weaver went undercover with them. That's where he met Ms. Webb. When he first went undercover, she was fourteen. She was occasionally seen, but didn't have any involvement in the club. That changed when she turned sixteen. She took over duties in the clubhouse, keeping the bikers fed and supplied with girls. She fully admits bringing in girls from off the streets to them."

"She was a madame at the age of sixteen?" I asked, surprised. "And you're just believing her?"

"There's video proof. She got involved with Weaver at that point." Mills looked disgusted. "Show her the tape."

Hartley tapped a button on his computer and turned the screen. I watched as a young girl was forced to her knees in front of Grant Weaver. He didn't look like a decorated detective in the video. Instead, he looked like a typical biker with a heavy beard, tattoos, and a hard look about him. He had a grip on her ponytail and a sneer on his face.

"What can I do for you, Daddy? How can I make you feel good?" the girl asked.

I felt as though I was going to be sick. "That's enough. I don't need to see more."

Hartley turned the screen back and shut the video down. "There is quite a bit of this kind of thing, but this was the beginning of Weaver's operation. He told Ms. Webb that he wouldn't arrest her if she made herself available whenever he wanted. From there it escalated. He started passing her on to buddies, drugs got involved... The investigation is still ongoing for us to determine everything they were tangled up in."

"And Finlay was definitely involved?"

"According to Ms. Webb, yes. We have traffic cam footage of him driving her between here and Santa Monica. I would have arrested him this week if he weren't killed. We were hoping to use him to gain more information on the rest of the group."

"Do you have the other police personnel's names?"

"Not yet," Hartley replied. "Ms. Webb is piecemealing the information to us. She claims she's trying to protect herself, but it's frustrating."

"She has described a few of the men who used her, and we're working to identify them, but she didn't know their names," Mills added. "So if you come across anyone you think might be a potential for your suspect, let us cross-check them."

"Okay. Thanks for filling me in," I said, thinking more about the case.

"We'd appreciate it if you kept what we've told you quiet. With various other officers out there who could be involved, I'd rather they didn't hear where we are in the investigation."

I started to stand and then paused halfway up. I didn't want to bring it up, but seeing as how many cops were potentially involved, I wanted to be sure of whom I could actually share the information with. "I can talk to my partner about what you've told me, right?"

"Reyes? Yeah, that will be fine."

I felt a wave of relief flood me as I sank back in my chair. I hated having to keep things from Angel, so I rarely did. There was one other person I knew I might need to share information with... at least, one I was willing to share with at any rate. I was bypassing Jordan, because I didn't willingly share anything with him anymore, and I hoped he wouldn't think to ask me about IA other than to make a jab about them calling me in.

"And Robinson?" I asked.

Mills and Hartley hesitated.

"Come on, he's my captain."

"It's not that he's involved. More—" Mills started.

Hartley interrupted, "It's fine. If you need to speak to Captain Robinson about what we've discussed, then do. We'd just like to contain the information as much as possible."

"I will. Was there anything else?" I asked, fully rising now.

"Not at the moment, Detective Kendrick." Mills stood and moved to the door, opening it.

"Have a good day," I said and then got out of there.

They had shared a lot more than I'd thought they would about their investigation, and I was appalled that any of it had happened, let alone gotten that far. Weaver was a complete scumbag. He'd taken advantage of that girl, used her for his own sick purposes, and all the while walked around the LAPD like the big man on campus for years.

Disgust filled me as I strode down the hallway. Weaver was lucky that IA had him locked up because after seeing that video, I totally had it in me to shoot the man in the balls. I wouldn't even be a little bit sorry.

7

DEDUCTIONS, SPECULATIONS, AND PROBABILITIES

MARCY

I found Angel in the incident room where I'd left him an hour earlier. I glanced up at the clock. It was only a little after two. We still had a few hours before we could go home. "Anything new come in?" I asked as I sank into the chair next to him.

"Nope." He popped the 'p'.

I grinned, despite the somber pictures on the wall and the active case we were working. "Anything in the report that could lead to catching our killer?"

He sighed. "Nada. Nil. Nothin'."

I picked up the part of the file he wasn't looking at and skimmed it, debating what to do next. There were a number of people I needed to speak to, if only to rule them out. The problem was that one of them I really didn't want to revictimize by asking her questions about one of her assailants, and the other... well. I had never liked him. Then there were Sam's other friends and family, whom I probably needed to get in touch with. As it was, I still had to inform Sam's family of his death.

I set the file down and said, "Come on, we need to go speak to Sam's wife."

"Bethany's his ex. We'll need to go to his parents."

I stopped moving toward the door and looked over my shoulder at him. "Since when?"

"It's been about two months since it was finalized."

"Why didn't it show up on anything?" I frowned as I recalled seeing pictures of him and Bethany on his social media. Nothing said he had divorced her.

Angel shrugged. "Don't know. But rumor is she got tired of him cheating and his verbal abuse, so she took the kids and left him. They've moved to Lake Tahoe, according to her Insta page."

I pinched the bridge of my nose. I couldn't believe I'd missed that. "Thanks for catching that."

"Still want to go see his folks?"

"Yeah, they need to be informed formally."

"And we should go check out his place. He kept the house in the divorce."

Half an hour later we pulled up to the Finlay residence on Estrada Street in the Boyle Heights neighborhood. It was a Spanish style home with beige stucco walls, white trim, and black iron fencing around the property. There was a beautiful flower garden on one side of the drive that led to the front door.

"Nice place," Angel murmured.

I nodded as I shut the car down. "Ready?"

Telling the loved ones of the victim's passing was always the hard part of an investigation. It was made doubly hard considering Sam was a cop. I couldn't help but be grateful that neither of his parents had been on the job. That would have made this even harder. We headed for the door, and I knocked.

After a moment, an elegantly dressed woman with styled gray hair opened the door. "May I help you?" she asked, a pleasant smile on her face.

"Mrs. Finlay?"

"Yes?"

"My name is Detective Kendrick. This is my partner, Detective Reyes. May we come in?"

Her brow furrowed and her breathing picked up. "May I ask what it's pertaining to?"

"It would be better if we could come in to speak with you where you'll be more comfortable, ma'am."

She opened the door wider, her eyes filling with tears. "Come in."

Angel and I stepped across the threshold into the foyer. She led us to the comfortable living room and gestured to the sofa. She took the chair.

"Ma'am, is your husband home?"

She nodded hesitantly. "He's in his workshop in the back garden. Should I... should I get him?"

"That might be best, ma'am."

We waited as she left the room and returned a few minutes later with her husband in tow. "What's this all about?" he asked as he took the second chair in the room, while his wife returned to the one she'd sat in earlier.

"Mr. and Mrs. Finlay, we regret to inform you that Sam has passed away."

Mrs. Finlay burst into tears.

"How?" Mr. Finlay asked, reaching for his wife's hand. "Was it in the line of duty? Did a gang member take him out?"

"We are looking into every possibility, sir. We will find out who did this to him." I paused, not wanting to tell these nice people that their son wasn't a good man. "I am afraid you may hear some negative things about Sam on the news, but we are trying to keep as much as possible from the public eye."

Mr. Finlay's face crumpled. "Negative things? What has he done?" His voice was barely a whisper. "What did Grant drag him into?"

Instead of answering him, I asked, "Were Sam and Grant close?"

He nodded. "Best friends, partners. When Grant was arrested, Sam—" His voice broke and he got choked up, unable to speak for a few moments. "Sam grew distant and wouldn't talk about it. He got angry at us when we questioned him about what we were hearing. I had a bad feeling... Does... was his death... did he suffer?"

"I hope not, but I'm afraid he may have."

Mrs. Finlay began crying harder. She got to her feet and rushed from the room.

I stood and Angel followed suit. "We'll let you see to your wife, sir. I am so sorry for your loss."

"Thank you." He paused, looking distraught. "Have you contacted Bethany yet?"

"No, but we will be doing that as soon as we return to the precinct."

"Would it be okay if we broke the news? I know Sam didn't treat her very well, but I think it would be better coming from us."

"Of course."

He walked us out and I got into the car.

As soon as Angel was in the car, I said, "God, I hate doing those."

"You'd think they'd get easier, but they never do," Angel replied.

We returned to the station. As I reached my desk, a voice shouted down the hall. "Kendrick!"

I gritted my teeth and spun around to see Jordan striding toward me. "What is it?"

"What happened with IA?" he demanded. "Are you suspended again? Do I need to reassign the Finlay case? Maybe you aren't qualified to run this case—"

I was pissed and seeing red. My fingers clenched. "I'm not in any trouble," I said, cutting him off. "If I was, I'm sure you'd be the first to know because you'd have been the one to send IA after my ass in the first place. And I am perfectly qualified to run the Finlay case, and you know it!" I shouted at him.

Heads swiveled toward us, and Robinson came out of his office looking irate. "What the hell is going on out here?" He stormed toward us, his face red.

"I was just asking Kendrick about the Finlay case and she went ballistic, sir," Jordan fumed.

I gaped at him for lying. It was obvious to anyone with ears that he'd started this.

Robinson narrowed his eyes. "I don't have the time nor patience for this crap. Brasswell, my office. Kendrick, Reyes, go home."

I nodded. He didn't have to tell me twice. I grabbed my purse and marched out of the office with Angel at my side. I was so pissed off my breathing was huffy.

"Don't drive angry," Angel said, slipping into the seat next to me.

I glanced over at him, and he grinned wide at me. I laughed. "Okay, Phil Conners. I promise not to drive us over a cliff like Punxsutawney Phil." I felt my anger leave me. Jordan was an ass, and he knew how to push my buttons faster than any person on the planet. That didn't mean I had to take the bait. I needed to work on that.

As I drove Angel home, he took out his phone and started texting. He had a slight smile on his lips.

"What is that about?"

"None ya." He typed a couple more words and hit send, then grinned, and slipped his phone in his pocket.

"Oooh, you chatting with your date from last night?"

"Yes," Angel replied, his eyes lighting up.

When I pulled up in front of his house, I noticed his car wasn't there. "Do you need a ride in the morning?"

"Yeah. Would you mind?" he asked.

"Nope. I'll see ya bright and early."

"Great." He got out and waved before heading up the walk to his place.

I headed home, but before I reached my apartment complex, my phone rang. I hit the Bluetooth button on my steering wheel and answered. "Kendrick."

"Hey, girl. Wondered what you were up to tonight. Wanna grab dinner?" Katrina, one of the women I'd bonded with in group therapy asked.

"Hey, that sounds good. I was just headed home. Let me change clothes and we can meet up."

"Great. How about Sushi A Go Go?"

"Perfect. See you in an hour?"

"I'll be there."

I hung up and pulled into a parking spot. I rushed up to my

apartment and made quick work of changing clothes, dressing in a fun sundress and sandals. I slipped my service weapon into my purse and headed back out. Forty-five minutes later I pulled into the restaurant parking lot and went in.

Katrina and I spent the entire meal catching up with each other. We both still did the group therapy Zoom calls, but we didn't really go into each other's lives on there. Mostly it was all about coping and dealing with feelings and the various things life was throwing at us. So spending time with her outside of those therapy sessions was nice.

"So, dating anyone new?" she asked, taking a bite of her spicy yellowtail roll.

I shook my head. "No. I haven't really been looking at dating, you know?"

"What about that hot partner of yours?"

Laughing, I rolled my eyes. "Angel is ridiculously hot, isn't he?" I grinned. "But you know I'm not going to become a cliché and get involved with my partner. Besides, I think he's dating someone. Well, I don't think, I know. At least he's been on one date with her and he's planning another. Plus, he's been texting with her."

"I don't know… with him as a partner, I might risk being a cliché," Katrina said, laughing, her eyes sparkling as she teased me.

"How about you?" I asked. "You dating again?"

"I've been on a few dates, but nobody special yet."

We finished up dinner and hugged as we made plans to do this again soon. I went home and settled on the couch with a glass of wine and the remote control. While I was watching a movie, my phone buzzed.

I looked down to see a text from Stephen.

You up?

Yeah. What's up?

A moment later my phone rang. "Hey, what's up?" I asked, turning the TV off.

"I heard about that cop being killed and I wanted to check in with you."

"Oh. Yeah. It's my case."

"You doing okay with it?" he asked, concern lacing his voice.

"Yeah, I'm alright. I mean it was a gruesome killing, but I'm not sure it had anything to do with him being a cop."

"So I don't have to worry about someone coming after you?"

I smiled. It was good to know he cared, considering he was pretty much the only family I had left. "No, you don't have to worry. I'm good."

"Good."

"How are you doing?"

"I'm okay. Work has helped."

We talked a little bit more about his search for Rick, which seemed to be hitting dead ends everywhere he turned, but he was determined to find the guy. After my sixth yawn, I said, "Hey, I'm gonna have to go to bed. Dinner sometime soon?"

"That sounds good. Be safe, little sis. I don't like worrying about you."

"I will."

"And let me know when you catch the asshole who killed that cop."

I smiled. I liked that he was confident in my ability to do that. "I will. Night."

I changed into my pjs, washed up and got into bed. I was asleep within minutes, but it was fitful. The stress of the job, and Sam's death, the way he died, led to nightmares.

I ran through the city, my heart pounding in my chest. I didn't have my weapon on me; I couldn't find it. I glanced down at my feet, bare and bloody, as I ran. I was only going to lead the killer straight to me. I had to get away.

I couldn't let them catch me. I glanced over my shoulder, but all I saw was a massive blackness coming for me. The flash of silver glinted in the moonlight. A knife. I pushed myself to run faster, but the figure kept the same pace as I did. I couldn't shake them.

"I didn't do anything. Why are you after me?" I shouted, but my words were carried away on the wind and faded.

"It's time to face what you've done, the actions you've taken." The words were faint, but I heard them all the same.

I was terrified.

The figure grew closer. It was catching up to me.

"What actions?" I questioned, not understanding. "I've been cleared for all my shootings!"

"Face what you've done," it said again, wielding the knife as it arched down toward me.

I screamed in terror as I tripped and fell to the ground.

8

CHERRY BLOSSOM PINK
MARCY

The nightmare had me waking up on my bedroom floor in a cold sweat. Luckily, it was before my alarm, so I had plenty of time to prepare myself for the day.

When we got into the precinct, I had a message from the coroner's office. Damien had made another discovery.

Angel and I headed there after I stuck my purse in my desk drawer.

"Oh good, you're here," Damien said, standing up from his desk. "So I did a more thorough examination of the body yesterday afternoon, and we got the tox report in just a bit ago too."

"So you've found something new?" I asked.

"I did." He led us over to the body and opened Sam's mouth. "See this?" He raised the upper lip. There was a smear of pink on the teeth.

"Lipstick?"

"Yep. Cherry Blossom by Revlon, to be exact."

"Okay, so he was with a woman wearing that lipstick.

How many in the greater LA area could possibly wear that shade? One hundred? Two hundred thousand women?" I deadpanned.

"Funny woman." Damien smiled.

A knock sounded on the door, and I turned to see Lindsey standing there, a file in her hand. "Hey. You here for Damien or us?"

"You, actually. We found something at the scene that may or may not have something to do with the case."

"Oh?" I raised my brows. "What is it?"

"There was a long strand of blonde synthetic hair in one of the blood pools."

"Now that is interesting. If it was in the blood, shouldn't it be part of the case?"

"Well, that's the thing. It's probable, but not absolute. It could have come from someone who worked in the bakery prior to it being shut down. You know, floated down from one of the shelves or something. But I'm leaning toward it came off Sam when he undressed."

"Have you found his clothes yet?"

Lindsey shook her head. "My guess is the killer disposed of them elsewhere."

"So we have a possible blonde wig-wearing woman with Cherry Blossom lipstick."

"It's a start," Angel added. "We should trace Sam's movements that night. Maybe we'll figure something out."

I nodded. "Anyone find his car?"

"Not yet. Want me to run a trace?" Angel replied.

"Yeah, and I'll find his phone carrier and see if we can get a data dump on his messages and voicemails," I suggested. I looked back at Damien. "What about the tox report; you said you got it in?"

"Yeah. Sam had both chloroform and ketamine in his system." He turned back to the body and pointed at a couple of red patches on Sam's cheeks. "See, this is from the chloroform. It soaked into his skin and caused it to rash up like that."

"So do you think he was awake for all this?"

"I think he was awake for some of it," Damien speculated. "Chloroform doesn't last long, which is why I think the killer added the ketamine. It takes longer to wear off. So he was probably dosed with both when the killer grabbed him and brought him to the shop he was found in."

It made sense to me. "So are we thinking this woman, whoever she is, was involved?"

"Hard to say. It could have just been a woman he hooked up with," Lindsey suggested. "He was a pretty notorious womanizer, you know."

"I'm becoming aware of that," I answered. "Well, thanks. Let me know if you discover anything else."

"We're still going through stuff from the scene. If we come across anything significant, I'll call you," Lindsey tossed over her shoulder as she left.

Angel and I weren't far behind her as we went back to our desks. We got started on our tasks for the day. I put a call in to the Finlays to find out if they knew what Sam's phone carrier was. It didn't take long to gain the information I needed, and I put in a call to the carrier. Before long I was sifting through thousands of texts. They'd also sent over his call list for the past month.

"I've got a trace on his car. He's got OnStar, so they're searching for it. Should have an answer soon," Angel shared.

"Look at this." I passed him the paper I'd been looking at

with text messages. "It's dated the night before he was found."

Angel took the paper and looked at it. He was just about to speak when his phone rang, and he quickly lifted the receiver. "Reyes," he answered.

I paused my reading to look over at him.

He hung up after thanking the person on the end of the line. "Got it. And it matches up with this text."

"So his car was left at Elixir."

"Wanna take a ride over there?" Angel asked.

I glanced at the clock. It was still early; there probably wasn't anyone at the bar yet. "Let's wait till after lunch. In the meantime, I want to do some digging into the ketamine. Maybe it's an angle?"

"You thinking the date rape angle? Think this woman with the Cherry Blossom lipstick is our killer?" Angel pursed his lips. "It's a bit unusual for a woman to use a date rape drug on a guy, but maybe as a revenge sort of thing?"

"Maybe so. I'll look into the ketamine, you keep going with the timeline using his texts and whatever else you can come up with, okay?" I handed over the paperwork.

We got busy, and half an hour later I had quite a bit of information on ketamine. "Listen to this."

Angel turned to me. "What is it?"

"It's from a blog called Future of Palm Beach about using ketamine to spike a drink." I cleared my throat and read, "'Ketamine can leave you unconscious very quickly or cause a loss of muscle function combined with a dream-like awareness of what's happening to you.'" I glanced over at Angel. "What if that's what happened to Sam? What if he was in some sort of dream-like state as he was tortured, unable to move or scream or anything?"

Angel shuddered. "It would explain why he didn't fight back."

"And according to Zinnia Health, you can buy one hundred milligrams of ketamine on the street for about twenty-five dollars. It looks like it could be bought just about anywhere on the streets, and you can even get it prescribed online from one of those tele-doctors." I was appalled. "How has Narco not shut this down?"

"What's it prescribed for?" Angel asked.

"Depression and anxiety. Various mental health reasons from what I can see."

"So there's no telling where our killer got theirs from, is there?"

I rolled my shoulders and sighed. "No, it doesn't look that way. Following it is a dead end. Maybe chloroform purchases in the last month might be easier to trace," I said, more to myself than to Angel.

"How easy is it to get?"

"I'll start digging." I closed out the tabs I had open on ketamine and started a new search, this time looking at chloroform. "Damn it," I muttered an hour later.

"What is it?"

"Look at this." My jaw ticked as I pointed at my computer screen.

"They just give you a how to guide on making chloroform?" Angel sounded as incredulous as I felt.

"Looks that way," I muttered. "Not only that, you can buy it with the right credentials. And how much do you want to bet it's sold on the street as well?"

"Damn near everything is these days, Marce."

"What is the point of banning stuff if this kind of thing is available for every crazy person on the internet to see?" I shut down my search. It was pointless and I was getting nowhere.

"How about lunch and then we go check out Elixir?" Angel suggested.

Frustrated with how things were progressing, I agreed.

Something in this case had to break soon, because I hated chasing dead ends. Surely this guy slipped up somewhere. He wasn't perfect, was he?

9

A POSSIBLE LEAD

ANGEL

"**S**o what sounds good?" Marcy asked as we got in the car.

"Burgers?" I suggested.

"D-Town or Jack in the Box?"

"Let's go to D-Town Burger Bar." It would give us a chance to sit down, and the burgers were the best.

Marcy didn't say much as she drove. I could tell she was still pissed off about the idea of those drugs being so readily available. I couldn't blame her when I knew at least the ketamine was used as a date rape drug. Narco needed to get on top of that. Maybe they would, now that one of their own had been dosed with it and then murdered.

She parked on the street near the burger place, and we went in. I ordered my burger with garlic parmesan fries and Marcy did the same.

While we waited for our food, we talked about the case.

"What do you know about Elixir?" Marcy asked.

"Never been, but I think a few of the Narco guys have

hung out there. If I'm going out though, I want a better atmosphere." I grinned.

Marcy laughed. "I should have known you'd never been to Elixir; you always go to The Short Stop."

I shrugged and gave her a rueful smile. She knew me well. "They've got great tacos right outside, there's no cover charge, and they have a DJ who plays good music. What's not to love about The Short Stop?"

She shook her head and smiled. "Did you take Callie there? You never did tell me about your date."

"I did meet her there, actually. We had a couple of beers, danced to a few songs, then got tacos. It was a work night, so we didn't stay late, but we really hit it off, I think."

"I noticed you'd been texting back and forth," she said as our food arrived.

"Yeah. She makes me laugh." She'd sent me some funny memes about living in California. She was originally from Indiana, so transplanting out here had been a big change for her.

"So when are you seeing her again?"

I shrugged. "I'm not sure yet. We haven't been able to match our schedules up."

"Well, I hope you get to see her soon. You seem happier."

She wasn't wrong. I felt happier overall. Things with Marcy were never going anywhere, so I had decided to leave things as they were between us. Maybe one day, if we were ever not partners, we'd figure things out, but as long as we worked so close together, I knew she'd never pursue a relationship with me. It didn't mean that I didn't still love her; I did, but she had been pretty clear that she wouldn't get involved with anyone she worked with. Jordan had fucked that up.

"Where'd you disappear to?" Marcy asked, eating the last of her fries.

I blinked and realized I'd stopped eating while my mind had been preoccupied with thoughts of Marcy and a relationship with her. I smiled and shook my head. "Just thinking about Callie." I finished my burger quickly and gulped down my soda. "We should go."

Marcy wiped her mouth on the paper napkin and tossed it on the tray before standing up with it. "That was good."

"It was better than good," I replied, pitching our trash in the garbage can as we went back to the car.

We arrived at Elixir within five minutes. Marcy parked next to Sam's car. "Crime scene is coming to get it, right?" she asked, looking at it.

"Yeah, I think they're sending a truck to come get it this afternoon," I replied as I pulled open the door to the bar.

We both flashed our badges as we walked in, and Marcy asked to speak to the bar manager.

The bartender nodded and headed to an office just off the bar. She returned a few moments later with a large man following her.

"Good afternoon. I'm Detective Kendrick. This is Detective Reyes. We'd like to ask you some questions about one of your patrons. Sam Finlay?"

"Yeah, I know him. He's here pretty often. What do you want to know?"

"What's your name?" Marcy asked.

The man crossed his arms over his chest, giving us a defiant look.

"Look, we're trying to keep things quiet, but Sam was murdered two nights ago, and we're tracing his movements. His car is in your parking lot."

"Sam's dead?" The man's arms dropped, and he looked shocked.

"Sir, what's your name?"

"Jack." He said it in an absentminded kind of way, as though he was suddenly unaware of what was going on. He blinked and came back to himself. "Sorry. Jack Hampton. I'm the manager. Sam was here two nights ago. He was here nearly until close."

"And you close at two?"

Jack nodded. "Law says we have to."

"Right. I only meant you didn't close any earlier," Marcy offered.

"No, we didn't close early. I'm not kicking nobody out until I have to."

"So was Sam here with anyone?" I asked.

Jack frowned, then looked over at his bartender. "Kindra, did you see Sam come in with anyone?"

"I think Parsons was with him, but he left around ten."

"Parsons?" I asked. "Derek Parsons?"

"Yeah, that's the guy." Jack picked up a dishrag and started cleaning the countertop.

Marcy arched her brow at me.

"Later," I mouthed. I looked back to Jack. "Did you see anyone else with Sam? Did anyone join him?"

"Maybe a blonde with Cherry Blossom lipstick?" Marcy added.

Kindra walked over. "Yeah, there was a blonde. I don't know about the lipstick though. She was all over him. Sam's big on buying drinks for women, and most of them will take him up on the offer. They probably would be better off if they didn't. He's got a temper and we've had to help a number of women get away from him over the last year."

That had me pausing. "Why? Did he hurt them?"

"He got handsy and wouldn't take no for an answer. We managed to get the women out of here and away from him."

"And the blonde?" Marcy asked, going back to the woman in question. "Did he get handsy with her?"

Kindra shrugged. "Yeah, but she was into it."

"Did they leave together?"

"I wasn't really watching; it was almost closing time, and I was cleaning up the bar. It's possible though."

"Do you have surveillance cameras?"

Jack nodded. "The whole place is covered."

"We'd like copies of the tapes from two nights ago, please," Marcy said.

"Sure thing." Jack dropped the rag on the counter and returned to his office.

"It's going to take him a few minutes to burn a disk for you. Can I get you anything while you're waiting?" Kindra asked.

"Got a cola?" I asked.

"Sure," Kindra replied and looked at Marcy. "You want one?"

"No, I'm good."

Kindra fixed my drink and set it on the bar top in front of me. "There you go."

"Jack said your name is Kindra?"

"Yeah, Kindra Martin."

I smiled. "Thanks, Kindra, I appreciate it." I tapped my glass. "Can you tell us if you've ever seen the woman before?" I asked as I lifted the glass and took a sip.

She thought about it for a moment. "No, I don't think so. But we get a lot of newbies in here that end up being one-offs. You know, they're just here to have guys buy them drinks. Probably make the rounds of the bars."

"I know Jack said Sam was here pretty often, but how often?" I asked.

"Nearly every night after his shift ended. He was a regular. Sometimes he didn't come in until eleven or twelve though, when he was working a case."

Jack emerged from his office with a DVD case in his hand. "Here you go. That's all the footage from every camera."

Marcy took it. "Thank you. We appreciate your cooperation."

"Sure thing. Do you know when they're holding the funeral?"

"No idea, but I'm sure it will be in the paper," I offered. "His parents will probably be handling everything."

"Before we go, was there anyone here, any patrons who were here that night?" Marcy asked.

Kindra looked at the few men who were drinking further down the bar. "Mike Bryant was, I think, at least for a little while."

"Mike," Jack called down the bar, "they're here about Sam. He was killed."

"Sam?" He stumbled off his stool. "Good guy, Sam, always bought me a pint."

"Yes, he did," Jack agreed. "Will you talk to them?"

"Don't talk to no cops," Mike slurred.

I pulled out my wallet and handed Jack a twenty. "That's for my drink, and get him a pint and keep the change."

Mike looked up as a pint was set before him. "Thank you. You're a good guy too. Just like Sam."

"Sam was here the night before last with a blonde woman; did you see him?"

"Yep. Pretty little thing. Ain't never seen her a'fore. Sam left with her."

"Did you hear him say where he was going?"

Mike guffawed, his eyes lighting with merriment. "He was goin' to fuck her outside." He pointed toward a side door. He picked up the pint and downed it in three gulps.

"Thanks, Mike. Are you hungry? Let me buy you something." I pulled my wallet out again and set another twenty on the counter as I looked at Jack. "Get him a good meal."

Jack nodded. "We'll take care of him."

I patted Mike on the shoulder and left with Marcy. We returned to the precinct and headed for the incident room. I put the DVD in the laptop, and we sent the footage to the big screen Marcy pulled down. We watched for a few minutes, speeding it up until we found Sam. I set it for four times the speed until the blonde came into the bar, then slowed it back to normal speed.

"She's tiny," Marcy murmured.

"She's definitely on the short, skinny side. What do you think, maybe five foot two?"

"Yeah. There is no way she could have taken Sam out on her own. If she's involved, she had help."

"So, we're most likely looking at the killer's accomplice."

"Yeah, and that's definitely a wig, and from her actions it's like she's not used to wearing it. See how she messes with it?"

I watched the woman smoothing her hand over the hair at her hairline. It was like she was checking to be sure that her real hair was fully covered. "She seems nervous."

"I agree. Can you grab a still shot of her and run her through facial recognition? Maybe we'll get a hit."

"Good idea." I pulled a screen shot of the woman and logged into the state database. I uploaded the image and waited.

"Tell me about Derek Parsons," Marcy said.

"Right." I turned in my chair to look at her. "Derek is a low-level drug dealer who works the Skid Row area. I've heard rumors that he was Sam's informant and that's why he's rarely picked up."

I saw anger flash in Marcy's eyes. I should have known it would piss her off. She wasn't a fan of letting people off the hook when they committed a crime. It was probably a good thing she was in Homicide and not Gang and Narco. Lines were blurred pretty often over there when they were going after the bigger fish.

"We need to bring him in."

"I'll see what I can do," I replied. Picking up the phone, I made a call to Gang and Narco. "Hey, Stone, it's Reyes. I'm looking into a possible connection to Sam's death, and I need to pick up Derek Parsons."

"What do you want with that scumbag?" Stone Murphy asked. "You thinking he had something to do with Sam's murder?"

"No, not really. He was seen in the bar with Sam the night of his murder, but he left around ten. Just need to clear him."

There was a pause on the line and then Stone offered, "Let me grab him up for you. I'll flip him to my informant since Sam's gone. It'll come better from me; he knows me. You go after him and he's liable to hit the wind."

"Thanks, appreciate it."

"I'll pick him up and have him at the precinct in an hour, that good?"

"Perfect." I hung up and looked at Marcy. "Stone Murphy is going to bring him in for us. He'll be here in an hour."

"Okay. Anything on facial recognition yet?"

I glanced at the computer screen, and it was still running. "No, still going."

"Then I'm going to start running names, see if anything pops on the people from Elixir."

"I'll call Lindsey about the status of the car, then check in with the people in Sam's life, see if I can fill out the picture."

We both got busy and shortly before four, Stone Murphy showed up with a weaselly looking little man who couldn't have been more than twenty-two. We joined them in an interrogation room and asked Derek about Sam and what he knew about the night Sam died.

"Look, man, I wasn't even there. I had nothin' to do with Sam getting killed. He probably pissed off the wrong gang-banger. He liked to shove people around, you know?" He sniffed and wiped his nose with the back of his arm.

"Kindra told us you were there that night, and we have the video footage showing us you were. So try again, Derek."

Derek looked at Stone, who nodded. "Fine, man, fine. I was just there to give Sam some info about a drop going down next week. Big shipment of oxy, coming up from Mexico. Soon as I got my payment and a few drinks, I was outta there. Sam was with some slut when I left."

"The woman, was she blonde?" I asked.

"Yeah, man. Long blonde hair, had bright blue eyes too. Didn't look natural."

"What do you mean?" Marcy asked.

"Her eyes were like super bright. Like, I don't know,

what's that color... you know," he snapped his fingers and then brightened, "like the shade of blue on the Royals' logo."

"The baseball team?" I asked.

"Yeah, man, I like baseball."

I looked over at Marcy, whose lips were pressed in a firm line.

"Sounds like she was wearing contacts," Stone offered. "You can pick up colored contacts with weird colors and decorations on them online. I've got some I use when I'm undercover."

"Anything else you remember about her?" I asked.

"Who?"

Marcy made a frustrated sound but stayed quiet.

"The blonde with the bright blue eyes."

"Oh, yeah, man. She had a bangin' body." He waved his hands like he was tracing an hourglass.

"Anything else?"

"I don't know, man. She was just a bar slut. There for the drinks and the booty call."

"Did she have an accent?"

"N-uh-uh. She sounded like all the other sluts around here."

"Okay. Well, thanks for coming in and talking to us, Derek."

"Sure." He looked at Stone and added, "Where's my money? You said there was a twenty in it for me."

Marcy's eyes blazed and her fingers gripped the pen she was holding hard. "You bribed him to come talk to us?" she gritted out.

"Not at all," Stone replied. "This is a doing business payment. I've got it covered." He handed Derek a twenty.

"Remember, you come to me now when you've got information."

"You got it." Derek took the twenty. "We leavin' or what, man?"

"Reyes, Kendrick, 'preciate it if you keep me in the loop on Sam. We're all pretty pissed it fell to you all to investigate, but we get it. We just wanna know who did this."

I nodded. "If we uncover something and it won't mess with our case, we'll let you know." I held my hand out to shake his.

Stone paused and gave me a hard look, but then a single nod as he gripped my hand. "See you around."

Once they were gone, we returned to the incident room and got back to work.

Ten minutes before five, my phone buzzed with a text from Callie.

> Hey, Handsome. :)

> Beautiful, how is your day going?

> Not bad. Actually getting off work early, thought maybe we could meet up for drinks?

> That would be great. The Short Stop at six?

> Perfect. I'll see you then! :)

> Looking forward to it.

As I slipped my phone back in my pocket, I looked up to see Marcy watching me, a grin on her face. "What?" I asked.

"You were texting Callie."

I laughed. "Yeah, I was. I've got a date after work."

10

GOING TO JAIL

MARCY

Angel still didn't have his car back, so I drove to his place to pick him up. After dropping him off last night, I'd continued to work the case from home. Not that I'd accomplished much. I went over witness statements, as well as all the statements Angel had gotten from Sam's friends and family. There didn't really seem to be anything in them.

I knew Sam was a dirty cop. He'd trafficked Selene, and possibly other women, he'd supplied them with drugs and who knew what else. It didn't seem like that big of a leap to think that he got involved with the wrong people and they took him out, but it didn't feel right to me. Besides, he wasn't working on any active cases, at least nothing deep. He'd run in a few low-level gang members, but they'd all bailed out within twenty-four hours. It was just busy work and an everyday occurrence for some of the offenders. Nothing that seemed to warrant a death like Sam's.

I pulled into Angel's driveway and honked. A minute later he ran out of the house, his jacket half on and his tie hanging loose around his neck. That was unusual for Angel. He was usually very put together. I arched a brow as he climbed in. "Late night?" I asked.

"Coffee. Need coffee."

Laughing, I waited for him to put his seatbelt on and headed for our regular coffee shop. "So how was your date with Callie?"

"Amazing. We danced and drank and talked until about one a.m. Probably would have stayed longer if we didn't both have to be at work today." He grinned as he tied his tie.

"She go home with you?" I tossed him a glance then looked back at the road.

"No, Nosy Rosy. She didn't and I didn't ask her to."

"I'm glad you had a good time." I pulled through the drive-thru and placed our order.

Once we had our drinks I pulled back into traffic.

He took a few swallows of his coffee and sighed. "So what's on the agenda for today?"

I pulled into the precinct and parked, but didn't open the door. I shifted in the seat and looked over at him. "I spent most of the evening going over all the witness, family, and friend statements. I think we're going to have to pursue the IA angle."

"You think it might be linked?"

"I can't see a gangbanger torturing him like that. They'd have just shot him. Same goes for a drug dealer—at least not the ones he'd been busting lately. They're all piddly misdemeanors, no major players trying to send a message. If this had happened after that shipment Derek spoke of, then I might lean more toward that, but..."

"It doesn't feel right," Angel supplied the rest of my sentence.

"Exactly. So that leaves us with his partner, and Selene Webb."

"So what do you want to do?"

"Let's go to the Metropolitan Detention Center."

"You want to talk to Grant Weaver?"

"Do I want to? No. But I think we need to. Maybe he'll have an idea of who might have wanted Sam dead."

"Then we need to call and make sure we can get in to see him." Angel pulled his phone from his pocket and dialed, then put it on speaker.

"Metropolitan Detention Center. How may I direct your call?"

"Hi. This is Detective Angel Reyes with the HSS unit. Is Warden Pelitars available?"

"Can you tell me what this is pertaining to?"

"We'd like to arrange a visitation with Grant Weaver."

"I'll let her know. One moment."

The phone buzzed and quiet music played for a minute or two as we sat there.

"Detective Reyes, I'm connecting you now."

"Thank you."

The phone clicked and a woman's voice came over the line. "Detective Reyes, why would the HSS need to speak with Weaver?"

"Good morning, ma'am. We're investigating the death of Detective Weaver's former partner, Sam Finlay. He was found murdered the other day."

"I see. We have Weaver in solitary for his safety, and he's being held without bond. We've allowed no visitors except for IA and his lawyer thus far. Considering these extenuating circumstances though, I think we can arrange it. He should be taking his morning meal about now. Can you be here within the hour?"

"We'll leave now." Angel nodded at me.

. "I'll see you soon." Warden Pelitars hung up.

"Should we go in first and check in with the captain or lieutenant?" Angel asked.

"Call Jason," I said, referring to the captain's assistant, "just to let the captain know where we are if anyone asks."

I pulled back out of the lot and headed to North Almeda Street. The morning traffic was heavy, so it took a bit longer to get there than I'd thought, but forty minutes later we were headed through security, after filling in the visitor forms, to speak with Warden Pelitars.

"Do come in, Detectives," she welcomed us.

I held my hand out. "Detective Marcy Kendrick, ma'am. It's a pleasure to meet you."

Warden Pelitars shook my hand. "The pleasure is mine. You're the detective who caught that serial killer, Nicholas Pound, the one who was mutilating his victims' faces?"

I nodded.

"I understand he's locked up at Atascadero State Hospital."

"He is. He was found to be criminally insane and will be doing life there, without the chance of parole," I shared.

"That's good to hear." She gestured to the hallway for us to walk back out with her. "I know you're wanting to speak with Weaver. I don't know how cooperative he'll be." She sighed. "He's a piece of work, that's all I'll say. Have you met him?"

"I know him," Angel replied, keeping his voice even and void of emotion.

"I know him by reputation, and I've met him on various

occasions where the two departments overlapped," I answered.

"I've arranged to have him brought to a private room. He'll remain shackled. Don't give him anything—not that I think you will, but I have to go over all the rules." She smiled and then continued to give us the rundown of how this would work. "Any questions?"

"No, I think we're good."

"Then you can leave your service weapons here," she gestured to the desk we were standing next to. "Officer Tooms will check them in, show you to the room where you can see Weaver, and when you're finished, he'll make sure they're returned to you."

I smiled at her. "Thank you, Warden."

"I hope you get what you need. Have a good day, Detectives."

I checked my Glock, pulled the magazine out and then handed both parts over to the officer while Angel did the same. Once they were locked up, Tooms led us through a locked glass door that I was sure was bulletproof, and then down the hall.

"Weaver is already inside," he said as he opened the door.

Angel and I crossed the threshold and Tooms closed the door behind us.

"Reyes. I wondered who was coming to visit me. They wouldn't say," Weaver said from the chair he was shackled to. "Funny, no one from my own department has been by to visit."

Angel stared at him. "This isn't a friendly visit, Weaver. We're here about Sam."

"That bastard? He hasn't been by at all." Weaver sneered.

"He's probably bangin' my wife. He dips his dick in anything wet and he's always lusted after her. With me locked up, he's probably fuckin' her like a rabbit."

I blinked. He thought his partner was having an affair with his wife? Could that have caused Weaver to put a hit out on Sam? Was that why we had a dead cop?

"Your wife and Finlay are having an affair?" Angel asked. His voice sounded neutral, as though he was making general inquiries.

"Who the fuck knows? I'm stuck in this shit can, for shit that shouldn't even matter. I didn't do anything but what she wanted."

"Who?" I asked, but I was pretty sure he was talking about Selene Webb.

"That little slut. I took care of her, and this is the treatment I get. Locked up while she plays the victim card. It's all bullshit."

I gave him a skeptical look. "Really? So you didn't rape her when she was just a teenager, get her hooked on drugs, and pass her around like a bottle of Crown?"

Weaver glared at me. "Who the fuck are you?"

"Detective Kendrick."

"Brasswell's bitch?" He snorted.

"His ex-bitch, actually." I stared at him hard. "So? You gonna answer?"

"You're not IA; I don't have to say shit all to you."

"True. You don't. So, if you don't want to talk about that, let's talk about Sam."

"What about him? What's the bastard done now? That bitch gonna get him the same as she got me? He was fucking her too."

"He was sleeping with her and your wife? He's a busy guy. How does he have time to work?"

"How the fuck should I know? I'm locked up in here."

"Right. Right, so... anyone else you know of that Sam's been fucking over?" Angel asked.

Weaver's brow furrowed. "Wait a minute, what's this about? Where is Sam? Did something happen?"

"You could say that," Angel replied. "Sam was murdered three nights ago."

Weaver's eyes grew wide and then a harsh look crossed his face. "Wow, wasn't expecting that, but maybe I should have."

"Why is that?" I asked. "What was Sam into?"

"You name it, Sam was into it."

"Yeah, but the way he was killed..." I trailed off and looked at Weaver. "It wasn't a hit. This wasn't gang related, or a drug deal gone wrong. It was personal."

"So we'll ask again, did Sam piss off the wrong husband?" Angel asked.

Weaver shrugged. "I couldn't say. It's possible." He had a look on his face that said he didn't quite believe that though.

"Or maybe there's someone out there who knows what the two of you were up to," I said softly, staring at Weaver, watching for any sign that he knew who killed Sam. "Someone who's decided to take the law into their own hands and make sure you pay for what you did to Selene Webb and the others."

Weaver's eye twitched just slightly and his lips tightened into a tense line. "Guess it's a good thing I'm locked up in here, then, huh? If that bitch is after payback."

"You think your victim is now planning her revenge on you and your buddies?"

Again, Weaver's eye twitched, but he didn't say anything further.

"Who are the others, Weaver? Who else was in your Circle of Justice?"

Weaver's eyes widened momentarily at my use of his group's name. "I'm not telling you shit."

"You don't want me to warn them that they could possibly be next?"

"If that biker slut is doing this, then she'll be the next one dead, not one of my guys. She's not going to get the drop on them."

"You don't think they deserve to at least know she's after them, or someone is?"

"And you don't know if that's true, so I'm not subjecting my boys to a witch hunt because of that biker slut's lies."

"Come on, Angel. I think we're done here." I stood and headed for the door.

"Wait."

I turned back and looked at him over my shoulder, arching a brow.

"How did he die?"

I turned back to the door, but Angel was still facing him as he said, "He was tortured until he bled to death."

I heard Weaver suck in a breath as I banged on the door for the guard to open it. A moment later we were back in the hallway.

11

DISAGREEMENT AND CAPITULATION
MARCY

"Did you get what you were after, Detectives?" Tooms asked as we walked back to the desk to pick up our service weapons.

"Not really," I replied. "The asshole is protecting his boys." I finger quoted the word boys.

"Don't know what good that's going to do. Selene Webb is talking to the Brass and the media, it's going to come out eventually."

I couldn't have agreed more. "I'm sure it will. The question is will it be too late by the time it does." I gave him a tight smile. "Have a good day, Officer Tooms."

"You as well, Detectives."

Angel and I reholstered our weapons and left the MDC. We got into the car, and I stuck the key in the ignition, but I didn't turn the car on. My mind was going over the interview. I wasn't sure what to do next. I knew what I probably needed to do, but I was extremely reluctant to do it.

Angel looked at me, obviously wondering why I was just sitting there. "Where are we headed, Marce?"

"Precinct maybe?" I said, thinking about our next step, or rather the step I wanted to avoid.

"We need to track down Selene Webb and talk to her."

I bit my lip. "No."

"What do you mean, no? Marcy, she's a key witness. This whole investigation could be turned around by talking to her."

"She's a victim, and accusing her of killing Sam or having any part in killing him is not on my agenda for today. I won't do it, Angel. She's been through enough."

"We aren't going to accuse her, but we need to talk to her. She's got pertinent information to our case. She may or may not be involved directly, but we won't know that until we speak to her."

I shifted in my seat, turning to face Angel. "The woman is fragile. Not only did she manage to break free of Weaver and his band of dickhole cop buddies, but she got herself sober and cleaned up and she's finally standing up for herself. She is going the right way about getting her vengeance on them, by taking it to the Brass and the media to hold them accountable. Why would she start killing them? That doesn't make any sense. I can't see how she would be connected to this except by the virtue of being their victim."

"All of that is true, it doesn't make sense, but until we talk to her, it could all be just for show so that she can take her real revenge. We won't know until we talk to her, Marce. You know this. You're empathizing with her, and I completely understand where you're coming from, but we're detectives, and this is our job. We have to question her."

I sighed. I knew he was right. I didn't want him to be right though. I wanted this case over. I wanted the cop killer caught. "Look, I know having a conversation with her is the right thing to do to catch whoever did this to Sam. And I don't like the idea that we may have more victims on our hands if we don't get that list and at least warn them. I'm sure IA has a few names, but they didn't share them with me. Maybe we could try them first?"

Angel tilted his head and just looked at me, his lips pursed. "Fine. We can try that first, but we need to see Selene at some point, and sooner is better than later."

"I know. We will. Just... not yet, okay?" I shifted back in my seat to face the steering wheel and turned the car on.

We drove back to the station in silence. Angel opened the door and strode toward the building without waiting for me. I hated when we argued. I knew he was pissed off at me, but he'd calm down eventually, and we'd be all right. We always were. And while I knew that he was angry with me, I also knew it was more out of frustration with this case. Neither of us wanted to see a cop killer get away with murder.

Following Angel at a slower pace, I entered the building and headed for the detective pool. I didn't see Angel and I wondered where he'd gone. Probably somewhere to cool off. I started toward my desk, but before I could reach it, Hummel looked up at me.

"Hey, Brasswell wants to see you. He was pretty adamant about it."

I shrugged. I didn't care what Jordan wanted. I wasn't ready to deal with him after just arguing with Angel. It wasn't even as though it was much of an argument, but it was still unsettling when we weren't on the same page. Pair that with the fact that we were all on edge about Sam's death, and it didn't make for a peaceful day.

I sat down at my desk and shoved my purse in the drawer.

"You aren't gonna go see him?" Hummel asked, surprised.

"He can wait. I've got things to do." I turned on my computer and waited for it to load. I was going to get my mind sorted before I went to see my ex-husband. I hated thinking of him as our lieutenant. I hated to think of him at all, honestly.

I pulled up my email and started going through it. I had a message from my therapy group about an upcoming session and sent in my acknowledgement of it. It was early in the morning, so I'd be there unless there was a new body and I got called to the scene. There was also a message from my friend Katrina about getting coffee after the session. Coffee sounded good, and maybe it would be better to get coffee with her instead of Angel tomorrow, considering he might still be mad at me.

It wasn't that Angel held a grudge; he didn't, but he could be stubborn. I knew I was as well, so I understood. And if the IA had what we needed, then I could put off the Selene talk indefinitely. That was my hope anyway.

"Kendrick! You were supposed to report to my office immediately!" Jordan's voice carried loudly down the hall as he stomped toward me.

I glanced up at him, leaned back in my seat and crossed my arms over my chest. "Don't speak to me like that." I didn't raise my voice and I tried to sound reasonable but firm.

"I'll speak to you however the fuck I feel! You're fucking worthless!" Jordan was screaming so much that spittle was flying from his lips and his face was turning redder by the second. "I don't know how the hell they don't fire you already. You cause us nothing but problems, shooting suspects, going off on your own, ignoring orders—"

"That is enough, Brasswell. My office, now." Robinson had walked up behind him and gripped his arm, turning him away from yelling in my face.

"But, sir—"

"Did I stutter?" Robinson's face was furious. "Now."

Jordan slunk off.

Robinson looked around, then turned back to me. "Where's Reyes?"

"Not sure, sir. He's here somewhere. We just got back from talking to Weaver at the MDC."

"Any breakthroughs with the case?" he asked.

"Not really, sir. We're still looking at possible connections from various parts of Finlay's job, but with the IA investigation, well, I can't help but think it all goes back to that. It's just a gut feeling. I think they're tied together; I just don't know how yet."

He nodded. "You are looking stressed, Kendrick. When was your last day off?"

I shrugged. "More than a week ago, I guess. Jordan's had me on call, on top of my regular shift."

"Right. Okay, take the rest of the day. Regroup and come at it fresh tomorrow. We can manage around here without you, and the Finlay case isn't going anywhere right now anyway. If anything comes up, I'll let you know."

I was surprised he was offering me the rest of the day off, since it was barely eleven. "Are you sure, sir?"

"Yeah. Tell Reyes. You both need the time." With a sigh, he turned back toward his office.

I smirked at Jordan, who was standing in Robinson's doorway looking mutinous.

"What's going on? I feel like I just walked in on the tail end of something, but I don't know what."

I glanced over at Angel, who looked bewildered, as every other detective got back to work. "Just Jordan being his usual assholish self."

Angel sighed. "Look, about earlier. I don't like arguing with you. It's just that I don't like knowing whoever killed Sam is walking around free and we've got a possible lead that we aren't utilizing. I also don't like knowing there are more dirty cops that we're basically trying to protect from possibly being killed." He shook his head, clearly frustrated. "It just sucks all around."

I blew out a breath. "Same. I don't want to go to her about it if we can get the info from IA."

"I get that. So did you put in a call to IA?"

"Not yet. Jordan was in a mood when I came in, so that kind of threw things off. You missed quite a bit actually, and now it's going to have to wait until tomorrow."

His brow furrowed. "Why?"

"Because Captain told us to go home."

His expression grew cloudier and more stormy, but he didn't say anything.

I knew how he was feeling. We normally didn't just take an afternoon off in the middle of a case. "Look, we're both stressed, and we've had a rough few months with, well, everything that's been going on. We need to decompress and come back fresh in the morning. Okay?"

He stood there for a moment, tense, and then after a moment said, "Yeah, okay." He seemed resigned to it as his shoulders deflated and his expression cleared. "I guess I can go pick up my car then."

"Is it ready?" I asked.

"Yeah. There was an issue with a couple of fuses. These newer cars have a shit ton of them, and when they go out it's like searching for a needle in a haystack. Anyway, that's where I was, talking to the mechanic. Think you can drop me off at their shop?"

"Sure thing."

I was glad that we were back to both being on the same page, at least for now. I've heard people compare cop partnerships to marriage, and they aren't far off. Of course, my marriage had sucked big time, but I wasn't against marriage. With the right person it could be really good. Partnerships were the same. When you had the right partner, it was great. Didn't mean you didn't argue occasionally—everyone did— but you usually worked it out, like Angel and I had.

"Wanna grab some lunch?" he asked as we left the station.

I smiled over at him. "Thought you'd never ask." I turned the car on and pulled out of the parking space.

As I pulled forward, Jordan stepped off the curb and in front of my car looking livid.

I slammed on my brakes and jolted in my seat. "What the hell?"

Angel looked up and noticed Jordan as well. "Brasswell. What's that jackass doing now?"

Jordan slammed his fists onto the hood of my car. "This isn't over, Kendrick! Not by a long shot!"

12

PUBLIC MISTRUST AND ACCUSATIONS

ANGEL

Watching Jordan storm off after assaulting Marcy's car had her pissed off. Me too for that matter. I didn't know what bug had crawled up Jordan's ass, but his behavior had escalated beyond anything that could pass for acceptable.

"You okay?" I asked, looking at Marcy.

"Yeah. I'm fine. Not so sure about my car."

"We can take a look at the repair shop when we get there. Get their opinion."

Marcy shrugged. "Yeah, okay."

She headed for an In and Out where we ate in the parking lot and then headed to the repair shop. When we arrived, I went in to talk to the mechanic while Marcy checked out the hood of her car.

By the time I returned, she was being seen to by another mechanic, who also happened to be the owner of the repair shop, Greg. I didn't want to interrupt, so I just waved to her as I claimed my car.

It was unusual to have a Thursday afternoon free, and I

didn't know what to do with myself. An idea struck me and, with a grin, I went to Giovanni's and ordered dinner for two. I knew Callie was working until close, but that didn't mean she didn't have time for dinner. I thought I'd surprise her. I also picked up a bouquet of flowers to bring her. She had said Gerber daisies were her favorite, and the florist had them in a variety of colors, so I had her build a nice bouquet of them.

I had texted her to see what her plans were first, so I knew she'd planned to eat a microwave meal around six, so at five forty-five I pulled into her salon's parking lot with the food and the flowers. I walked in and her receptionist stared at me curiously.

"Is Callie available?" I asked, looking around the salon floor and not seeing her.

"You must be Angel. I'm Rebecca. She's shampooing a client. Just a second and I'll get her for you." She rose from the chair and walked toward the back of the shop. A minute later she returned. "She'll be right up. Why don't you have a seat?"

I nodded and took a seat by the window. The salon was busy. Only one stylist seemed to be free, and she was flipping through a magazine. I noticed Callie with an older woman as she escorted her to a salon chair. She put a cape around her shoulders, met the woman's eyes in the mirror, and then pointed to me. The woman nodded and I could see her smile in the mirror.

"Hey. I wasn't expecting to see you tonight." Callie came over and hugged me. "Are those for me?" Her eyes lit up as she eyed the bouquet. "You remembered my favorite daisies." The smile that crossed her lips was angelic.

"I also brought dinner for two. I thought maybe we could commandeer your breakroom?"

"That sounds great. It won't take me long to fix Miriam's hair, if you want to go in and set everything up?"

"Sure, I can do that. Where do I go?" I asked.

"Hey, Rebecca?" Callie looked at the receptionist. "Can you show Angel to the breakroom?"

"Of course."

Callie turned back to me. "Give me ten minutes and I'll join you."

"Perfect," I replied.

We spent her break enjoying the meal and talking about our days. I told her how frustrated I was about not following the lead we had, but she actually sided with Marcy, saying the less trauma Selene was put through would be better for everyone involved. I could see her and Marcy's point, but that didn't mean we should just ignore the lead. The woman had the information we needed, and it was just frustrating that they didn't want to go after it.

Of course, I knew it was possible that IA had the same information and they were being just as tight lipped about it. Marcy had already been to see them once; they could have shared the information then. That gave me pause. It was possible that Selene hadn't given them more than Grant Weaver and Sam Finlay.

After the meal, I hung out at the salon and then followed Callie to her home where we watched a movie. I left around midnight and headed home. It had been a really nice day overall, and by the time my head hit my pillow I was out.

I woke at five and got ready for work. I felt more rested than I had in a while, and I knew giving us the afternoon off had been the right call by the captain. I had really needed it. I switched the TV on to listen to the morning news as I shaved. I spread shaving cream on my face and raised my razor to my cheek, drawing it downward just as the newscaster spoke.

"We have a breaking story this morning. Our investigative reporter Bill Meeks is here with Selene Webb, daughter of Stafford Webb, the former president of the Serpents Motorcycle Club, who was taken down by LAPD a few years ago. Bill broke that story as well, and now he's back with more sordid details of what happened to the rest of the people from the club. Bill, what can you tell us?"

I whipped around to stare at the TV.

"Well, Sheila, I'm here with Selene Webb, who was still a teenager at the time the Serpents were taken down," Bill said. "She has quite the story to tell, don't you, Selene?"

"Yes. It's not just my story, though. There were several of us women, girls really, who were coerced into a life of prostitution and drugs by the very men who took down my father's motorcycle club."

"Are you saying that LAPD officers forced you into a life of prostitution?"

"Specifically, Grant Weaver and Sam Finlay, yes. They called themselves the Circle of Justice. I was just a girl. I didn't understand what was going on and I begged them to not arrest me when they arrested my dad and his friends. All of us girls did. Grant said he'd let me go if I agreed to do—" She stopped and got teary. She shook her head and choked on her words.

"It's all right. Continue when you're ready."

"Thank you," she replied and then took a steadying breath. "They—Grant and Sam—would take me and some of the other girls to various apartments between LA and

Santa Monica and they would... they would offer us to their friends like... like we were a free pizza. They gave us drugs to keep us high and from fighting them off. We were literal prisoners."

"It is my understanding that you were able to get away and into a rehab facility."

She nodded, dashed a few tears from her cheeks. "I had help. A neighbor got me away and took me to northern California where I was able to get clean. Part of my therapy was to have the courage to step forward and face my captors. So I went to the Internal Affairs department and told them my story."

"And Grant Weaver has already been arrested and is facing numerous charges."

I clicked the TV off. This was going to blow up in our faces. I finished getting ready and rushed to my car as I hit the call button to see if Marcy had seen the news. I set it up to be able to speak through the radio and headed to the coffee shop.

"Yeah, I saw it," Marcy said instead of greeting me.

"This isn't going to be good for morale, or for the public," I muttered.

"I know. We're going to have to talk to her."

"I said that yesterday." Yes, it was an *I told you so,* and I didn't care.

"Yeah, you were right. I just didn't want to make it worse, but it doesn't seem like it can get much worse, does it?" Her voice was crackly as it came through my car speakers.

"I'm headed for coffee. You want me to grab you one?"

"Yeah. I'll meet you at the station. I'm nearly there. I'm going to call IA and see if they have what we need, but when you get here, I want you to call Selene. See if you can set up a time for us to speak with her."

"Sounds like a plan. See you in thirty." I hung up.

I pulled into the shop's parking lot and parked. The drive-thru line was long and I wanted to grab a pastry as well anyway, so I went inside. I got in line and waited my turn. When I reached the counter, Tina, the barista, smiled.

"Detective Reyes, what can I get for you?"

"Detective?" a voice said from behind me. "You're not serving these assholes here, are you? They're prostituting women and hooking them on drugs."

I turned around to see a young woman with pink, spikey hair, and a nose ring. She was wearing cutoff jean shorts and a white tee with Mickey Mouse on it. She couldn't have been more than twenty.

"There are a few cops who are involved in that, and I am not one of them. If you wouldn't mind, I'd like to order my drink and be on my way." My tone was sharp as I glared at her. I turned back to Tina. "I'd like my usual along with Detective Kendrick's usual, and I'll take two of the apple crumbles."

"Of course, Detective," she replied.

"If you're going to serve him, then I'm leaving. You've just lost a customer." The pink-haired young woman slammed open the glass door and walked out.

I sighed. "I'm sorry. I should have just gone through the drive-thru."

"No, it's not your fault. You haven't done anything wrong. Some people just like to make trouble."

She handed me my order and I put a twenty in her tip jar. "Thanks, Tina. I'll just use the drive-thru tomorrow anyway."

She gave me a small smile and turned to the next customer.

As I walked out to my car, I noticed there was spit coating the windshield and I sighed. Opening the car, I set the bag and cup carrier on the passenger seat and grabbed a few napkins from the center console. I wiped off the windshield and then threw the napkins in the trash by the door to the shop.

I headed for the station and felt the stress I'd been carrying for the past month descend on my shoulders again. Normally I loved my job. I loved solving puzzles, finding the one piece that unlocked the case and blew it wide open so we could find the perpetrator. Today wasn't one of those days.

"Why do you look like someone just ran over your favorite flower bed?" Marcy asked as I set her drink and apple crumble donut on her desk.

"Ran into a cop-hating woman at the coffee shop. Kind of ruined my good mood."

"Yeah? Well, get back in a good mood, Mr. Grumpy. I called IA."

I arched a brow. "Did they give you anything?"

"No, they confirmed that there are more officers involved. However, the only names Selene gave them so far are Grant and Sam. Grant was the first name and Selene apparently gave his name and told them that once he was arrested and she could see that they could be trusted, she'd hand over another name. That's how they got Sam. She said she'd release another name after he was arrested. They'd planned to do that the morning he was found murdered. So that put a kink in the plan."

"Without his being arrested, Selene decided to do a press interview?"

"Yes, and IA is worried that it will tip off the others involved and they won't be able to find them all. They'll get away with it." Marcy had a look of disgust on her face. "Anyway, they did mention that Selene didn't know all of the men's names. She was going to ID them by looking at police academy photos, and now that is out the window as well."

"She's stopped speaking to them? She doesn't want justice?"

Marcy shrugged. "I don't know what she wants. In her interview she said that IA had let her down. She claimed Weaver was going to get out and we were going to *back the blue*. Probably why you faced off that woman this morning."

"Probably."

"Eat your donut and then try and call her. Sympathize with her and tell her that we're on her side. We aren't backing the blue. We want the bad cops arrested because they're just making those of us who do our jobs look bad."

I nodded and picked up my powdered sugar-coated donut and took a large bite. It was filled with apple pie filling along with the crumbly cake. I finished it off in three bites, wiped my mouth and then picked up the phone. I dialed Selene Webb's number and waited.

"Hello?"

"Ms. Webb? This is Detective Reyes—"

The phone clicked and she disconnected.

I sat staring at the phone, then looked over at Marcy. "She hung up on me."

"Damn. I was afraid of that." Marcy pursed her lips and tapped a pen on her chin. She dropped it to the desk and yanked open her desk drawer, pulling out her purse. "Come on. We'll drive over to her apartment and see if we can get her to talk."

"Good plan." I grabbed my coffee, and we headed out to her car.

Almost an hour later, we pulled up to her apartment building. "She's in 104," Marcy said.

We found the right apartment and I knocked then stepped back next to Marcy.

The door opened slightly, and Selene Webb looked out at us. "Whatever you're selling, I'm not buying," she said and started to close the door.

Marcy stuck her foot in so she couldn't close it. "Ms. Webb, we aren't here to sell you anything. I'm Detective Kendrick. We'd like to talk to you about—"

"I'm not talking to no cops. I already talked to your watchdogs and look where that got me."

"Please. We aren't with IA, and we aren't part of Grant Weaver's crew. We're with HSS, Homicide Special Section unit."

Selene opened the door a little wider and tilted her head at us. "I'm not talking without my lawyer and Bill Meeks present. I promised him an exclusive."

"I understand you wanting a lawyer with you—that's your right—but a journalist? I don't know that our captain is going to allow that."

Selene crossed her arms over her chest and stared at us. "You want to talk to me, then those are my terms."

"We'll put it before our captain and then give you a call. Please don't hang up on Detective Reyes when he calls. I don't want to make another drive out here."

Selene smirked. "Then don't have him call. You call me."

Marcy sighed. "Fine. I'll be in touch, Ms. Webb."

Selene closed the door without another word.

We strode down the hall and back out the doors to the car. The drive back to the precinct was mostly quiet and I suspected that Marcy was trying to come up with a way to encourage the captain to agree to Selene's terms. I didn't think we should. The woman wasn't just a witness, she was a possible suspect in Sam's death. Though I wasn't sure how she could have done it. Maybe if she'd come at him from behind? But she was tiny. How she was able to then maneuver his dead weight after knocking him out was much harder to imagine.

"So?" I said, breaking the silence.

"We'll try to get the captain to agree. We need to know what she knows. She's really the only lead we've got. None of Sam's associates know anything. His team are closed mouthed and closing ranks. They aren't giving anything up. Probably they think they're on IA's hit list already and they don't want to draw any more attention to themselves."

"Can't say I blame them. Were someone in our department doing what they did, I don't think I'd be opening my mouth to volunteer anything other than I wasn't involved."

Marcy tossed me a look.

"What?"

"You and I both know that neither of us would sit quiet if that was going on in our department and we found out about it. We'd both be in IA's office telling them who, what, when, where and why because neither of us are going to support dirty cops. This whole back-the-blue-no-matter-what thing is just trouble. It makes us all look bad. I'm all for the thin blue line, but not when dirty cops are involved."

I shrugged. She was right. I wouldn't be able to sit quietly and let it happen either. "Yeah, alright. I wouldn't be able to allow it to go on if I found out about it."

"That's why we make good partners. We share the same values."

An hour later, after leaving a very grumpy Captain Robinson's office, Marcy called Selene and set up a date and time for us to interview her. I wasn't so sure we shouldn't push to speak to her immediately, but Marcy wanted to be accommodating to make her happy.

"When did she agree to meet with us?" I asked.

"Tuesday morning. That's when her lawyer and that journalist can be there."

"Great, so we have to sit on this over the weekend?"

"Looks that way."

13

A FUNERAL FOR A BLACK-HEARTED COP

MARCY

Saturday morning, I dressed in my formal blues. I was headed to Sam Finlay's funeral and then to the family's repast at their home in Boyle Heights.

Normally I wouldn't attend the repast for a cop I didn't know, but Angel and I were working the case, and everyone knew that usually the murderer put in an appearance. I might not recognize them as being the murderer, but then that wasn't actually the point. The point was to go and see who behaved oddly and if they were our possible suspect. I hated doing that to Sam's family, but it couldn't be helped. Besides, it would also give me a chance to speak to his ex-wife, who I assumed would be there.

Angel was picking me up to go to the funeral, which was being held at New City Church on Spring St. It was one of the larger churches in Los Angeles. It needed to be, since any cop who wasn't on duty would probably be there. Normally, the mayor would have an honor parade for the fallen cop, but with Sam's name currently mud because of Selene

Webb's accusations and public sentiment toward the LAPD at the moment, he'd decided not to hold one.

We arrived at the church well before the funeral was to start, and found a place to sit about midway in the congregation room. The pews filled up quickly and soon it was a sea of officers in their dress blues, standing at attention as Sam's casket was brought down the aisle to the altar. I could hear his mother sobbing at the front of the room, but I couldn't see her with so many people there.

I kept my eyes open for anything that seemed off, but as I did, I noticed some officers I didn't recognize. That wasn't unusual. There were nearly ten thousand officers in Los Angeles. We had the third largest municipal police department in the United States. The difference was, these officers weren't wearing the LAPD badge.

I tilted my head toward Angel and whispered, "Did Sam work for another city before coming to LAPD?"

"He worked on a task force with Santa Monica for a while. Why?"

"I noticed them." I nodded toward the two officers with the different badges.

"Yeah, they're from Santa Monica."

Santa Monica was only about thirty minutes toward the coast. Still, we didn't often interact with them. They did their thing, and we did ours. It was nice that some of them came out for Sam, even considering he was a black-hearted bastard.

The older of the two caught my eye. He was very handsome, with salt and pepper hair that was a little longer than his collar. He was close enough that I could see his eyes were light in color, but not what color they were. He was freshly shaven, but I suspected that when he had a five o'clock shadow, it would be the same mix of black and gray. He looked stern. A bit like the strong and silent type. I didn't know how true that was, since I hadn't met him, but that was the impression I got from him.

As the preacher continued the service, I let my eyes wander over the crowd, looking for anyone and anything out of place. However, I continually returned my gaze to the cops from Santa Monica. There was just something about the tall, broad-shouldered man that drew me.

We followed the procession to the Finlay home and parked on the street. Not every cop would be coming here, only those who knew the family or were friends or acquaintances with Sam.

Mrs. Finlay greeted us at the door with puffy eyes and a sad smile. "Hello. You're detectives, aren't you? The ones investigating Sam's death?" She sniffled and wiped her nose with a tissue.

"Yes, ma'am. I am so sorry for your loss."

"Thank you. Sam would be so happy with the turnout. He very much loved being a cop."

I gave her a tight smile. "It was a lovely service."

She nodded. "Please come in and help yourselves to the food."

"Thank you," I murmured as we slipped past her and into the foyer.

"Grab a plate and mingle?" Angel suggested.

"That's my thinking."

There was a huge buffet stuffed with various casseroles, finger sandwiches, crockpots with soups and meats, and desserts. There were pitchers with tea and lemonade and coolers full of water and soda. I filled my plate with a few finger foods and grabbed a bottle of water.

Angel and I walked around, listening in on the various conversations, murmuring various platitudes along with everyone.

The hair on the back of my neck rose and I began to scan the room to see if I could figure out why. It was the hiss of an argument coming from the two officers from Santa Monica. The deep timbre of the older officer's voice made goosebumps rise on my arms. Something about it turned me on and I was appalled at how inappropriate it was for me to notice that. Instead, I focused on the two men and what they might possibly be arguing about at Sam Finlay's repast.

"You said those two were from Santa Monica. Who are they? Were they close to Sam?"

Angel looked over at them. "Those are the Maldon brothers. They come from a long line of cops. They both work in the Gang and Narco Division in the Santa Monica branch. It's much smaller than ours, so sometimes there's crossover, especially with the gangs and drugs. I'm sure they often worked with Sam, which is why they're here. I know them from before, when I was working that serial that spanned the California coast about ten years back."

"Oh, that's right. I forgot you had set up in Santa Monica for that."

"Well, we weren't partners then." He shrugged. "I wouldn't do that now. I'm not working any task force you aren't on." He smiled.

I smiled back. "So, what do you think they're arguing about?" I wondered as the younger brother took off for the door. The older one watched him with an almost anguished look on his face.

"Don't know. Want to meet him?" Angel asked.

"Sure," I agreed, almost giddily.

We walked over and Angel touched the man's forearm. "Hey, Frank, how have you been?"

The man was taller than I thought. He was nearly a whole head taller than me and had a few inches on Angel. He gave us a half-hearted smile. "Hey, not bad, Reyes. How about you?"

"Pretty good now. Had a major car accident a few months back that filled my leg with metal, but I'm nearly back to normal. Was that Daniel I saw a few minutes ago?"

"Yeah, yeah. He's... he's having a rough time."

"Oh, I'm sorry to hear that," Angel replied.

Frank's eyes flitted to me with interest. "And you are?"

"Sorry, should have introduced you," Angel apologized. "This is my partner, Marcy Kendrick. Marcy, this is Frank Maldon."

"Kendrick. I know that name... You're the one who was all over the news a few months back, right? That serial killer case," Frank started. "Good work on that."

"Thanks. Yeah, that's me." My toes curled at the fact he knew of me.

We conversed for a little while longer, but Frank seemed distracted, his gaze repeatedly going toward the door. Eventually, he excused himself and left.

Angel and I made our rounds, speaking with Sam's ex-wife, Bethany, and his parents and siblings.

Nothing really stood out to me about the people who'd come to pay their respects. Well, other than Frank, but that was for an entirely different reason and had nothing to do with the case. I wondered if he was seeing anyone, and if he wasn't, would he want to see me?

14

MENTALLY AND EMOTIONALLY EQUIPPED

MARCY

Since we'd had Thursday afternoon off, and Sam's funeral and repast on Saturday, Angel and I were back in the precinct Sunday morning, bright and early. I wanted to go over who had been at the funeral and who hadn't. And those who hadn't, I wanted to know if it was because they were on duty, or if they'd chosen not to attend for some reason. Not everyone, of course. I meant of the people we'd expected to see, not Joe Smith who worked patrol and had only been a cop for five minutes.

"What are your thoughts about the funeral?" I asked Angel as we studied our board in the incident room.

"I expected to see more officers from Santa Monica. Only the Maldon brothers were there. I thought Jimmy Long and Marty Flint would be there too."

"Could they have been on duty?"

"Maybe. I'll text Frank and ask."

"You have Frank's number?"

"Yeah." Angel said it like of course he did and it's not weird.

"I didn't know you two were that close."

"We're not. It's just still in my contacts from before."

I stared at him, incredulous. "Do you not delete things ever?"

He shrugged. "Rarely." His phone pinged with a text message. "Frank says they were both on duty, so we can mark them off the list."

We continued going over various names until Hummel stuck his head in the door. "Hey, Brasswell is looking for the two of you."

I rolled my eyes. "Great." I gritted my teeth, fully annoyed now. "After what he did to my car—if it wasn't for the kindness of the mechanic, I'd have had a large bill to pay to fix that dent he left."

"He didn't charge you?"

"No. I told him my ex-husband did it to scare me and he said no man should ever behave that way and that he'd take care of it. When it came time to pay for it, he said it was no charge." Recalling the conversation, I smiled. "I told him he's now my mechanic for life."

Angel chuckled. "That was the owner, Greg Harris. Larry is his partner; that's who I was dealing with. They're both good guys and great mechanics."

"That's good to hear." I smiled and then sighed. "We might as well go see what he wants."

We both rose from the table and walked down the hall to Jordan's office. I knocked and waited for him to tell us to come in.

"You wanted us?" I asked when we entered the room.

Jordan was seated behind his desk. He had dark circles under his eyes and a tenseness about his shoulders. I could see new wrinkles forming on his forehead and he'd gained more gray in his hair. He looked as though he hadn't been sleeping and he was under a lot of pressure. I'd half-thought maybe he was calling us in to offer us—okay, me—an apology for damaging my car, but that was just wishful thinking.

"You haven't given me an update on the case in days. Where are you with it?"

I gave him the rundown of everything we'd been doing, whom we'd eliminated and where the case was taking us. Every word out of my mouth made Jordan's features tighten as though I was turning a screw too tight on him. It was odd, to say the least.

"So basically, you're nowhere. I should have known you weren't mentally and emotionally equipped to handle this case. I should reassign it."

"What? No, you can't just take us off this case, Jordan. It's ours."

"You can't handle the media circus that is about to be unleashed. It's beyond your capabilities, Kendrick. I'm reassigning it and that's final," Jordan said, but he was avoiding my eyes.

I knew he was hiding something, but I didn't know what. It didn't make any sense for him to pull us now. And his mention of the media just made me even more suspicious. I didn't know what was going on, but I didn't like it. Still, as the lieutenant, it was his prerogative to pull us from the case, unless the captain intervened.

I gritted my teeth. "Fine." I turned on my heel and marched down the hall.

"Who do you want us to give the case to?" I heard Angel ask.

I paused my steps, wanting to hear the answer.

"I don't know yet."

I rolled my eyes and continued down the hall to my desk. I was so pissed off I was seeing red. I sat there sulking until Jason walked up twenty minutes later. "What's up?" I asked, trying to keep my annoyance from my tone. He didn't deserve any of that.

Jason held out a slip of paper. "Brasswell told me to send you and Angel out. There was a drive-by shooting."

"Great," I murmured, taking the paper. I grabbed my purse and glanced over at Angel. "Ready?"

Angel nodded.

"You can drive."

I was too angry to get behind the wheel. I knew I would be aggressive driving with as much anger as I was holding. I needed to find a way to release it. I should have just gone to the range and shot a few hundred rounds. It would have calmed me down, but it was too late to do that now.

We headed for Saint James Park and the Portland Street Café. As Angel drove, I sat in silence, my mind whirling over the case we'd been yanked from. On a regular day, Jordan was an ass to me, always finding little things to pick at me over, but since this case had started, he'd been even nastier to me. I had to think him taking the case from us was personal, not because of the media circus, as he claimed.

He knew I wasn't mentally and emotionally lacking. I was extremely well adjusted. My therapist had even said so in his report to Captain Robinson. Sure, I'd had a little bit of a break-down, but I'd been holding onto a lot of guilt over Henry's death, and who wouldn't after something like that? As my therapist had said, it was natural to have some feelings of guilt. I'd worked through most of it and had been given the mentally sound all-clear, and was able to return to work doing what I loved. Jordan was just an asshole.

It took the rest of the morning and most of the early afternoon to interview everyone who'd witnessed the drive-by shooting and to get BOLOs out on the make and model of the car. Nobody had managed to get a license plate number, so it was doubtful we'd find them. We stopped for lunch at the Jack-in-the-Box and then returned to the precinct.

It had been a long and frustrating day so far and I was just ready for it to be over. As soon as I sank down into my chair, I looked up to see Jordan hovering over my desk, a scowl on his face.

I sighed. "What now?"

"I thought it over and I'm giving the case back to you."

My fingers clenched into fists. This man was going to drive me insane. Maybe that was his intention. To mess with me until I had myself committed. I took a few deep breaths. "Excuse me? You were adamant that I wasn't... what did you say? Mentally and emotionally equipped to handle the case."

"You aren't. However, you're back on it anyway." He spun on his heel and strode down the hall. A moment later his office door slammed shut.

"Nobody would take it," Hummel said.

I turned to look over at him. "What do you mean?"

"Jordan asked us if we wanted it and we all told him to basically pound sand, we weren't touching it. Then Robinson came out to see what was up, got pissed you weren't here, and Brasswell had to backpedal. He told the captain you needed a break from the case and it was too much for you."

"Bastard."

"Captain disagreed and told him when you got back you better be back on the Finlay case."

"I almost wish I'd been here to see him try and cover for himself pulling us off it."

I was darkly amused at Jordan getting his ass handed to him again. Though it made me wonder what was really behind him trying to pull me and Angel off the case in the first place. What was he hiding? It bothered me that I thought he might actually be hiding something pertinent to the case. But what on earth could that be? I knew he couldn't be involved in the whole prostitution angle; he wouldn't dare, because that would have messed up his chances of becoming lieutenant. He was always very driven to achieve. He wouldn't ruin it by becoming involved himself.

So maybe it was something else he was hiding. Was he covering up for someone else?

That was a very distinct possibility.

15

COLOR ME IMPRESSED

MARCY

My mind was still on Jordan and what he might be hiding as I got back to work on the case. I was determined to figure out who in Sam's life was connected to his death. Someone had to be. Someone had to know about his involvement in the Circle of Justice. Or maybe they were also involved, and I just had to make that connection. So I started doing a deep dive into every friend, relative, and cop who had ever worked with Sam and Grant.

It wasn't exactly my job to look into the Circle of Justice per se, but with the connection to Sam's murder, I couldn't just leave it to IA. While their job was looking into those cops who might have participated in Grant and Sam's prostitution and drug rings, I needed to know who was trying to either shut Sam up, or get vengeance for those he'd taken advantage of.

A thought occurred to me that I might also need to look into people close to Selene Webb who might want to take revenge on her behalf. So I added looking into her friends and family to my list of things to do.

"I'm going to grab a snack. Want one?" Angel asked, getting up with a tired sigh.

I glanced up at him. "I'm good for now. Besides, we only have about thirty-five minutes left on shift."

"I know, but I'm hungry and I need a break." He shrugged. "I'll be back in a bit."

I gave him a nod and typed another name into the computer. Devon Adders, age 27, LAPD patrol officer. He had been one of the officers who'd helped with the Serpents bust. I dug into his life. Married a year earlier, a daughter born two months ago. Pretty wife, modest home... nothing hinky popped up about him. I moved on to the next name.

As I began typing, someone walked up to my desk and stopped.

I trailed my eyes up the thick thighs encased in denim, hard torso wrapped in a white T-shirt that fit like a second skin, to the handsome and rugged face of Frank Maldon. Only problem was that his face was wracked with concern and worry. I tilted my head and said, "Frank? What's up?"

He ran a hand through his thick salt and pepper hair, his lips pressed in a thin line as he looked about the detective pool, then back down to me. "You're working Sam's murder."

"Yes," I said cautiously.

He glanced around the room again, looking agitated. His voice dropped a little as he said, "Can we go somewhere private and talk?"

I leaned back in my chair and studied him for a moment before getting up. "Okay, sure. Come with me." I led him to the incident room Angel and I were using. There wasn't anything there that we needed to keep from him. At least I was fairly certain. His name hadn't popped up as anyone associated with Sam and Grant's activities.

"Do you have information about Sam?" I asked as I closed the door behind us.

"I have information on some of the men who are part of the Circle of Justice," he said quietly, his dark eyes looking troubled.

His words surprised me. "Have you told IA? I'm not investigating the Circle."

He narrowed his eyes. They became hooded as he stared at me. "You and I both know that Sam's death is related to that damn Circle. Don't play me, Detective Kendrick."

My lips twitched. "Okay, you're not wrong. I am pretty damn sure that Sam's death had something to do with him being involved in that group. However, I don't know if his killer is looking to avenge those women or was trying to shut him up and keep him from talking." I crossed my arms over my chest. "You really need to take this information to IA."

He ran his large hand through his hair again, letting it flop over his forehead. "That's where I just came from. I've already told them everything I know."

I was impressed that he had the guts to come forward. It wasn't easy to go to IA with information on bad cops. It was a good way to get you labelled a rat. Not that I cared all that much, but there were others who did or would care. I was never one of those who stood quietly just because it was a cop. Still, I was impressed that this cop in front of me had the guts to come forward. "That's good. The sooner we can get these dirty cops out, the better for all of us."

"I know. It's been a struggle though. Look, I want to talk to you about it and what it might mean for your investigation, but I have to get back to Santa Monica. I'm expected for dinner at my folks' place, and I can't be late. Can we meet up tomorrow?"

I was disappointed that he didn't want to talk now, and I hesitated.

"I'm not trying to drag it out, I promise. It's just a lot to go over and I'm not really comfortable sharing what I know with you here at the precinct. Too many people might make the connection between me being here and IA coming out with more names soon."

Slowly, I nodded. "You want to keep your involvement quiet. I can respect that. Okay, we can meet tomorrow after work, if that works for you?"

"Name the time and place and I'll be there."

I didn't want him to have to drive all the way into central LA to meet with me, so I suggested a place about halfway between Santa Monica and central LA. "How about Blue Bottle Coffee on Santa Monica Boulevard around six-thirty?"

"Yeah, that works for me." He held out his hand.

I put my hand in his and felt a spark of electricity jump between us. I smiled at him, and we lingered with our hands linked for a moment longer than necessary. "See you tomorrow?"

He nodded and, with seeming reluctance, pulled his hand free. "Until tomorrow, Detective Kendrick."

"Marcy. Please," I offered.

"Marcy." His lips curved up into a roguish smile.

The way my name rolled off his tongue had heat pooling in my stomach. I swallowed hard and felt my cheeks getting hot. "Bye," I murmured.

He opened the door and gave me a two-fingered salute as he left.

I followed and walked to my desk in the detective pool,

enjoying the view as I stared after him. He had a very nice backside. And that spark that I'd felt when he'd held my hand... he had my libido doing a tap dance. Of course, I knew in my head it was a bad idea to get involved with another cop. Been there, done that, have the divorce papers to prove it was a bad idea. Still, there was something about the man.

"Was that Frank Maldon?" Angel asked, walking up next to me with a bag of popcorn.

I took a handful and popped it in my mouth as I nodded.

"What did he want?"

My eyes traveled the room, noticing others listening in on our conversation. "Nothing, really. He wanted to see what we had on Sam's murder."

Angel frowned, his brow furrowing. "Why? He and Sam weren't exactly friends."

I shrugged and then, because I didn't like keeping things from Angel, I added in a hushed whisper, "He's got information for us, but didn't want to share here."

"Oh," Angel breathed out as I took another handful of the popcorn. "You know I'd have gotten you a bag if you'd said you wanted some." He snatched the bag out of my reach.

I laughed. "I just want a few pieces. Come on, Angel, share." I pouted at him.

Sighing, he handed over the bag. "You got plans tonight?"

"Dinner for one, a glass of wine, and a hot bath. You?"

His smile grew to a full-blown grin. "I'm meeting Callie at Le Petit Paris."

"Fancy, fancy. Things getting hot and heavy between you

two?" I queried, arching a brow at him as I stole another handful of popcorn.

He rolled his eyes. "We're taking it slow, but I really like her. She's special."

The fact that Angel had found someone special warmed my heart. He deserved to have a good woman in his life. I did feel a pang of jealousy that it wasn't me, but even if he had been interested in me, I still didn't think it was a good idea for us to date. We had a good partnership. He was pretty much my best friend. I didn't want to ruin it by getting involved with him in that way.

As I thought about relationships, Frank's face flitted through my mind. The man was sexy and pushed all my buttons in the right way. The only thing working against him was that he was a cop. Granted, he was Santa Monica PD, not LAPD, so if things blew up, I wouldn't have to see him every day. Of course, that was even if he was interested in me in the way I was thinking about him.

I wondered if we could make a relationship work with us living and working in different areas. I rarely made it over to Santa Monica. As pretty as it was, it just wasn't all that convenient for my life. My days off were generally filled with errands and cleaning up my apartment, or spending time with Stephen, Katrina, Lindsey, or a handful of other friends. I supposed I could find time to spend with Frank, but did I really want to? That was the question.

"You okay?" Angel nudged my shoulder.

"What?" I blinked and then realized I must have spaced out for a minute. "Oh, yeah, I'm fine." I glanced at the clock; it was two minutes to five. "Let's clean this stuff up and head out."

"Sounds good." Angel crumpled up his popcorn bag and tossed it in the garbage can.

I set about straightening my desk and then turned off my computer. I debated taking some of my research home, but figured it would still be waiting for me in the morning. I grabbed my purse and walked out with Angel. "See you in the morning. Have a good time with Callie."

Angel grinned. "I plan to."

Climbing into my car, I turned on the radio. I spun the dial until it got to 113 so I could listen to some power rock from the eighties and nineties. As I drove and sang along to Bon Jovi's "Living on a Prayer", I debated what to eat for dinner.

Just as I was about to pull into the parking lot near Hollywood Burger, my phone rang. I hit the Bluetooth button as I pulled into a parking space and answered. "Hey, Lindsey, what's up?"

"Hey. I wondered if you were busy. I was headed to grab food and thought you might wanna meet me if you didn't have plans."

"Sure, where at?" I asked, pulling back out of the space and onto Palm Ave.

"How about Anajak?"

"The Thai place on Ventura Boulevard? Sure, that sounds great. I'm over in West Hollywood, so it will take me about thirty minutes." I got back on Santa Monica Boulevard.

"See you there."

I hung up, pulled back onto the 101, and turned the car toward Ventura. Suddenly my evening wasn't looking so bad. Good food, good friend, good conversation—who could ask for more?

Unfortunately, that wasn't how my evening went. Halfway to Anajak, I had to slam on my brakes to miss hitting the car in front of me. They yanked hard on their steering wheel, but it wasn't enough to keep them from hitting the group of cars in front of them.

"Shit!" I muttered, grabbing my radio. "This is Detective Kendrick. Accident on Ventura, seven cars, possible injuries. Send patrol. Tell them I'm on the scene." I dropped the radio back in its holder and rushed to start helping people.

16

A NIGHTMARE OF A CALL

MARCY

Someone shook my shoulder and I opened my eyes to see my brother hovering over me.

Stephen put his hand over my mouth and held his finger to his lips. "Come with me," he whispered, pulling me from my bed.

Trembling, I climbed from my bed as I heard Mom scream. My eyes widened. I opened my mouth to call out to her, but Stephen wrapped his arm around my neck and put his hand over my mouth as he dragged me into Mom's bedroom. I struggled against him, wanting to go and help her. I knew I could. I was an LAPD homicide detective. I had a gun. I could deal with whoever was attacking her.

Suddenly I found myself shoved under Mom's bed. A moment later Mom ran into the room and attempted to shut the door against whoever was out there. They were strong though, too strong for Mom. I gasped as I recognized Nicholas Pound standing in the room.

"Marcy, come play with me," he called. "We're the same, you

and I... You know you want to play with me." His voice was a
seductive whisper.

A phone rang somewhere in the room. Persistent. I wondered
if it was mine.

Nick, Stephen, and my mom faded away, but the ringing
continued. I slid my hand along the floor, looking for the phone,
but it felt wrong. It was soft and squishy, not hard wood. The
sound of the phone stopped, and I began to move, wiggling about
on the squishy floor, but my legs were bound, and I was strug-
gling. I heaved myself forward and suddenly I was falling . . .

I woke with a pounding headache. I was on the floor, my
legs tangled up in the sheets from the bed. My cellphone on
the bedside table started ringing with the chorus of *Calling
All Angels* by Train.

I shoved the tangled sheets off my legs and sat up.
Reaching for my cell, I said, "Angel? What's going on?"

"Sorry to wake you, but we've got a problem."

I rubbed my face, trying to wake up more fully. I glanced
at the clock; it was two forty-three in the morning. "Do we
have another body?"

"No, we have video footage of the killer torturing Sam on
social media."

I gasped. "What?" That definitely woke me up. "Where?"

"It's everywhere. It's really ugly, Marce. Sadistic. Tech is
trying to work with the various sites to get it taken down, but
it keeps getting reuploaded."

I stood up and headed for my laptop. "What do I type in
to find it?" I logged in and pulled up my Facebook account.

"LAPD Cop should do it."

I typed it into the search and sure enough the video
came up. "Found it. Don't hang up."

"I won't."

I took a deep breath and clicked the video. It started with a shot of a man and a woman getting hot and heavy against a building. A moment later, I watched as the killer wrapped a towel around Sam's face, then injected him with something, possibly the ketamine. The film was very shaky as the killer struggled with the body. I noticed there wasn't any sound, but I could tell that the woman had been a part of this. She didn't scream or try to get away; instead, she helped the killer with the body. The problem was that her face was blurred out and replaced with a smiling emoji.

I paused the video. "So we were right about the woman being involved."

"Looks that way, at least in the beginning. Keep watching."

I pushed play again and the film continued. Once Sam's body was in the back of a van, the killer handed the woman a stack of money.

"Fuck," I muttered.

The film jumped time and suddenly we could see Sam tied to a chair. Not only that, there was now sound. I paused it again, pushed it back ten seconds and began to listen.

"What is the Circle of Justice?" a voice asked, but it was computerized, so nothing we could use to identify the killer.

When Sam didn't answer, the killer tazed him, shocking his body until it convulsed.

Suddenly my phone buzzed in my hand. I hit pause on the video as I looked at it. "Hey, Captain is calling. One sec," I said into the phone and then clicked over to answer the captain's call. "Hey, Captain Robison. Angel's already got me on it."

"Good. Tried your landline earlier. You didn't answer. Was afraid you were out."

"No, just sleeping pretty rough. Sorry I didn't get it in time."

"No problem. As long as you two are on it. We've already got the tech department trying to take down the videos, but they keep popping up from other accounts."

"I'm just watching it now. Haven't seen it all the way through yet."

"It's not pretty, I can tell you that."

"Angel said the same, sir."

"I'm already at the station. Come see me when you get in."

"Will do, sir." I clicked off with him and back over to Angel. "I'm back. Captain wanted to make sure I knew what was going on."

"Yeah, he said he tried calling you first, but when you didn't answer he called me."

"I was out cold. Hey, what were you doing up?" I asked suspiciously.

"I'd just gotten home about twenty minutes before. Hadn't gotten to bed yet."

"And now you aren't getting to bed at all," I replied.

"Nope, probably not. Worth it though."

I could hear the smile in his voice. "We'll talk about that later," I said with a laugh and then glanced at the frozen video on my computer screen. With a sigh, I murmured, "Okay, let me finish watching this."

"I'll be here."

I clicked the button to continue the video.

"Answer the fucking question!" the robotic computer voice said.

"You already know! It's just a group of cops—" Sam gasped as the knife made another cut, this one along his groin.

"*What did you and this Circle do?*"

Sam shook his head, his breathing labored.

"*Answer me!*" The knife was dragged down Sam's bicep, digging deep as Sam screamed.

"*You know what we—*" Sam started to say, but the film jumped again, as though the killer cut out something Sam said. "*Stop! Stop... please...*" He had several more slices on him that were pouring blood.

Something flashed on the screen and his body convulsed again. It took me a moment to realize it was the wires from the taser. The killer had tased him again.

"*Admit what you did! Admit what a perverted, disgusting human garbage heap you are!*"

Tears ran down Sam's bloody cheeks. "*I'm garbage. I hurt those women, okay? I admit it. Please—*"

"*You don't deserve mercy. You deserve death.*" Another cut was made along Sam's thigh.

Sam screamed and screamed before eventually passing out, then slowly—and what I was sure would have been painfully were he conscious—he bled out.

The camera then showed a masked face. I couldn't make out any features, not even the color of the killer's eyes, because they were blocked. It was just a black humanoid-shaped head. "*I'm coming for all of you. Death will find you wherever you are, and you will pay for what you've done.*"

The video feed ended with a final look at Sam posed in front of the bakery window for everyone to see before ending.

"Shit." I blew out a harsh breath.

"Yeah. Did you notice anything in the video feed we can use to find this guy before he kills again? Because from the sound of it, he's not done," Angel asked.

"No. I'll watch it again. We need to get the tech guys on it, see if we can find some metadata in that video, maybe figure out where it was uploaded from. Maybe get an IP address?"

"Sounds like a plan. You headed into the station?"

"I need a shower first, but then I'll be on the way."

"I'll pick up coffee. Pretty sure we're going to need it."

I hung up with Angel and closed down my Facebook account and then shut down my laptop. Taking a shaky breath, I headed for the bathroom and a hot shower to loosen my tense muscles. The dream I'd had prior to Angel's call had already messed with my head, then watching that video... yeah, it was going to be a crap day.

I stood beneath the hot spray of water until it turned cold. Feeling somewhat more human, I blow-dried my hair, got dressed, throwing on a pair of black pants, a lavender blouse, and a blazer. I added my holster, checked my weapon, and slid it into place on my hip. I ran a brush through my hair, put on some mascara and lipstick, then put on my socks and shoes.

With one last glance around my apartment to make sure I'd turned everything off that I needed to, I headed out to my car. As I got behind the wheel, I couldn't help thinking back over the video. I felt like there was something I was missing. I would need to watch it again.

Instead of turning on the car, I pulled my phone out of my purse and typed LAPD Cop into the search bar again. Sure enough, about seven references popped up with the video feed. I watched the entire thing again, studying the scenes as it played out. I noticed that the first scene, where Sam was taken from, was in a parking lot. It looked a lot like the delivery area for the fish market over on Towne Ave, which was right next door to Elixir.

Was it possible that the woman and the killer had been caught on cameras out there? I'd have to check with the fish market to see if they had outdoor security cameras pointed toward Elixir. Maybe we'd catch a break and get a glimpse of the woman's face, or even the killer's.

I continued to watch and realized the van was white with some sort of logo on the side. I'd have to ask the tech guys if they could zoom in and search for that logo. When the film picked up again, Sam was already in the freezer. I recognized it from the scene. I played through that part again a couple of times, trying to look for clues, but I just wasn't seeing much. The film was trained on Sam, the knife and the taser. There were no reflections of the killer in any of the equipment or shelving in the freezer. Nothing that could tell me even if the killer was a man or a woman.

I thought back to the first part of the film, but again, even as the towel was wrapped around Sam's face and the shot was given, the person's hands were gloved and were just average in size, not really large or really small and slender, so it was hard to say if it was a man or woman. Given the struggle they'd had with Sam's body, it could have been a woman, or it could have been a slender man.

Sighing, I clicked the video off and set my phone aside. It was a good thing Angel was bringing coffee. I needed the caffeine fix like a junkie needed his next heroin fix. With my thoughts still on the video, I headed into work.

17

COFFEE SHOP TALK

MARCY

I arrived at the station in record time. Who knew traffic at nearly three forty-five in the morning would be almost non-existent? I dropped my purse in my drawer and picked up the coffee Angel had set on my desk, taking a blissful drink of the heavenly nectar as I sank into my chair.

"Is it still warm?" he asked.

"It's perfection. And yes, it's still warm." I glanced over at him. "Shower took longer than I intended."

"No problem. Captain wants to see us."

I nodded and took another sip of my coffee, before standing up again. "Let's go."

We were the only two from the morning crew in. I got a couple of nods from a few of the night shift detectives— Thompson, Reed, Ortiz, and Flores. I raised my coffee cup in greeting. We didn't often cross paths, but they were good detectives, and I was happy to have them on the team.

I strode past Jason's desk, since he wasn't in yet, and knocked on Robinson's door.

"Come in," Robinson called.

"Sir?" I poked my head in.

"Have a seat, Kendrick, Reyes."

I moved into the office and sat down in the far chair. "Has tech had any luck with the video?"

Robinson shook his head, rubbing his temple. I noticed that his wedding ring was missing, and he had dark circles under his eyes. A glance around the room told me the pictures he used to have of his wife were also missing.

"No, they're still working on getting all the videos down. For every one that gets taken down, three more pop up. We're not sure how whoever this is, is able to do that. They'll figure it out."

"Do we have someone looking at the metadata yet?"

"Not yet. Did you notice anything of importance in the video?" he asked.

"A couple of things, sir." I took a breath and told him what I noticed about the area from where Sam was taken as well as the logo on the van. "So we'll need someone to zoom in on it and see if we can trace that van. And we'll need to get over to the fish market and see if there are any cameras in that parking lot."

"Good idea. Maybe we'll get lucky," he said, sounding tired. "Anything else?"

I frowned and looked over at Angel. I arched a brow, asking if he had anything.

"Only that the killer was pretty well disguised, as though they knew that we would be studying the video and did everything they could to keep us from identifying them. Hell, at this point I couldn't even tell you if we're dealing with a man or a woman. I know statistically that it's most likely a man, but we can't be a hundred percent sure."

"My thoughts too," Robinson said. "That and the fact that we might have more bodies soon. More dead cops."

"Dirty cops," I muttered.

"Be that as it may, it's not a good look for LAPD," Robinson replied.

"I know, sir. None of this is a good look for LAPD, it's just... we have no idea who those other cops involved are. And now that this video is out for anyone and everyone to see, they may even go to ground."

"You're not wrong, Kendrick. Go have a talk with IA. See if they've got any more information on who was involved in this Circle of Justice. We need to know."

I nodded. It was a good place to start. "I'll see if I can get them to cooperate, sir."

"Aren't you meeting up with Frank Maldon today?" Angel asked.

My eyes flashed to him.

"Frank Maldon? Why are you meeting with a detective from Santa Monica?"

I turned back to the captain. "He stopped by yesterday, said he might have some information toward our case, but he didn't want to talk here. He was afraid he would look like a rat if others knew he was talking to me about Sam."

"If I remember correctly, Sam has worked with a task-force from SMPD on occasion. See what Frank knows, and if it's anything pertaining to the IA's case, try to get him to talk to them too."

"He said he was already talking to them, sir. That was originally why he was here, not to talk to me." I felt my cheeks heating.

"See if IA will fill you in."

"I'll give it a go, sir."

"Dismissed." Robinson tilted his head toward the door, signaling us to leave.

"Yes, sir." I stood and followed Angel out of the room.

"Let's go check in with tech, then maybe grab breakfast?" Angel suggested. "We can't do much else until IA gets in. And I think the fish market opens at six. I can go check that out while you talk to IA."

"Sounds like a plan."

We checked in with tech, who was stretched thin trying to get those videos down, but they were finally making headway.

"It's been downloaded about three million times though," Howard Bennet, one of our techs, said, pushing his black-framed glasses up his nose. "Not sure what to do about that."

"Nothing we can do," another tech answered over his shoulder.

"Howard, can we pull you to look at a couple of elements from the video?"

Howard looked over at his commander, who nodded. "Sure thing. What do you need me to look at?"

"So, at the beginning of the video, just before they toss Sam into the van. There's a logo on the side. I was hoping you could zoom in on it. See if we can locate the company and maybe find out where that van came from."

"No problem."

He began by finding the image, then took a screenshot and zoomed in on it. It was a colorful picture of several liquor bottles and the words Lake Arrowhead Liquors Inc. over the image of a lake. I'd never heard of the company, but

I knew Lake Arrowhead was near the San Bernardino Mountains. Originally it had been called Little Bear Lake, until it was bought in 1920 and renamed by the cooperation that bought it and the area surrounding it. It had been turned into a tourist destination.

Howard typed the name into the computer and then turned to us. "It's fake. There is no company called Lake Arrowhead Liquors Inc."

"Then how did they get a label like that?"

"Give me a second." He started typing away, clipping away parts of the logo and searching. "Okay, see here?" He pointed at the screen. "These are all stock photos, easily accessible to the public for a small fee. Looks like whoever made the label just used these images to make the fake logo."

"So there's no way to trace who created it?"

"Not really. I can try and do an online search for the label image and see if any printing companies have used it in their advertising, maybe as something they created, but that's a shot in the dark and it may take a while."

"Okay, well, can you give it a try and let me know if anything comes back?" I asked.

"Sure thing, Detective."

Angel and I left him to it and walked down the hall. Back in the detective pool, I grabbed my purse from my desk drawer, tossed my now empty coffee cup and we went out to his car. I climbed into the passenger seat and leaned my head back against the headrest. We decided to head for West Hollywood where we knew Norms Restaurant would be open and serving breakfast. They had buttermilk hot cakes that were delicious and calling my name.

After a very filling meal, we returned to the precinct, and

I went to speak to Lieutenant Hartley in IA. I knocked on the door and was welcomed in.

"Detective Kendrick, what can I do for you?"

"Good morning, sir. I'm sure you are aware of the video that's gone viral."

He nodded slightly, just a short and sharp bob of his head. "We are aware."

"So you can see why I'm here, then."

"Why exactly are you here, Detective?"

"Because we're going to have more dead cops soon, if this killer has his way."

He stared at me, his expression bland.

"I'd like to keep that from happening, if at all possible."

"And what does that have to do with IA?"

"You have to have the names of the cops who were invol—" I stopped as he shook his head. "What do you mean, no?"

"We don't have any more names. We're in the same spot we were in when last we spoke."

My brow furrowed. "But..." I hesitated. Had Frank lied to me? He had said he'd spoken to IA. "Did Frank Maldon come see you?"

That seemed to pique Lieutenant Hartley's interest. "What do you know about Frank Maldon?"

My heart started beating a little harder in my chest. "He said he came to speak to you yesterday afternoon. Did he not?"

"Oh, he did."

"And?" I dragged the word out.

"He came here. He said one of the cops involved had confided in him and gave him some information which he did share with us; however, he didn't tell me the name of the cop who had confided in him, nor any of the other officers' names who are involved. Makes it a little difficult to investigate, but I can assure you we're working on it."

My heart sank. "So he didn't tell you who was involved?"

"No, but I'm hopeful that he will come back and speak to us again. I'll give him a little time."

I thought about it for a moment. "You don't think he was involved?"

Hartley shook his head. "At the moment, I don't think so. We're looking into various others who are connected to him, trying to work out who might have confided in him, but the list is long and it's going to take us a bit to go through everyone."

"He said he might have information that will help my case, help me find whoever might be doing this."

"Did he?" He arched a brow. "What kind of information?"

"He wouldn't say. We're meeting this evening to discuss it."

"You come across anything we need to know, I'd appreciate a heads-up."

"Of course, Lieutenant."

He smiled. "You know, Kendrick, you ever get tired of chasing serial killers, you'd make a good IA officer."

"I'll keep that in mind, sir." I gave him a tight smile and then headed out.

I met up with Angel back at our desks. He'd gone to the fish market to find out if there were any cameras. The look on his face told me the answer to that before I even asked.

"So they had nothing?"

"Oh, they had cameras, but they weren't pointed anywhere near Elixir. They were pointed at their doors and toward the street. Only thing it captured was the van leaving, driving past on the street."

"So no view of the attack at all."

"Nope."

"Great." I sighed. It was going to be a long day.

I wasn't wrong.

We spent the rest of the day checking more into the friends and various people Sam ran around with, but came up empty handed. Tech got nothing from the logo search. And at the end of the day, we were still as lost as we were when we walked in the doors this morning. It made for a very frustrating day.

After work, I went to meet Frank. I headed down Santa Monica Boulevard, listening to soft jazz because it was relaxing. I pulled into the parking lot next to Blue Bottle Coffee and parked.

Frank was already there at a table when I walked in. I headed for the counter, placed my order and, once I had it, I went to join him.

"Hey." I set my plate and cup down on the table, then took a seat across from him.

"Hi." He ran a hand through his hair. "Saw that video."

"Nearly everyone on the planet has, I would imagine."

"Yeah." He sighed and looked toward the window. "It was awful."

"It was."

"You deal with that kind of stuff a lot?"

I shrugged. "Some."

"I guess most of your killers don't leave you video of them doing their killings though, huh?"

"Nope. Not usually." I picked up my coffee and took a sip. It was good. "So..." I started but as I said it, a busload of people poured into the shop, making the place not only loud but overcrowded. I glanced at Frank's face and he looked almost panicked.

"Can we go somewhere a little..." he trailed off.

"Less crowded? Sure, but where?"

"Would you mind following me to my place? I don't live too far from here; about fifteen minutes."

I hesitated. It wasn't as though I thought he'd try to harm me, and even if he did, I had my service weapon, and everyone knew I wasn't afraid to use it. I shrugged. "Alright."

He seemed relieved as he gave me the address, just in case I lost him in traffic. "I'll see you there."

I pulled out onto Santa Monica Boulevard, following him in his hunter-green Jeep Wrangler. He wasn't wrong. It took about fourteen minutes to reach his bungalow, a cute little sandstone house with a chain-link fence around it. I pulled into the driveway behind his Jeep and parked. I'd eaten my muffin in the car, but I still had coffee left, so I brought it with me as I got out.

"Um, welcome to my place," he murmured as he opened the gate for us. His keys jingled as he put one of them in the lock and opened the front door. He flipped on the hallway light and said, "Sorry, it's a little messy. I didn't know I'd be inviting anyone over." He started grabbing various bits of clothing from the furniture and picking things up.

I smiled. "It's fine. I'm not here to inspect your house-keeping, Frank."

He dropped the clothing he'd gathered into a pile on one of the comfortable-looking chairs and rubbed the back of his neck. "Yeah, I know. Errr... want to sit?" He gestured toward the sofa.

I took the offered seat and looked at him expectantly.

When he didn't say anything, I decided to just ask straight out. "So, what's going on? I went to speak to IA today, given the video, and I thought they'd have something after talking to you, but they said you didn't really give them much."

Frank frowned and looked down at his feet as he sat next to me. "No." He looked up at me, anguish in his eyes. "I gave them some information, but I didn't give them the name of the cop who told me. I... don't... I don't know if I can do it."

I reached for his hand and held it in mine, feeling that spark of electricity jump between us, but I couldn't focus on that right now. I needed to make Frank realize that by protecting whoever it was who confided in him, it could be exactly what got them killed. "Frank, I know it's hard to talk to IA about those who aren't doing what they're supposed to be doing. The thin blue line is a tough one to cross, but don't you see? This killer isn't going to stop with Sam. Every officer involved in the Circle of Justice is on their hit list."

"His."

I frowned. "What?"

"*His* hit list. The killer is a man."

I pulled back and stared at him. "How do you know that?"

His lips pressed firmly together, and he seemed to have an internal debate before pulling out his phone. "Watch." He sped the video up until he got to a point where the killer was cutting into Sam. Then he paused it. "Did you see it?"

"Play it again." I had no idea what he was talking about. I watched as he played it in slow motion. A hand covered in black latex-style gloves dragged a knife down Sam's bicep. "It looks like a hand. Average sized, could be a man's or a woman's."

"No." He paused it again. "Right there. See it?" He

pointed to a flash of silver that was only visible for a moment as the sleeve of the killer's sweatshirt moved.

I narrowed my eyes as I watched. "Can you slow it down more?"

Frank did as I asked.

"It's a watch."

"Yeah. A men's watch."

I frowned at him. "Are you sure?"

"Pretty sure, yeah. Look at the size of the face. Look at the band around the wrist. It's wider than a woman's."

"Okay, I can go with that. It's a men's watch, but... still could be a woman."

"Maybe. But I doubt it. Did you also notice the dark arm hair?"

He hit play again and, on super-slow motion, I noticed the narrow bit of flesh with the coarse dark hair showing for a micro-second. The skin was tanned as well.

"See?"

"Yeah, I think you're right. The killer is a man." I glanced at him as he put his phone away. "That still doesn't tell me why you wanted to see me."

"I know. I just... well, I was going to talk to you about what Sam was into. The person who confided in me told me Sam was the one who was driving these women between LA and Santa Monica. He was also the one providing them with drugs. That it was still going on after Selene got free, and... that there may still be women stashed somewhere."

"What?" I gasped. "Frank, we need to find them."

He pursed his lips. "I know. I'm trying to get my friend to turn themselves in and share what they know, what they're involved in. I already gave IA the location of where my friend said the women were. Or where they thought they were. I'm hoping they will recover them."

I stared at him. "Do you think Selene already gave them the information?"

"No, my friend said Selene wouldn't know the location. It was new, only used after she escaped. Weaver expected Selene to spill her guts, and he didn't want anything that she could actually tie to him. Still, she must have given IA something because they arrested him."

I nodded. "They were about to arrest Sam too."

"That's what they told me when I spoke to them. I just couldn't give them any names. I can't rat out a fellow cop; it doesn't seem right."

I grabbed his hand again and moved closer, our knees touching. "Look, Frank, these aren't fellow cops. They're dirty. They're worse than the criminals we go after every day. They give those of us who take pride in doing the job right a bad name. We're here to protect and serve the people. These cops aren't. They're using their positions to use and abuse women."

"I know, but you don't understand how hard it is... I've... I've known them a long time. They aren't a bad person, they just... they got in over their head..."

I sighed, squeezing his hand in mine. "If they weren't directly involved, they might just lose their job and not face any criminal charges, but Frank, you can't keep this secret for long. It's going to come out. If anything, telling IA might protect them from whoever this killer is."

Frank nodded. His thumb stroked over the back of my hand thoughtfully. "I know you're right."

"Please talk to Lieutenant Hartley. He's a good man."

His lips twisted up in a half smile. "I almost feel a stab of jealousy."

I bit back a smile. "Oh?"

He nodded. "I like you, Marcy. You're a beautiful, strong, smart woman. Brasswell was an idiot to let you go."

"Yeah, well, he didn't have much of a choice when I served him with divorce papers." I snorted.

Frank smiled. "His loss."

I drew my hand free of his and stood up. "I should probably go."

Frank stood up as well. "Sorry, didn't mean to make it awkward."

I put my hand on his arm, noticing that he also had dark hair on his forearm, but no watch. Plus, he was taller than the person in the video, from what I could tell. My eyes flashed up to his. "You didn't. I like you too, Frank. I just think you have some things to think over and maybe right this moment isn't a good time to do this?" I waved my hand between us.

He gave me a rueful smile. "I get it. Bad timing. You're not... are you seeing anyone?"

I smiled as I moved to the door. "I'm single, if that's what you're asking. Goodbye, Frank." I opened the door and waved to him as I headed to my car.

He stood in the doorway and watched until I could no longer see him in my rearview mirror.

I hoped that he made the right decision and told IA who had confided in him. I wanted him to have a clear conscience and I was afraid that whatever he knew was going to eat at him until it drove him mad. I really didn't want to see that happen. I liked him too much. Much more than I would have imagined for having known him for such a short amount of time. I wondered if he was as interested in me as I was in him.

Then it occurred to me that it might be a bad idea getting involved with someone connected to my case. Take Henry for instance. He'd gotten killed because of me. I wasn't sure if my heart could take another death like that, but maybe dating Frank would be different.

I had to have hope, right?

18

A TERRIFIED VICTIM

MARCY

"So where are we headed?" Angel asked the next morning as we pulled out of the parking lot.

"Selene is staying at the Holiday Inn by LAX. She wasn't feeling safe at her friend's apartment. She's in room 304."

"Wonder how she's paying for that," Angel muttered.

"My guess is with what she's been through, there's a lot of people willing to help her." I frowned and glanced over at him. "What's the matter with you?"

He sighed. "Sorry. Just all this is taking a toll."

"I get that, but we aren't going to victim blame. You're usually better than that. I don't understand what has you acting like she doesn't deserve our compassion."

He shifted in his seat to look at me. "Callie's getting some flak for dating a cop."

I shifted my eyes from the road to him. "She break up with you?"

"No, not yet."

"You think she will?"

He shrugged. "I don't know. I hope not. Just hard with all this going on. She says we can still talk and see each other, but she doesn't want me coming by the salon for a while. It's almost like we're sneaking around, and I don't like it."

I could understand that. Dating someone should never feel like a dirty little secret. Especially when the man was such a good one like Angel. I really hoped Callie would figure that out and not break his heart. "I wouldn't either."

I pulled off the 405 onto La Cienega Boulevard. The Holiday Inn was on our right. I found a parking place and we headed in, catching the elevator up to the third floor.

Angel knocked and a moment later the door was opened by Bill Meeks, the journalist Selene had been speaking to. "We're here to see Selene Webb."

"Come in." Bill opened the door wider.

We stepped into the small standard room. It held two double beds, a desk, an entertainment center, as well as a small table and chairs in front of the windows. Selene and a woman in a business suit sat at the table.

The woman stood and held her hand out. "Good morning, Detectives. I'm Adrianne Glass, Ms. Webb's lawyer, and I am sure you are familiar with Bill Meeks."

"Yes, hello. We're Detectives Kendrick," I gestured to myself and then to Angel, "and Reyes."

"I understand you have questions for my client. Shall we have a seat?" She gestured to the table and two extra chairs.

Bill sat at the chair by the desk, leaving the open chairs for me and Angel. After sitting, Selene moved slightly away from Angel, a look of terror on her face that she tried to disguise.

"Angel, switch chairs with me," I murmured.

He rose and said, "Why don't I let you handle this, and

I'll just wait over here?" He tilted his head toward the far side of the room.

I nodded as Selene began to relax a little more. "Ms. Webb. We aren't here to make you uncomfortable. Nor are we looking to accuse you of anything. We are looking into the death of one of the men you've accused of being your captor."

Selene glanced at her lawyer and then back to me. "Yes. Sam called himself my handler, like it was somehow better than kidnapper or abuser or drug dealer." Her voice was monotone, and her eyes seemed almost dead as she spoke of him.

She'd been a bit sassier the last time we spoke, and I wondered if something had happened between then and now. Had someone threatened her? Was that why she'd left her friend's apartment?

"Before we continue, Ms. Webb, has someone tried to intimidate you into keeping quiet?"

Her eyes flashed for a moment, and she turned to her lawyer.

"Ms. Webb has had a few threats, and we are taking every precaution to keep her safe," Ms. Glass replied.

"I'm sorry to hear that. I can assure you that we will do what we can to keep you safe as well," I told her.

Selene snorted. "Yeah, right. I know all about you cops and your thin blue line. You'll back each other up and I'll end up with cement shoes at the bottom of the ocean."

Shaking my head, I explained, "Absolutely not. I will not stand by and allow anyone, cop or not, to hurt you anymore. We are here to protect and serve the public, not each other. I don't condone what any of those who hurt you did, and I won't protect them from the justice that is being brought against them. However, I also have a duty to the public to find whoever killed Sam Finlay. And I need to make sure he doesn't kill any others."

Selene seemed to shrink in on herself. "What happened to Sam was awful. He deserved to pay for what he did to me and the others, and maybe even deserved death, but that was... that was heinous." She shuddered. "My dad... he was a violent man. I grew up in that life, but I never liked it."

"Selene, I know you've spoken to IA, but you've been reluctant to give them the names of all the men involved in the Circle of Justice. We really need to know who they are."

Her eyes flashed to her lawyer again and they seemed to have a silent conversation. "I don't know." She drew herself in even tighter, as though trying to make herself as small as possible. "They haven't even found the other women yet."

"Someone has come forward, so the police are searching for the women now."

"Someone came forward?" She sounded surprised.

"Apparently the cop who came forward was confided in by one of the men involved, and he went to Internal Affairs about what he'd learned. He wants those women found just as badly as you do."

"How do I know that they'll stop hurting the other women? You could just warn them and let them get away."

"I won't allow them to get away. They are going to pay for everything they've done. I promise you, Selene."

Her brow furrowed as she thought about my words. "I guess... if you'll promise me that they will face justice, I will give you the list of those I know. It's not all of them. There were several who took advantage of us, used us, but weren't part of the operation. More like Johns, but I never got their names."

"Would you be able to identify them by their pictures?" I asked, curious.

She hesitated for a moment. "Maybe. But it would be my word against theirs. The ones on the list I have proof."

"That might be true... however, you're proving exactly how big this operation was and you have proof of the major players. Your word should hold more weight than theirs." I glanced over at Angel.

"If those officers took advantage of you or any of the women, they should at minimum lose their badges. We don't need cops like that on the LAPD."

"Not all of them are LAPD. Several are cops in Santa Monica," Selene said softly. "Sam would drive me and the others to an apartment there where we were given heroin and cocaine to get us high, and then they'd..." She looked down at her folded hands.

"I'm glad you were able to escape and get help."

"I was lucky."

"I think that is enough for now." Ms. Glass pulled a paper from her briefcase and handed it over. "It's the list of officers my client can identify as being part of the Circle of Justice inner workings."

I took the list and glanced at it before handing it over to Angel. "Thank you for cooperating with us, Selene. I really appreciate it."

She nodded.

"If you think of anything else, don't hesitate to contact me. And I hope, if I have any more questions, I can reach out to you."

"Please contact me first," Ms. Glass said as she gestured toward the door to walk us out.

"I can do that." I put my hand on the door and turned

back to her. "Thank you for helping her. I can't imagine you're getting paid to do so."

Ms. Glass smirked. "We have an understanding. Ms. Webb will be suing the city and once we win, I will be getting a small paycheck. The majority of it will go to help others in her situation. Perhaps not trafficked by cops, but by powerful people just the same."

"I'm glad to hear it. If I can help in any way, I would be happy to," I murmured.

"You are helping, Detective, by making sure these men pay for their crimes." She smiled. "Have a good day, Detectives."

Angel and I headed to the car in silence.

My stomach was churning, and I just wanted to get out of there. I'd only had a glimpse of that list, but I had recognized a few of the names.

19

CONNECTIONS AND ASSOCIATIONS
MARCY

"Please tell me that my eyes were deceiving me," I muttered as I climbed into the car.

"Afraid that's not possible."

"George Peck, Glen Jefferies, Daniel Maldon, and Byron Steiner? I just can't believe it." I shook my head.

"There are notations on what they did," Angel murmured. "Steiner helped Sam acquire the drugs, while Maldon gave them to the women; Jefferies, like Maldon, was another who kept them high and locked up in those rooms. Wait—" Angel frowned and looked at the list again, rereading. "Sorry, no, Maldon wasn't involved in keeping them locked up, but he did give them drugs occasionally. She's got him listed as mostly a John."

"And Peck?" I asked as I turned the car on.

"Looks like he was part of recruitment. He brought the others in on it. Selene wrote that he was also the money man, whatever that means."

"How many other names are on the list?" I asked.

Angel took a moment and dragged his finger over the

page. "Five more are listed, but that includes Sam and Grant, so three others whose names I don't recognize, and they appear to be minor players. They're all listed as Johns."

"And the others—Steiner, Jefferies, Peck, Nilsson, and probably Maldon, since he was giving them drugs too—were all major players in the Circle of Justice with Grant and Sam?"

Angel nodded. "Looks that way."

"I don't want to take this to Jordan," I said, glancing at Angel. "Something's up with him."

"Yeah, I noticed. Let's just go to the captain."

Sighing, I let my shoulders sink. "Is that really a good idea? The man is a wreck."

"He's still the captain, divorce or not. We have to go to somebody and if we aren't going to Jordan, we need to go to the captain."

I knew he was right. I just didn't like it. "Okay. You're right. I'm just worried about him." Instead of getting on the 405, I turned toward West Century Boulevard and went East on it, then hopped on the 110 and headed North toward the precinct. It took about forty-five minutes to get there, which honestly wasn't too bad.

With the list in hand, we headed for Robinson's office. I stopped at Jason's desk. "Is he in?"

Jason glanced over his shoulder toward the door and then looked back at us. "Is it important?"

"Yeah."

The look on my face must have decided it because he picked up the phone and spoke quietly into it. A moment later, he said, "Go on in."

Angel and I moved past him, and I knocked gently on the door, then opened it. "Sir?"

"Come in." Robinson looked drained, rundown, and miserable. The couch in the back corner had a blanket and a pillow on it, like the captain had been sleeping here. That was worrisome. He looked up at us, his expression almost bleak.

"Sir, we've just come from the interview with Ms. Webb. She gave us a list of officers who were part of the Circle of Justice."

It was almost as though he didn't register what I was saying. He just stared blankly.

"Sir?" Angel prompted.

"We didn't want to take this to Jordan, considering he's been acting strangely since the news broke, and well, there are names on here..."

"Brasswell?"

"Well, no, he's not on the list." I handed it to the captain.

Robinson scanned the list, and his eyes widened a little. "No, you were right to bring this to me. Kendrick, any of these names you recognize as close to Brasswell?"

"I know Jordan knows several of them, but I couldn't say how close he was to any of them, sir."

"Look into it. Might explain his behavior. Keep him out of the loop. He'll want to know about the interview, but keep the list of names quiet."

"We can do that, sir," Angel replied.

"And make sure IA has a copy of this list; they're going to need it too. I want these men prosecuted within every inch of the law. If I could have them pitched into solitary confinement for the rest of their days, I'd do it." His tired eyes rose up to look at us. He looked back down at the list with disgust. "Decorated officers... never should have happened," he muttered.

"No, sir, it shouldn't have," I replied.

"Keep this list close to the vest. Your eyes only, aside from IA. Got it?"

"Yes, sir." I took the list back, folded it and put it in the inside pocket of my blazer. "We'll go fill Jordan in on the rest of the interview."

"Did you learn anything else? Other than the list?" he asked, perking up a little.

"Not exactly, sir. Ms. Webb doesn't really trust us, but then who could blame her after what she's been through?" Angel sighed and ran a hand through his hair.

"No, I'd imagine she doesn't. She's not involved in Finlay's death though, right?"

"I doubt it, sir. Someone has been threatening her, which is why she moved to the hotel. Her lawyer and that journalist, Bill Meeks, were very protective of her. She's pretty scared," I shared.

"Okay, well, at least you've ruled her out."

"For the most part, sir." I turned toward the door. Reaching for it, I turned back, "Get some rest, sir."

With that, Angel and I left and walked down the hall toward Jordan's office. I wasn't looking forward to this. I almost thought about letting Angel handle it, but I didn't want to give Jordan the satisfaction of knowing he'd cowed me. I shoved my shoulders back, straightening my spine as I knocked on his door.

"Enter."

I pushed open the door and saw Jordan sitting at his desk.

Jordan's gaze flicked to us then immediately went down to stare at his computer screen. "What is it?"

"Just wanted to update you on the interview we did with Ms. Webb."

"Did she do it? She's the only one who knew who those men were. It had to be her."

I gritted my teeth. "She isn't the only one. There are a number of people aware of who they are. So to say that she was the only one—"

"Don't argue with me, Kendrick. I said I wanted her alibi; does she even have one?"

"First of all, you didn't ask us to get her alibi. We've seen the video, and it was a man who killed Sam Finlay, not a woman."

"Besides, the woman is terrified of male cops. There's no way she got close to one voluntarily," Angel said.

"She's a whore and probably a good actress. If she doesn't have an alibi, she's probably guilty," Jordan sneered, but continued to avoid giving us eye contact. "She could have hired someone to do the job."

"But—" I started to argue.

"I don't want to hear it, Kendrick. Do what I said. I want you looking into every single person she knows and is connected with. She probably has ties to other MC clubs, considering who her dad is. She could have easily gotten one of them to do this for her."

I stared at him. The man was tilting at windmills if he believed that. "Fine. We'll look into her connections."

"Anyone she's associated with is a possible suspect. Find them, Kendrick. Yesterday."

Rolling my eyes, I couldn't even bring myself to speak anymore. I looked at Angel, pleading with him to finish this.

"We'll get right on that, sir," Angel said as he turned toward the door and shoved me out into the hallway. He kept a hand on my arm as we moved quickly away from Jordan's office. "Don't," he muttered.

He must have known I was ready to explode. Instead of stopping in the detective pool at our desks, he kept going, pretty much dragging me out of the doorway into the main area of the precinct and then out to the parking lot. A moment later we were next to the passenger side of his car.

"Get in."

"What?" I blinked.

"We're getting out of here and getting you fed before you lose your shit and get suspended."

I smiled. Blowing out a breath, I got in, sinking into his passenger seat. "You're buying," I said when he got behind the steering wheel.

He chuckled. "I figured."

He started the car and we headed away from the station.

I had no idea where we were going but the farther from the precinct we got, the more my shoulders relaxed. Interacting with Jordan stressed me out and made me want to drink. It was too bad it was only noon and we were still working.

20

A NIGHTTIME CONVERSATION

MARCY

After work, I headed home to a microwave meal and a date with my television. I clicked on an episode of *Death in Paradise* on Prime—one I'd seen a hundred times, but something about the show was relaxing. Maybe it was the Caribbean setting? Either way, I was able to let it play as I ate and contemplated Sam Finlay's murder.

I knew there would be more murders if we didn't find this guy and soon. IA hadn't been much help, even after I'd given them Selene's list of dirty cops. They'd been grateful, of course, but closed mouthed about anything they'd uncovered. I knew how meticulous they were when putting together a case. They had to cross every 't' and dot every 'i' in going after cops who were dirty. It was a tough gig, and I didn't envy them, but I really wished they could help me out a bit.

I knew the cops who had the most to lose—Weaver for one, but he was already locked up. Sam would have been second if he hadn't already been murdered. I supposed, from

Selene's list of cops who were part of the upper echelon of the circle, George Peck was next in line of hierarchy. He'd been around forever. He was currently on night shift in our department. If I recalled correctly, he'd gotten into trouble a few times for coming to work drunk.

I recalled, back when Jordan and I first married, that Peck and a couple of the others on the list had been to our place for game days. Jordan had always expected me to cook appetizers and play hostess. After the first few times when they'd all treated me like a second-class citizen with boobs, I'd stopped doing it. Whenever he had the guys over, I'd made sure I was on shift or out with one of my friends.

I should have known that was the beginning of the end of us as a couple. Jordan had gotten more belligerent and controlling as our marriage went on, but I'd put up with it until I caught him cheating on me. That was the last straw. It was one indignity too much. I deserved better. So much better than what he'd given me. Looking back, I should have left him well before he started cheating, but I'd thought it was just the way husbands were and it was my fault for marrying him. I'd been naïve when we first married. It wasn't as though I'd had a good example of what a marriage should be. Mom had never married because she'd been a prostitute and had both Stephen and me with different men.

After her murder, we'd spent the rest of our youth in a group home, since they'd deemed us too screwed up to be sent into foster care. That kind of upbringing didn't exactly teach me how good relationships should work. I'd had to learn that on my own through trial and error. I was still learning and probably always would be.

With everything that had gone on over the last eight months, I couldn't believe I was as sane as I was. I had therapy to thank for that. And good friends like Angel. The thought of him made me smile. He'd been Jordan's friend before he'd become my partner. I was pretty sure I'd gotten custody of Angel in the divorce. He rarely spent time with Jordan anymore, and he complained about Jordan's behavior almost as much as I did now.

The show on the TV ended and I pushed the button to play the next episode. Re-gathering my thoughts, I focused back on the case as the theme music played. So, after Weaver, Finlay, and Peck, next in line had to be Byron Steiner, Glen Jefferies, Daniel Maldon, and Carter Nilsson. I'd done a little digging earlier that afternoon to see exactly who Nilsson was, and found he was just a first-rank detective with Gang and Narco out of Santa Monica. He was in his early thirties, and had never been in trouble with IA. According to Selene, he'd been one of the cops who brought them drugs, food, and lingerie occasionally. I wondered if that made him basically the group's gopher.

I knew I should probably ask Frank about him, but I was avoiding Frank at the moment because I wasn't sure what to say to him. His brother's name was on that list as well. I had a feeling it was Daniel who had him all tied in knots about going to IA. Daniel was listed as a mid-level member who was mostly a John. One of the men who took advantage of the girls as prostitutes, but he wasn't a high-ranking member of the Circle as far as Selene was aware. She had written that he did sometimes administer drugs to them though, giving them the shots of heroin, or cutting the coke for them.

I supposed I could understand Frank not wanting to give IA his own brother's name, and wanting to encourage him to go on his own. Of course, it was too late for that now. Selene had given me the names and I'd passed them on to IA, even knowing that in doing so I could be destroying any chance I had with Frank. Still, I wasn't going to sit on it just because I liked the guy.

Honestly, I was just glad not to see Frank's name on that list. I would hate to have to go after him as a suspect in Sam's murder. Speaking of suspects, I needed to make a list. I reached into the side table drawer and pulled out a notebook and pen. I began listing all the names from the list Selene had given me, and then added Selene as well. Even though she had been forthcoming with the list and seemed frightened of male cops, I couldn't say one hundred percent that she hadn't put someone up to doing the murders on her behalf. I needed to look more into her, even though I was fairly certain she was innocent.

Of course, she did have ties to some pretty dangerous people. If one of them got wind of what had happened to her, it was possible that they were acting on her behalf without her knowledge. I needed to look into the Serpents and see if any of them had gotten out on early parole or if any of them had escaped justice for some reason. There were also the other MC groups that the Serpents had done business with who might have a reason to look out for Selene.

I started a new page with exactly what my plan for tomorrow would be. Starting with the Serpents and their affiliates. Next, assuming I got nowhere with that, I would start checking into alibis of the top-tier members of the Circle. I supposed I needed to have conversations with each of them as well.

At midnight, I shut down the TV and headed to my room. I was still wired. My mind just wouldn't shut down, but I knew I needed to sleep. I got ready for bed and set the alarm on my phone. Just as I turned off the light, my phone buzzed.

Curious, I picked it up.

It was a message from Stephen.

> Hey, you up?

> > Yeah, can't sleep. Why are you up?

> Couldn't sleep either. Saw that video of the cop. Has me worried about you.

> > You don't have to worry about me. He was killed because of what he was doing.

> I know you're a good cop, sis, just still worry about you.

> > Thanks, and you know you don't have to.

> So are you investigating his death?

> > Yes. It's my case.

> Think he's going to kill again? He said there would be more.

> > Not if I can find him first.

> I hope you do.

> > Me too.

> Wanna meet for lunch tomorrow?

> Sure, what time?

> How about around one at El Pollo Loco?

> Sounds good. See you then. Gotta get some sleep.

> Okay, be careful, yeah?

> Of course. Love you.

> Love you too.

I clicked the phone off and set it aside. I lay down and closed my eyes, but my mind continued to sift through the facts of the case. I kept hitting on the fact that Frank's brother was on that list. I felt bad that I'd told IA without telling him that I was doing so. I knew I had no reason to feel that way, but I did.

I grabbed my phone and clicked on his name. We'd exchanged numbers during our conversation at his place, but I hadn't texted him yet. It was getting close to one a.m. now and I knew it was a bad idea, but guilt was eating at me. I needed to tell him.

> Hey, are you awake?

I set my phone on my nightstand. If he answered, I'd hear it. It wasn't like I was going to actually get any sleep. Still, I tried. I closed my eyes and started counting backwards from a hundred. I made it to seventy-two before my phone buzzed. I grabbed it and clicked the message.

> Hey, what are you doing up?

> Can't sleep. Came across information today and I had to give it to IA.

> Oh?

> Frank, you could have told me your brother was the one who confided in you.

I sighed as I hit send. This was either going to blow up any chance we had of getting together or he would be the kind of guy I thought he might be and understand. Still, it was his family who would be affected, so I wouldn't blame him if he never wanted to see me again. I set the phone down, half-expecting him to not answer me.

Closing my eyes again, I started counting once more. This time I made it to sixty-one before my phone buzzed. My heart was pounding in my chest as I picked it up and read his text.

> You understand why I couldn't though. I hate that IA knows, but I can't blame you for taking it to them. You're an upstanding cop and what Daniel got involved in isn't anyone's fault but his own. I'm still trying to talk him into coming forward and speaking to IA before they come for him. Maybe if he knows they have his name, he'll do the right thing.

I blew out a relieved breath. I really liked Frank, and I didn't want things to be messed up before they even really had a chance to begin.

Glad you're not mad.

At you? Nope. Myself? Yeah. Daniel? Hell yeah. But you and me? We're good. You should get some sleep. Don't you have to be in at seven?

Yeah. Seven-to-five shift. You?

Same. Talk tomorrow?

Sure. Goodnight.

Sweet dreams.

I smiled as I set my phone aside. I felt a little more relaxed and sleepy now, knowing we were good. Maybe I actually would be able to sleep after all.

21

RESEARCH AND DEVELOPMENTS

MARCY

I was already at my desk Wednesday morning when Angel walked in, two steaming cups of coffee in his hands. "For me?" I asked, hopeful.

Angel handed one over, his lips quirking up in a smile. "Of course. How long you been here?" He sat down at his desk and leaned back in his chair as he took a sip.

I raised the cup to my lips and gulped the warm goodness, my eyes closing at the heavenly nectar. "So good," I murmured and then looked over at him. "Got in about thirty minutes ago. I didn't get much sleep and wanted to get a jump start this morning. Didn't even stop for coffee, which was a bad idea."

Angel chuckled. "That is always a bad idea. Coffee should always come first." He winked. "So what's on the agenda for today?"

"I'm looking into the Serpents and their affiliates."

Angel's eyebrow quirked up. "Why?"

"As I was going over things at home yesterday, I started thinking that maybe we've looked at this the wrong way.

Selene wasn't the only woman from that MC club that Grant and Sam kidnapped and trafficked. So maybe one of the Serpents or someone who was connected to them found out what was going on and is now going after the cops?"

"Not a bad hypothesis. How can I help?"

"There's a lot of names here. I've gotten through about four of them. Wanna take half the list? These are just the Serpents, but they were affiliated with another, smaller, MC club as well, one called—" I glanced at my notes, "the Sidewinders."

"Let's get through the Serpents first, then we'll look at the others. Sound like a plan?"

"Yup." I passed him a sheet of paper with a list of names.

We spent the next few hours running down each and every member. Most were still in prison serving life sentences, but there were a handful who'd been released on parole. Of those, three had been killed, two were no longer in the US, and four were missing. That could mean they were dead or had managed to change their names and were either still living here in California or had moved God knew where. If they were still in California, it was possible one of them was out there getting revenge for Selene and the other women.

That meant I needed to have another conversation with her. I turned to Angel. "Hey, I'm going to call Selene. See if she can tell me about these four. Wanna start on the Sidewinders?"

"Sure thing." Angel took the list I offered him and turned back to his computer.

I glanced at the clock. It was going on eleven thirty. My coffee was long gone and my lunch with Stephen was still an hour and a half away. I got up and stretched. "I'm gonna get another coffee and a snack before I make that call. Want one?"

"I could use something. I saw the beignet truck out there this morning. Might still be there." Angel tilted his head toward the door.

"That would be better than the crap in the breakroom. I'll go see." I grabbed my purse and headed outside. Sure enough, the gold and brown truck was parked a block away. I ordered eight beignets, four with powdered sugar and four with cinnamon, and then two coffees.

After enjoying my snack, I picked up the phone and called Selene's lawyer, Ms. Glass, to explain what I needed from Selene. She gave me permission to call Selene directly, which I did. She answered after two rings.

"Selene? It's Detective Kendrick."

"Hello. Yes, Ms. Glass said you were going to call. What can I do for you, Detective?"

"I had a few questions I wanted to ask you about your father's motorcycle club, if you are willing to answer?"

She hesitated and I could hear her murmuring to someone with her. A moment later she said, "That depends on what you want to ask."

"Mostly about some of the members. I understand you were just a teen at the time and probably weren't privy to the goings-on at the club."

"I wasn't privy to anything there but that didn't stop Weaver from threatening to have me thrown in prison for life," she muttered.

"What did he say he was going to arrest you for?" I asked.

"He said he'd have me charged with prostitution, drug and gun running if I didn't do what he wanted. He told all of us women that. A few called his bluff and I think he did have them arrested, but I don't know what happened to them."

"Do you have any names?" I asked, my pen poised to write.

"I only know what they went by at the club. Holly, Pepper, and Taffy. They were older and had been around the club for as long as I can remember."

I wrote the three names down. I'd have to do some digging. "Okay, thanks for that. Can you tell me about a couple of men who were members?"

"Maybe."

"Casey Waters? I think he went by 'Digger'?" I asked.

"Digger? Yeah, I know him. He wasn't a bad guy. He was always nice to me. I think he went down for running drugs? Got like five years? He's probably out now."

"Yes, I've found that out. I'm wondering if you've seen him since then or if you know where he might be?"

"No, I haven't seen anyone from the club. If you can't find him, it's because he don't want to be found. Bet he's gone off-grid."

"Right. I wondered if you'd have any idea of how or where he might have done that?"

She gave a dry laugh. "I wasn't told anything about anyone's boltholes. Dad didn't even share his. Always said that I didn't need that information 'cause he'd take care of me. Worked out great, didn't it?" Her tone was pure sarcasm.

I asked her about the other few names, but she didn't have any information on them either. "Any chance any of them might be avenging you and the other women?"

Selene's laughter was almost a cackle. "There is no way those guys would avenge any of us. Not even for Dad. We were just the whores, or in my case the bar help to them.

Cannon fodder. Women weren't worth much in Dad's club. I'm not saying Dad isn't fond of me, or doesn't love me, but I'm not important to him, not like his brothers in the club. I doubt he even knows what happened to me. He's probably pissed off that I haven't been to see him."

"I'm sorry to hear that," I replied, and I was. Not only because it was a sad way to grow up, but also because that meant that this line of inquiry was probably a bust. "Okay, well, thank you for your time."

I hung up and turned to Angel. "I don't think this killer is one of the Serpents or from the Sidewinders. You?"

Angel shook his head. "After looking into these guys, I'm pretty sure they aren't who we're after."

I knew we needed to fill Jordan in, but I'd save that for later. It was getting close to one now and I was ready for a real break. "Let's head out for lunch, then we'll pick back up with the names on the Circle of Justice list Selene gave us, and there are a few women from the club that Selene mentioned I want to look into as well."

"Sounds good. I'm meeting Callie for lunch," he said, but he didn't sound as excited as he had before when he spoke about her.

"How are things going with her?"

"She's still taking heat for dating me. So far, she hasn't said she wants to stop seeing me, but I feel like she may any day now." He sighed.

"I hope she doesn't, but I get the stress she may be feeling from whoever is in her life pushing her to break things off with you."

He nodded. "I do too. It just sucks. I hate this. I hate that we are being blamed for the acts of a few bad apples."

I patted his shoulder and headed out to meet Stephen.

We got a table and ordered queso cheese for our chips as we studied the menu.

"So how is work going?" I asked.

"It's been okay, busy." Stephen dipped his chip in a bowl of cheese and salsa mix. "Having any luck finding your killer?"

"Not so far. Doing more ruling out possible suspects than tracking down the guy. We've got a list of cops who could be on the killer's hit list, but IA doesn't want us going to them to warn them, so I'm feeling a bit tied up at the moment. We need definitive proof before we can go see anyone on the list."

"What if you go after them as the person that you believe is doing the killing. That wouldn't be warning them, would it?" he suggested.

"No, that's a good point. I suppose we could do that. I just hate stepping on IA's toes. I deal with them enough; I don't need them having a vendetta against me."

"But you'd be doing your job."

"True." I nodded as the waiter appeared. I ordered the chicken quesadilla combo, and Stephen ordered the shredded chicken nachos.

As we ate, Stephen asked, "How's Jordan been lately? Still treating you like crap?"

I shrugged. "Pretty much. He's been weird though since all this came out. Like he's under more stress than normal. He looks like he's not sleeping at all, and he's been short tempered with everyone, not just me."

"Why do you think that is?" Stephen asked.

"I know he was friendly with some of the men who've been accused. I don't know if he was close to any of them, but..." I paused and decided to share one of my actual fears.

"I have to wonder if he was a member of the Circle. I mean, the way he's been acting... it's beyond abnormal."

"You said he was friendly with some of the accused men. Could he be covering for them?"

"Yeah, it's possible, but I don't know who he'd go to so much trouble for or why. He's always been extremely ambitious, so I can't imagine him doing something to hurt his chances of advancement. That's what makes his behavior so bizarre."

"Maybe you should see if he was closer to any of those men than you thought. Maybe they have something on him? I mean he cheated on you; is it possible he took advantage of one of those women? Maybe he's being blackmailed?"

"Yeah, you could be on to something." I finished eating and paid the tab. "Thanks, you've given me a few more paths to look down than I'd thought of."

Stephen smiled. "Glad I can help, and anything that interferes with Jordan's life, I am all for doing. The bastard never deserved you."

I grinned. "Thanks. I feel like we didn't really talk about you. You sure you're doing alright?"

Stephen nodded. "I'm good. Dr. Faulkner is amazing and I'm making good progress. Work has been good, keeping busy helps. I'm still looking for Rick too. I might have a bead on him."

"Really? I'm glad." I looked at him, suddenly concerned for no real reason other than he was my only family and I'd nearly lost him not too long ago. "You'd tell me, right? If things were off?" I hugged him and then looked into his eyes.

"I would. I promise."

Smiling, I hugged him again. "Okay. I'd better go. Same time next week?"

"Barring any murders that might interfere, sounds good." He chuckled.

"Right." I waved and, after getting in my car, headed back to the precinct.

Angel had beat me back and he seemed to be in a good mood, so I assumed things with Callie went well. "How's your brother?" he asked.

"He's good. He also gave me an idea," I said quietly. "Is there anyone on that list that Jordan might be closer to than I initially thought?"

Angel considered the list. "Maybe. George and Jordan have always been pretty close. Jordan tried to get him into a few AA programs, but you know George, always on a binge when he's not working."

I tried to remember Jordan having George over for anything, but I couldn't recall much. "Really? They're so different."

"They went to the Academy together, were partners when they first started. George made detective before Jordan, but he never had the ambition Jordan did. There was a pretty rough case, and I think it's what really got to George, turned him from an occasional drinker to a binge drinker."

"Happens to too many of us, unfortunately," I replied. "So, what if Jordan is trying to keep us from investigating his friend? What if he's sent us on this wild goose chase with the Serpents and Sidewinders and Selene all to avoid us questioning George?"

"It's a possibility," Angel agreed.

"Or, what if he's involved somehow," I said, keeping my voice hushed. "What if Jordan was part of the Circle and Selene just didn't know his name?"

Angel sucked in a breath, his eyes widening. "That would explain some of his erratic behavior..."

"Maybe George needs to be our next interview?" I suggested.

"Yeah, I think you've got the right idea," Angel replied.

"Kendrick, Reyes, Captain asked if you would go out on this call," Jason said from across the room. "Shooting in Koreatown. I'll text you the details," he added.

I grabbed my purse from my desk. Looking into those women Selene mentioned would have to wait. "On it," I called back and looked at Angel. "You can drive."

22

ANOTHER ONE BITES THE DUST

I was happy with how everything had gone with Sam Finlay's death. I'd meticulously planned it out and, so far, it seemed as if I'd gotten away with it, which was good because I had a lot more work to do.

I knew how the LAPD worked, what they'd look for. I was determined not to make any mistakes. With that in mind, I'd planned the next killing. It was a little easier this time. I knew this one better than most. He was apathetic and easily manipulated. It was how he'd gotten involved in that stupid Circle of Justice in the first place.

Carter Nilsson was a good ol' boy. He had a bit of a beer belly, and was pretty out of shape. Killing him wouldn't be a problem, but first, I wanted him to admit what he'd done to those women. He was a disgusting pervert. The world needed to know.

I watched as Carrie led Carter to his car. She'd found him in a bar in Santa Monica. I'd gone in to observe, sitting in a darkened corner out of the way as I kept an eye on them.

It was easy for Carrie to get up close and personal with Carter; he was such a letch.

It hadn't taken her long to convince him that she wanted him. She'd practically fucked him right there in the bar before she suggested they take it back to her place. When they'd left the bar together, I'd gone out a side door. I rounded the building and got in my van just as they reached Carter's car.

I watched as she snatched Carter's keys and shoved him into the passenger seat. Just like I knew he would, Carter didn't balk at her manhandling. He was fairly drunk. When Carrie pulled the car into traffic, I moved to follow them.

She drove through the streets of Santa Monica and pulled up outside a warehouse on Main Street. She turned into the alley, and I parked on the curb. I could see them, even though it was dark between the two buildings. She was supposed to be telling Carter that she had a loft apartment in the building. She didn't, of course. I'd already scouted the location though. It had been empty for a number of years. The best part was it had a large glass window that faced Pacific Street where I could pose him for everyone to see his humiliation.

Carrie led Carter toward the building. He started to hesitate, but Carrie was a pro. She wrapped herself around him and started kissing him, making him desperate to get horizontal with her.

I smiled as I climbed out the van. I'd already prepared myself, putting on my GoPro camera, mask, and gloves. I grabbed the baseball bat from the passenger seat and crept down the alley as they pushed into the building through the steel door that I'd already broken in so it would be easy for her to get him in.

While they were inside, I set my bat on the ground next to Carter's car and opened the driver side door. I pulled a small packet of wet wipes from my pocket and wiped down the steering wheel, the leather seat, the door, the center console, and mirrors. Anything Carrie might have touched.

I shut the door, picked up my bat, and waited a moment before I moved to the building and opened the door to follow them in. I watched as Carter slid his grimy hands over Carrie's body, pushing at her top to get to her breasts. Softly I moved toward them. I lifted the bat and swung, hitting him on his upper back and his head. I didn't really care if I fractured his skull or caused a concussion; he would be dying later anyway. I just needed to knock him out or daze him for a moment so I could administer the ketamine.

Carter stumbled and fell to his knees, but wasn't completely out. "What the fu—" he started to slur, his hands coming up to his head where I'd hit him.

I shoved the needle into his neck and a moment later he dropped to the cement floor.

"It's about damn time. His breath was foul." Carrie gagged.

"Well, you don't have to do anything else with this one." I pulled her fee from my pocket and handed it to her. "You can go. I've got it from here."

She put the money in her purse. "How many more? I don't know how much more I can do to help."

"I've got a few more, but you only need to help with one. Then you can take that money and disappear. Start a new life somewhere away from here. Maybe go to some island and just have a nice life."

"I'll think about it." She patted her purse and turned to

go. "Just one more?" She paused and looked over her shoulder at me.

"Yes. One more."

She nodded and left without another word.

I turned to the barely breathing body lying on the floor in front of me. I had some big plans for Carter. He thought it was funny to gang-rape several of the girls, well, he'd see just how funny it was when it was him on the other end of the interaction. I kicked him in the ribs and shot my taser at him just for the hell of it and watched his body jump and piss itself.

Smiling, I grabbed his leg and dragged him to the room I'd prepared ahead of time.

"Let the fun begin."

23

THE BROKEN BADGE KILLER
MARCY

The shooting in Koreatown yesterday afternoon had been between two teens in a dispute over the ownership of a mountain bike worth about ten grand. It had turned out that the bike had been stolen by the teens, and then one attempted to cut the other out of the payoff. They both ended up in custody, though one was currently in hospital with several gunshot wounds to his stomach and legs. It was questionable if he'd even be able to walk again. All over a stupid bike.

The entire thing had taken us most of the afternoon to clear up, so Angel and I had missed our opportunity to speak to George Peck. Because of that, we had planned to do it first thing this morning before we even went to the precinct. I picked Angel up and we headed for coffee before making the trip to George's house.

"Think he'll be sober enough to even talk to us?" Angel asked, looking out of the windshield.

"Is he really that much of a drunk?" I glanced toward him.

Angel shrugged. "From what I've heard, yeah."

The radio crackled to life and a voice said, "Detective Kendrick, we've had a call-in for a 187 in Santa Monica related to your case. SMPD is requesting you and Detective Reyes join them at the scene. SMPD patrol are holding the scene."

Angel grabbed the radio and answered, "Ten-four, dispatch, send the address." He set the radio down and picked up the siren, putting it on the dash and turning it on. "Guess no coffee then."

Dispatch gave us the location for the corner of Main and Pacific in Santa Monica.

As I turned the car west, I glanced at Angel. "You know that means we're about to find another cop."

"Yeah, it's gotta be the same killer. Otherwise SMPD would be handling it."

"So whoever it is must still be recognizable. I wonder if anything else pointed to the same killer."

"Guess we'll find out when we get there."

It took us nearly thirty minutes to reach our destination, despite the siren and the fact that I was going well over eighty-five miles an hour on Santa Monica Boulevard. Many of the travelers on the road no longer paid us the courtesy of pulling over to the side to let us by and I had to weave through traffic. I parked and we got out, heading for the patrol officer standing behind the yellow crime scene tape.

I pulled out my badge and held it up for the officer. "Detectives Kendrick and Reyes. We're expected."

"Yes, ma'am. Detective DeMarco is waiting for you." He nodded toward an older warehouse.

"Thanks," I answered as I ducked under the yellow tape and quickly walked toward the building. I noticed several news vans pulling up as well as crowds gathering to see what was going on.

The warehouse was mostly empty except for some steel barrels and piles of old wooden pallets. There was activity coming from one of the front rooms, so we hurried in that direction.

"DeMarco, what have we got?" I asked, holding up my badge as we found the detective who had to be in charge of the scene.

"You're Kendrick, right?" He looked at me, as though checking.

"Yes. This is Reyes." I tilted my head toward Angel.

"It's Carter Nilsson. He was SMPD, patrol. Looks like he was killed by the same psychopath who killed your guy, the one in the video."

"Sam Finlay. He wasn't ours; he was Gang and Narcos, but yeah," I clarified. "He was on our list."

"Guess you can cross him off as a suspect. He obviously didn't do that to himself." The man blanched and looked like he might be sick.

I was almost afraid to move forward and see what we were dealing with. "Coroner here or on their way?"

"Here. Waiting for you."

"I'm assuming he was set up on display for people to view? Sam was."

DeMarco nodded. "We blocked off the window as soon as we could. Not sure there weren't recordings made prior to that though."

I glanced at Angel. "Ready?"

Together we moved forward with DeMarco. As I took in the scene I had to suck in a breath and turn away for a moment. Carter was bent over the back of a chair, his ankles tied to the back legs, his arms tied to the front legs. A large, oblong, and wide object had been inserted into his rectum and another into his mouth. There were various cuts all over his body, as well as what looked like taser marks, similar to the ones Sam had.

"Damn," I muttered and had to look away again. "Get him untied and under a sheet."

"Figured you needed to see the scene before we moved the body," DeMarco murmured.

I wanted to vomit, but I pulled in a shaky breath and pressed my lips together hard. Nodding, I gave DeMarco a tight smile. I couldn't speak yet. I took a few steps away, trying to tamp down the urge to lose the contents of my stomach, not that there was anything really to lose since we hadn't even gotten coffee before being called out here.

"You okay?" Angel murmured next to me.

"Yeah. I'm good." I turned back to DeMarco. "Anything left at the scene?"

"His badge was smashed on the floor next to him, but we haven't found anything else yet."

That alone pretty much told me we were dealing with the same killer, even if the stab wounds and taser marks didn't. "Who found him?"

DeMarco pulled out his notebook and said, "Dennis Sheffield. Owns the gym across the street. He was there to open up for the day. Saw the light and got curious. Found Nilsson... well, like you saw, and called it in. Patrol was the first to arrive and they recognized him."

"Okay. I'll need his full statement, as well as those of the officers who were first on the scene. I want to know what has been dusted for prints, and where he was actually killed. Have you swept the building yet?"

"Yes, ma'am. We've found the room we believe Nilsson was murdered in. Do you want to see it?"

"Please."

Angel and I followed DeMarco out of the front room, through the large main room to another room at the back. There was blood splatter everywhere. Puddles of it. And around those puddles were various shoe prints.

"Please tell me your team did not walk through the scene and make all of these?"

DeMarco looked uncomfortable. "Sorry, ma'am. They didn't see the blood because it was dark and the power was out."

I practically growled. "I need the shoes of everyone who was in this room. I want every single shoe print accounted for."

"Yes, ma'am," DeMarco said.

"Get crime scene in here to photograph everything."

"They're on their way."

"I want the body transferred to Damien Black for the autopsy."

"I'll make sure that happens, ma'am." DeMarco hesitated.

"What is it, DeMarco?" I asked impatiently.

"Will you excuse me, ma'am? So I can go see to all of that?"

"Go." I waved my hand, gesturing for him to get on with it. I looked at Angel as I pinched the bridge of my nose. "I want to call Lindsey in."

"You don't trust the SMPD crime scene techs?"

I shrugged. "I don't know them. I trust Lindsey."

"Call her. Get her take. She may know the team here."

I pulled out my phone and dialed her number.

"Hey, chick, what's up?" Lindsey asked cheerfully.

"Linds, I'm out in Santa Monica with another body, another cop."

"Well, shit."

"Yeah, my thoughts exactly. What's your thoughts on the CSI team here?"

"They're good. Tell them everything you want images of, and if you want anything special, and they'll be all over it. I'll contact Jazz, er, Jasper Treavers. He's head of CSI there. I'll have him send me everything so we can compare it to the previous scene."

"Okay, thanks."

Angel and I spent the next hour going over everything with Jasper, who told us to call him Jazz, and he seemed to know his stuff. His team confiscated all of the patrol officers' shoes so they could rule them out of the scene, and they dusted everything for prints. No cameras were found anywhere around the building, inside or out. Though we did come across a car that was registered to Carter Nilsson, so it looked as though he drove himself here.

"I want it dusted for prints too. Maybe his killer was in the passenger seat," I suggested. "Go over it with a fine-tooth comb. Anything that looks out of place, I want to know about it."

"We'll take care of it, ma'am," Jazz replied.

"DeMarco," I called, seeing him walking back over to us, "send someone to inform the family and take their statements. And if you would, send me a copy of them?"

"Yes, ma'am."

After that, I released the scene to him, and Angel and I went outside. As we headed for my car, several reporters shouted at us.

"Was Officer Nilsson part of the Circle of Justice?"

"Was he killed by the Broken Badge Killer?" two more shouted.

That had me pausing. How did they know about the badges being left smashed at the scene? "We have a leak," I muttered.

He subtly shook his head. "Not necessarily. Remember both bodies were on display. Someone could have noticed the broken badges, and it was in the video too."

I let out a frustrated breath. "Yeah, okay. You're right, they could have seen it either of those places. But really, do they always have to come up with a fucking name for the killer?"

"It sells more papers, or whatever," he said, rolling his eyes. "Come on, let's go."

The reporters were still trying to get us to say something, but I just looked at them, a blank expression on my face as I said, "No comment."

I started the car and headed back to the precinct. Talking to George would have to wait. Carter Nilsson's murder took precedence.

I just hoped we'd get to him before our killer struck again.

24

LISTENING TO INSTINCTS

MARCY

Driving back from Santa Monica took longer than normal for a Thursday morning because there was a six-car accident that had traffic backed up for several miles. I was starving and dying for a coffee by the time we reached the parking lot. Luckily, the beignet truck was back, and I was able to get a cup and a snack before heading in.

That didn't improve my morning though. Jordan was waiting for us the minute we set foot in the door. I didn't even get to enjoy my treat while it was warm. "My office, now," he demanded before I could even put my purse away.

I set my beignets down on my desk and my purse in the drawer before heading down the hall with my coffee in hand. He could make me leave the food, but not the coffee. It was the only thing that was going to make me civil while speaking to him. I glanced at Angel; we'd already discussed in the car what we were going to tell Jordan. His erratic behavior lately had me worried that he was somehow involved in this case, but we weren't sure exactly how he fit in yet. Angel was just as concerned as I was, and he'd said we needed to listen to our instincts.

"Why did you drive out to Santa Monica? It's not your job to see to every murder victim. They have their own detectives—" Jordan began to rant.

I held up my hand to stop him. "We were called because of who the victim was and the manner of his death. SMPD immediately recognized that they were dealing with the same killer we are and called us in as a courtesy because the case is high profile and ours."

Jordan's lips tightened in a flat line, and he avoided meeting my gaze. "So? Who was it?"

"An SMPD patrol officer named Carter Nilsson. He died of multiple stab wounds, just like Sam Finlay. SMPD's crime scene techs are working with ours, and the body is being brought here for Damien Black to autopsy, since he's working the case with us."

"They have a perfectly capable coroner in Santa Monica. I don't know why you authorized the expense of bringing the body to LA."

I gritted my teeth and attempted to explain it to him like he was a five-year-old. "Captain Robinson approved it. As I am sure you are aware, any murder that is part of our case at HSS is given to Damien Black as the leading medical examiner for the greater Los Angeles area. He knows the details of the case and what we are looking for and he will be better equipped to make the comparisons needed, especially since both bodies will be in the same location."

Jordan grunted, not really acknowledging what I said, but he did more or less drop that line of questioning. "Do you have any leads on who this killer is? Have you brought Selene Webb back in for questioning?"

His question reminded me I still needed to look for the three women Selene had mentioned, but I wasn't about to bring them up in front of Jordan. From the way he was acting, he'd start demanding that I find them and charge them with these murders.

"No, we haven't questioned her again," Angel answered, clearly seeing how frustrated I was getting. "We did run down every connection she had to the Serpents and Sidewinders, and Kendrick did speak to her about the men who are unaccounted for."

"And?" Jordan prompted, sounding irritated.

"Ms. Webb denied any connection to those men."

"Of course she did. She's a whore. She's probably lying," Jordan snorted. "Bring her in."

"She's a victim and she's been cooperative. I'm not bringing her in and subjecting the department to an even bigger lawsuit," I replied. "We have other leads that we're following. Mutual associates between Nilsson and Finlay. If we exhaust those, then I will speak to Ms. Webb again. However, at this time, we've got nothing tying her directly to either murder."

Jordan huffed and glanced at his computer screen, his face turning pale as he stared at something. "Who spoke to the reporters?"

"Nobody that we are aware of. Why?"

"Because they have information they shouldn't," Jordan practically shouted. "Who told them about the smashed badges at the scene? Why are they calling this killer the Broken Badge Killer?"

"We know. They asked us about that this morning."

"Well?" he demanded.

"The leak could have come from the civilians who saw the scene prior to patrol arriving," Angel said, his voice calm.

"And it was in the video the killer released," I added.

"I want all comments shut down. No talking to the reporters, got it?"

"We haven't and we won't," I gritted out.

"Find me a viable suspect, Kendrick, or I'm yanking you from the case," Jordan threatened. "Go!"

I was really pissed off at him, but I kept my mouth shut as I stood up and walked out of the door with Angel on my heels. "One of these days," I muttered.

"Deep breaths. He's all bluster. He's not going to take the case from us. The captain won't allow it. He's already tried to do it once and look where that got him."

I knew Angel was right, but that didn't do much to shake my anger. "Clearly his anger management classes didn't work. He's a bigger ass than he was before he went." I slammed myself into my chair and picked up a beignet, biting it in half as powdered sugar went flying.

"What did that beignet do to you, Kendrick?" Hummel asked as he passed by my desk.

I rolled my eyes at him and dusted the sugar from my shirt. "Don't you have better things to do?"

Hummel shrugged. "Not really. Been a slow morning on our end. Heard you were called out to Santa Monica. Who got whacked?"

I stared at him.

"Another cop?"

I gave him a slight nod.

"Damn, that bites. Same killer? What was it they called him? Badge Smasher?"

"Broken Badge Killer."

"Yeah, that's it. Was it him?"

"More than likely."

"Better your case than mine," he muttered as he returned to his desk.

"I'll get started on mutual acquaintances between Sam and Carter, but considering what we know, I don't know why we're bothering," Angel said, keeping his voice low.

"We've got a while before Damien or Lindsey are ready for us, so we might as well keep busy with this. Stick to the names on our list, see if we can make connections between them and Carter and Sam. They're our most likely. Jordan doesn't have to know we're working from this list."

He nodded and started digging into the lives of several officers who had worked any aspect of a case Sam was connected to.

I decided to dig into George Peck's life, starting with his years in patrol and how he became a detective. He'd been connected to numerous high-profile cases over the years, but as the years went by, those cases got fewer and farther between. It was more or less busy work as we waited for the results of Carter's autopsy and Lindsey's analysis of the crime scene.

It was well after lunch, which we ate at our desks while we worked, before we finally got the call to join Damien in his lab. I grabbed my purse and we headed to the medical examiner's office. I knew pretty much what to expect, but I wanted out of the office. I felt a weight lift from my shoulders the moment we reached the floor with Damien's lab.

Knocking on the door, I said, "You ready for us?" I smiled at him as he looked up.

"I am. This killer is getting a little more aggressive."

"So he got his feet wet with Sam and now he's got a taste for it, you think?"

"I don't know if I'd say he's got a taste for it, but he's definitely more sure of himself. The cuts are very precise. The taser marks are strategic, and well, the additions..." Damien paused. "This was what was used to sodomize him." He held up a plastic oblong vase that was about twelve inches long and three inches around at the base.

"Was he alive, or was that after?" I asked, seeing Angel pale next to me.

"From the tearing and blood residue, I'd say alive. While Sam was tortured with just the cuts, Carter was subjected to more."

"He had something in his mouth as well," I said, hoping to get this part of the inquest over quickly.

"Another vase, smaller in scale." Damien nodded toward the table that held the smaller vase.

It too was about three inches wide at the base, but was only about seven inches tall. "Anything unique about them?" I asked.

"Lindsey is running down that aspect, but I'm pretty sure they're not rare or anything. They're pretty cheaply made from what I can tell."

"So we're definitely dealing with the same killer?" Angel asked.

"I'd say yes. Knife marks are the same, just more sure. There was one other interesting thing. Carter was hit on the back of the head and upper back, I'd say probably with a baseball bat, judging by the bruising, or something of similar shape and weight."

"What does the tox screen look like?"

Damien picked up a sheaf of papers and flipped through

them. "Ketamine in his system, but no chloroform this time. No other opioids or drugs. Stomach contents were pretty common foods. Pretzels, beer, and a bit of beef. I'd say he ate and drank all that about three hours prior to his death."

"So he was more than likely at a bar." I looked over at Angel. "How much you want to bet he was picked up at a bar by the same woman Sam was?"

"Yeah, I'm not taking that bet. I'm sure he was. I'll start calling around when we get back to our desks."

"If that's everything, I think we'll head back to it." I glanced at Damien.

"That's all I've got."

"Thanks, Damien." We headed out and went to the elevator.

Lindsey jogged over, a report in hand. "Hey, Marce, Angel. Wait up a sec."

"What's up?" I asked.

"Initial report of the scene. We've ruled out all of the footprints. None that can't be accounted for."

My teeth clamped together tight. "Not one stray footprint?"

"Nope. Every single print came from the cops on the scene."

"How is that even possi—" I stopped, and my eyes widened. "Is it possible our killer worked the scene?"

Lindsey's jaw dropped and so did Angel's.

"No way they'd be that diabolical, would they?" Angel asked.

"I want the name of every single officer who left prints. I want to run every single one under a microscope. If I even get a whiff of them being connected to the Circle of Justice, I am bringing them in."

Lindsey shrugged. "That won't be hard. It's all in the report. Every officer who walked through the blood, as well as a few who didn't, but we wanted to rule everyone out, so we got everyone's shoes and names."

"Good." I was seething. "What else can you tell me?"

"Car was wiped down No prints on the driver's side, the mirror, center console or door. Not even on the roof of the car."

I frowned. "What about the passenger side?"

"Well, that was interesting. Carter's prints are all over it. As well as a few others we haven't identified yet, but we're working on it. However, it was his print on the seatbelt and the door handle."

"So you think he rode there as a passenger in his own car and whoever drove the car wiped it down?"

"Looks that way for now." She nodded. "We didn't find any prints on the door into the building either. It was completely clean, like it had been wiped down. This killer is meticulous. We're not even finding a stray hair."

"Keep looking, especially in that car. Maybe they missed something."

"We'll do that. It's always possible." Lindsey held the file out to me. "Anyway, here you go."

"Thanks." I pushed the button for the elevator. "You got plans for tonight?" I asked her.

She smiled. "I've got a date." She raised her eyebrows a couple times as her grin widened.

I laughed. "Good for you."

She winked as she started back down the hall.

As we stepped onto the elevator, Angel asked, "You at loose ends tonight?"

"Not really. I mean, no real plans or anything, but that's

probably a good thing. I think I'll make it an early night. Just me, a glass of wine and a movie in my pajamas." I smiled. "How about you? Seeing Callie?"

"No, it's her late night at the salon. I'm going home for an early night too."

I glanced down at the file in my hand. "I need to look into those women Selene mentioned. I've been wondering if one of them might be helping our killer. We also still need to see George."

"Should we tell Jordan about either of those?" Angel asked skeptically.

My gut was screaming at me that telling Jordan was the last thing we needed to do. "No, not if we can avoid it. I don't want him jumping to conclusions about the women. They could be completely innocent. As for George, if Jordan's as close to him as you think, I don't want him giving George any warning. I don't know what's going on with him, if he's part of this or just covering for someone, but I don't trust him with this."

"Yeah, I don't either. I don't think he's part of the Circle, but he has been acting very strangely. It's concerning."

"Very."

25

MACABRE VIDEO RELEASE
MARCY

My early night in turned into a nearly sleepless night once again as at about three thirty a.m. my phone rang, disturbing my sleep. The ringtone was "Ride Captain Ride", so I knew it was important.

I hit the button to answer. "Yes, Captain?" I said sleepily as I yawned and attempted to wake up.

"Kendrick, another video dropped. I've got tech all over it, but I'm sending you a copy of it. It's disgusting, but maybe with the other, you'll be able to figure something out about this killer."

"Okay. Thanks, Captain." I sighed.

"I'll see you at the station in a few hours."

"You're already there?" I questioned.

"Never left, Kendrick. I'm sure you noticed I've been sleeping in my office."

"I did notice, sir, but I didn't want to pry."

"It's not prying. I'm offering the information. Cheryl kicked me out and I haven't found a place yet. Things have been a bit stressful."

"I'm sorry, sir."

"Why? You aren't the one who's having an affair with your Pilates instructor."

I could hear the frustration in his voice as it cracked. "I'm just sorry you're going through this. You know if you want to talk, I've been there."

He took a moment, and I could hear him breathing deeply. "Thanks. I'll let you go now so you can get a look at the video."

I could tell that he was done talking about his marriage, or rather the end of his marriage. "Okay, sir."

A moment after we hung up, my phone dinged with the video file he'd sent over. I wasn't sure I wanted to watch it. Not without being fully awake and a coffee handy. Or maybe a trashcan for me to vomit in considering I'd seen the aftermath of whatever was on this video.

I decided to take a quick shower and get dressed for the day. Once that was done, I still couldn't bring myself to hit play on the video. I set about making my bed and cleaning things up, then went to the kitchen and made coffee. I procrastinated as much as I could, but eventually I knew I needed to see the video.

I took a couple of gulps of coffee and sat down on the sofa, my phone in my hand. Figured watching it on there, with it small, I wouldn't see too much. I was wrong.

"You like that, Carter? It's too bad I only have one of these to use on you, unlike what you and the others did to those girls. Taking turns shoving your cocks in every orifice they had while they screamed for you to stop." He laughed as Carter screamed and begged for him to stop. *"Just like you're doing now, you cocksucker."*

I hit pause halfway through. I couldn't watch. I fast-forwarded until I saw the flash of the knife.

"Admit it. Admit you're a perverted, cock-sucking pedophile," the killer demanded.

"Yes, okay? I admit it! Let me go!" Carter cried.

"It's good for you to cleanse yourself by admitting what you've done. Now you can die with a clear conscience," the killer murmured as he stabbed Carter in the neck, severing his carotid artery. Within a few seconds Carter was dead.

The voice didn't help because once again it was distorted. I did notice something in the video though. There was plenty of light and the killer was careful not to disturb the blood splatter on the floor. I could see it in the video as he dragged the chair with Carter tied to it from the scene. I wondered if there were still drag marks on the floor that were somehow missed because of the officers walking through the blood.

I finished my coffee and glanced at the clock. It was only four forty-five. I thought about going to the precinct, but I couldn't really do much there at this time of day. I wasn't going to go track George down on my own before the sun was even up. I also hesitated to call Angel. At least one of us should get a decent night's sleep. I decided to go have breakfast at Norms again and then go in.

I took my time eating, trying to put the images from that video from my mind. In the end I didn't even get through half my plate before my phone started ringing off the hook with various reporters requesting an interview. I had to shut my phone off just to get some peace as I drove.

When I pulled into the precinct at six thirty, I noticed a slew of news vans parked along the curb. As I got out, the reporters rushed forward shouting questions at me about the Broken Badge Killer and the latest video drop. Apparently, me hanging up on them didn't give them the hint that I was not going to speak to them.

"No comment," I said I as maneuvered through them toward the door. *What a great start to the weekend,* I thought, *not that I'd get to enjoy it at all.*

"Detective, you're the lead investigator. Can't you tell us if this has any connection—"

I didn't hear the rest of the question as the door closed behind me.

Angel met me at the door to the detective pool. He looked drained. "You saw it?"

I nodded. "You?"

"Captain called early. Sent me the video."

"Damn, I was hoping at least you'd get some sleep. Sorry, should have told him."

"It's fine. I thought maybe you went back to bed and didn't watch it yet," he murmured.

"Of course I watched it. Then went to Norms and ate, or tried to anyway." I sighed. "I guess we need to fill Jordan in on the video."

"Um. About that." Angel put his hands on my arms to stop me from moving. "Maybe we should just keep it to ourselves for a while? You know, just leave him be?"

Something about the way he was acting had me suspicious. "What's going on? Is he on a rampage again?"

"No... not... no..." Angel sighed and dragged his hand through his hair. "Come with me." He slid his hand down my arm to my wrist and led me to Jordan's office. Quietly, he twisted the knob and opened the door.

I stuck my head in and caught a strong whiff of alcohol. I

blinked and looked the room over. It was a shambles, and Jordan was passed out on his couch with his shirt unbuttoned, his tie loose around his neck, his jacket balled up under his head for a pillow. He had one shoe on, and the other was on the floor with his sock next to an empty whiskey bottle.

I backed up and shook my head. "What the hell? Does Robinson know about this?"

Angel closed the door. "No, I don't think anyone does," he said softly.

"Screw it. He doesn't need to know. Let's just get to work. How many bars did you make it through yesterday?"

"About seven."

"How many left?"

"About thirty."

"Okay, we'll get on those. I want to find where Carter was picked up."

We got to work, calling all around Santa Monica looking for whatever bar Carter had been drinking in. As it neared lunch we finally got lucky. If you could call it luck, seeing as it was one of the last three bars in the Santa Monica area for us to call.

I hung up the phone. "We got a hit. The bartender at Shipwrecked said he knew Carter and that he'd been in there."

"Wanna head over there?"

I sat, staring down the hall toward Jordan's office. He had yet to make an appearance. I knew he hadn't because I'd been watching. "No. Not yet anyway."

I was feeling a bit spiteful now, thinking about how often Jordan called me unprofessional and threw things in my face that were merely me doing my job, when he was lying in his office drunk as a skunk. I stood up and started toward Robinson's office.

"Marce?" Angel said.

I paused and glanced at him over my shoulder. "I'm telling Robinson."

Angel opened and closed his mouth and then simply nodded. "I've got your back."

I strode forward feeling a little more confident. I stopped at Jason's desk. "I need to see the captain."

"Is it important?" he asked, hesitating.

"Yes."

He frowned and then picked up the phone, hitting the button to buzz Robinson. "Sir? Detective Kendrick wants a word. She says it's important." He paused and flicked his gaze to me for a moment. "Okay, I'll tell her."

I waited as he put the phone back in the cradle, my arms crossed as I tapped my foot impatiently.

"He has three minutes, so make it quick." He tilted his head toward the door.

I gave him a nod and moved to Robinson's door, knocking twice before opening it. "Sir?"

"Come in, Kendrick. What do you need?"

I shut the door behind me and turned toward his desk. It was covered with stacks of paperwork and there were several boxes and suitcases stacked against the wall. I didn't comment, but I was pretty sure this meant he'd moved completely, or nearly completely, out of his house. "May I?" I asked, gesturing to a chair that had a box in it.

He nodded. "I have a meeting with the deputy mayor in five minutes, so make it fast."

"Yes, sir. I wanted to talk to you about Jordan."

Robinson's expression fell and he looked weary. "I know he's been acting erratically—"

"No, sir. I mean, yes, he has, but that's not what I meant. I went in to speak to him this morning about the video that was released and... sir, have you seen him this morning?"

Robinson paused. "No, can't say I have, and it's been pretty quiet. He is here, isn't he?"

"Oh, he's here, sir. Passed out drunk, half-dressed in his office."

Robinson blinked and then gritted his teeth. "He's still there?"

"As far as I know, sir. I haven't seen him come out. There was an empty bottle of whiskey on the floor."

Robinson stood up from his desk chair and started toward the door. "Come with me," he muttered.

"Yes, sir." I got up and followed him as he strode from his office toward Jordan's.

The captain threw open the door. Jordan was exactly where I'd seen him before, only he looked even more disheveled. And there was a second bottle of whiskey tucked in next to him that I hadn't noticed before. Robinson marched in and shook Jordan's shoulder.

"Wh-what?" Jordan muttered groggily, his eyes still closed.

Robinson's hand went to the bridge of his nose, and he looked stressed. He flicked his gaze at me. "If Reyes helps you, can you get him to your car and take him home?"

I didn't want to. I wasn't his wife anymore. It wasn't my job to clean up after him, but I could see how stressed Robinson was and I didn't want to add to it. "I guess so, sir, but only this once. I'm not married to him anymore. He's not my responsibility."

Robinson nodded. "I know, Kendrick. I won't ask it of you again. He'll either clean up his act or he'll be out of a job. I'm not going to have my lieutenant drunk off his ass at work. The deputy mayor is going to be here any minute and I can't let him see this." He gestured to Jordan, who'd passed out again.

"No, sir."

"If you wouldn't mind, give me ten minutes, and then get him out of here. That should be enough time to make sure the deputy mayor is in an office and not out where he'd see you getting him out of the building." Robinson turned and headed for the door.

I closed it and stood there wondering how I was supposed to get Jordan out of the building. Shaking my head, I picked up the phone on his desk and hit the button to call Angel's desk.

"Reyes."

"Angel, it's me. Can you come down to Jordan's office?"

"Sure. Why are you calling me on his phone?"

"Never mind that. Just come down here."

"On my way."

I hung up and started to pick up things in the office. I tossed the empty bottle in the garbage, then grabbed the other bottle from the sofa where it was tucked into Jordan's side. In his stupor, he attempted to grab it back, but for once, I was stronger than he was, and his hands fell away from the bottle. As I set it on the desk, a knock sounded at the door. I moved to it and opened it a crack, but seeing Angel, I let him in quickly and then shut it again.

"What's going on?"

"Robinson asked me to get Jordan out of here and drive

him home. He asked if you would help me get him to the car."

"Sure. But why you?"

I shrugged. "Because I was the one who brought Jordan to his attention?"

"We should fix his clothes. Then we can try and get him on his feet," Angel suggested.

"I've never seen him like this. What's going on with him?" I murmured.

"I don't know, but whatever it is, it can't be good."

We got Jordan's sock and shoe back on his foot, straightened his shirt and rebuttoned it, then fixed his tie. He was still mostly out of it, but we got him into a sitting position, and I was about to suggest we make him stand when I recalled I didn't have my keys, or my purse.

"Shoot. Can you stay with him for a minute? I need to go grab my stuff."

Angel nodded. "Check and see if the deputy mayor is already in Robinson's office. I'm sure Robinson doesn't want this seen."

"You're right about that. I'll check."

I hurried out of the door and as I passed Jason's desk, I noticed the captain holding the door open for David Combs, our deputy mayor. He was in his mid-thirties but looked older since he was already balding. The captain waved his hand at me in a shooing motion that I took to mean hurry it up. I rushed to my desk, grabbed my purse and slung it crossways over my shoulder, and returned to get Jordan.

"Okay, let's go," I said as I opened the door. I moved to Jordan's left side, slid my arm around his waist and draped his arm around my shoulders.

Angel did the same on his other side and we got him on

his feet. "Jordan, we're going to get you to Marcy's car. She's going to take you home."

Jordan merely grunted, his head hanging forward so his chin rested on his chest.

"This will be fun," I huffed.

It took us almost twenty minutes to get him out of the building and into the passenger seat of my car. Anyone who questioned us, we just told them Jordan was ill. I was sure the captain didn't want it getting around that Jordan had been drinking on the job.

"Do you want me to go with you?" Angel asked. "I can skip my physical therapy appointment."

I glanced across the roof of the car at him. "Nah, I'm good. Katie will help me get him in the house."

"Well, if you're sure. If something happens, call me."

"I will. Can you shut down my computer? I'm probably not going to make it back in until later this afternoon."

"Sure thing." He waved as I got in the car.

I put my seat belt on and headed out of the parking lot. Jordan had sold our old house and bought a newer, nicer, and more expensive one for Katie when he married her. It was in a gated neighborhood and had an inground pool. It was also a forty-minute drive to get there. I really hoped that Katie would be there when we arrived because I hadn't thought to call her to make sure.

"Such an idiot," Jordan muttered, his head lolling against the passenger window.

"Who?" I slid my gaze to him, but his eyes were still closed.

"Fuckin' George," he slurred. "Draggin' me into shit."

Of course, it sounded more like, *Fooken Jorg, dragooning my inna shi*—so it took me a moment to decipher it.

"George Peck?" I questioned.

Jordan snorted. "Fooken Pecker."

I wondered exactly what George had dragged Jordan into. Was Jordan admitting he was part of the Circle of Justice? Had he partaken in the drugs and prostitutes Weaver, Finlay and Nilsson were trafficking? The idea of it turned my stomach.

"Ne'er wanna know 'bout it," he mumbled and then drifted off to sleep, loudly snoring.

Eventually, I pulled into his driveway and parked. I glanced over at him, wondering how I was going to get him out of the car. I shook his shoulder, but he didn't wake. Sighing, I got out and went to the front door. I knocked and rang the bell.

A moment later, Katie, dressed in a pair of yoga pants and a crop top, her feet bare, answered the door. "What are you doing here?" she asked, looking at me with suspicion.

"I brought Jordan home. He's passed out in my car."

Her eyes widened and she looked surprised. "Is he okay?" She rushed down the step and over to my car. "Jordan? Baby?" She yanked open the door and squatted down next to him. "What did you do to him?"

I rolled my eyes. "Nothing. He did this all by himself. Didn't you notice he didn't come home last night?"

"Well, yes. We had a fight. We've been having a lot of fights lately, since we lost the baby," she said, but then paused and looked up at me. "Thank you for bringing him home."

"Sure. Let me help you get him inside." I ended up having to push him from the driver's side while she pulled, but we eventually got him out of the car and into the house. "Where?"

"Let's take him to the living room. We can put him on the sofa. It's closest."

I followed her lead, and we ended up in the room to the left of the front door. It was decorated in shades of gray and cream. There were expensive looking crystal decorations with gold accents sitting on the tables. It was all a bit too much for my taste, but to each their own. I dropped my half of Jordan on the sofa and backed up.

"Well, I'll leave him to you," I murmured as I turned back toward the door.

Katie got up from where she'd collapsed on the sofa next to Jordan. "Let me walk you out."

I gave her a tight smile and made a beeline to the open front door. "See you," I said with a half-wave.

"Thanks again, Marcy. I... you didn't have to do this." She looked embarrassed.

"It's fine." I started toward the car and then hesitated and looked back at her. "Tell Jordan when he's sober that he'd better clean up his act because Robinson is pissed."

She sucked in a deep breath and nodded. "I will."

On my way back to the precinct I grabbed a sandwich and fries as well as a Coke. I needed the caffeine. It was nearly four by the time I sat back down behind my desk.

Angel came in shortly after I did, sinking into his own chair wearily. "Did you get him in okay?"

"Yeah. Katie helped, but I have to tell you something."

He looked at me with curiosity. "What?"

"Jordan was muttering to himself on the drive there. He kept talking about George and how he was dragged into something and didn't want to know."

Angel's eyebrows shot up to his hairline. "You think he was talking about the Circle?"

My lips twisted as I hesitated. "I think so, yeah."

"Damn."

"I know—" I started, but then my phone rang. I held up a finger and answered, "Detective Kendrick's desk."

"Detective Kendrick? It's Selene Webb."

I straightened in my chair. "Selene, what can I do for you?"

"I— I didn't know who else to call. Bill said I should call you."

"Has something happened? Are you alright?"

She sniffled. "Yes, I'm okay. It's just... I've been getting threatening phone calls, and a little bit ago... well, he showed up here at the hotel." Her voice was barely a whisper and I had to strain to hear her.

"Who? Who showed up there?" I asked, suddenly concerned.

"George Peck. He said he could get to me wherever I was... I don't know what to do."

"Listen to me, Selene. The first thing you are going to do is check out of that hotel, go to another, and register under a different name. Stop using your cellphone and only make calls from the hotel to trusted people."

"But I can't afford—"

"Then borrow from a friend. If I could get you into protective custody, I would, but that's gotta be up to IA. You're part of their case, so I'll see what I can do, but I make no promises where they are concerned."

"Okay, thank you. I'll change hotels. How... how will you reach me?"

"I'm assuming you'll tell Bill where you are?"

"Yes, he's here now."

"Great. I'll call Bill when I have information. If you don't hear from me before you find a place, you can call me on my cell."

"Thank you, Detective Kendrick."

"Do you want to press charges against Detective Peck for harassment and intimidation?" I asked, hoping she'd say yes.

"I... I don't know. Can I think about it?" She sounded frightened and I was afraid she wouldn't do it.

"Of course. Let me know what you decide."

"I will," she murmured.

"I'll talk to you soon." I hung up and looked over at Angel. "George Peck has been threatening Selene Webb."

"We really need to go see him," Angel said, frowning.

"Let's take a drive by his place," I said, pushing keys on my computer to shut it down.

"You don't want to call first?"

"And give him a chance to deny us? Nope."

With a nod, Angel stood up and we left the precinct.

26

ANOTHER FUNERAL AND A MISSING GEORGE

MARCY

Driving by George's house had been a bust. He hadn't been home, and we couldn't find him anywhere. He wasn't in any of his usual haunts and seemed to have fallen off the face of the earth. By six we'd given up and called it a night.

On Saturday, we'd continued searching for him, with no luck. He hadn't shown up for work the previous evening, and nobody had seen or heard from him. I was worried that our killer had gotten hold of him before we could, but we didn't get any calls about a mutilated body, so my fingers were crossed that George was just passed out drunk somewhere and we just hadn't figured out where yet.

Arrangements had been made for Nilsson's funeral to take place today, Sunday afternoon, at West Angeles Church after their regular services. I'd dressed in my blues, which were getting an unfortunate workout this month. It was rare for me to wear my dress uniform more than once a year. Twice in a month was almost unheard of.

I was really hoping that George would show up to the

funeral, but when we got to the church, it was almost mass hysteria. There were protesters lining the streets, shouting profanities, and carrying signs calling for the LAPD to be defunded and all of us put in jail. I could see LAPD patrol doing their best to keep the peace, but there were clashes happening all over between them and the crowds of protesters, who were dressed in all black and wearing face paint and masks. I didn't envy patrol having to deal with that.

In the church, the pews were packed and there was barely even standing room along the walls. Everyone was dressed in their blues to honor Nilsson, who really didn't deserve it considering what he'd done, but because he'd died before he could be charged with anything, he was still getting a state-funded funeral with all the accolades. I wondered how that affected his pension and if his wife would be eligible to receive it. He hadn't been on duty when he was kidnapped and murdered. I seemed to recall some-where in the back of my head that because he was off-duty, she'd get nothing. I hoped he'd had life insurance.

"Nilsson was married, wasn't he?" I murmured to Angel and then realized that I'd never gotten the statements from the family from DeMarco.

"Yeah, he was, had a wife and three-month-old daughter."

"Did you get the statements from DeMarco?"

"Yeah, they came in while you were dealing with Jordan. I went over them before I went to therapy. Sorry, should have told you."

"No, it's fine. I was just thinking I hadn't gotten them yet, and I was gonna track him down and read him the riot act over it." My lips twitched as I tried to stifle my smile. It wouldn't be appropriate here.

"No need, Dirty Harrietta. We got them. Nothing really in them though. Sandra Nilsson, the wife, is twenty-three. That's her," Angel said, his voice soft, nodding toward a pretty blonde at the front dressed in black, holding an infant.

"Right, should have known that was her. What about the older couple with her?"

"Her parents maybe? His are deceased and he had no siblings."

"Okay. Thanks," I murmured, tuning back into the service.

We were standing toward the front, but off to the side. I could see most of the faces in the crowd, but not all of them. I was scanning to see if I could see George anywhere, but so far, I hadn't even caught a glimpse of him. I did make eye contact with Frank, whose lips curved up as he saw me.

As the funeral ended, I felt my phone buzz through my purse on my hip. I pulled it out to see a text from Frank.

> Going to the repast?

> Yes, but basically working. You going to be there?

> Daniel and I will be there. I'll find you.

> Okay, see you there.

"Who was that?" Angel asked, glancing at my phone as I slid it back in my purse.

"Frank Maldon. He asked if I was going to the repast."

Angel's eyes narrowed. "Did he?" He sucked his teeth.

I arched a brow at him. "Problem?"

He took a breath and then, after hesitating for a moment, shook his head. "No. No problem. Frank's a decent guy."

I studied him for a moment, before saying, "Come on, let's head over to the house. I still want to speak to the wife, since I haven't had a chance to do that myself yet."

We left the church and headed for Santa Monica Boulevard. They'd opted not to do a graveside service because of the baby. I wanted to give them time to get ready to receive guests before we showed up at their house, so I made a stop at the Blue Bottle Coffee shop.

There were vehicles lining the street when we got there, and it took another twenty minutes to find a place to park and walk back to the house. The door was standing open when we arrived, and people were entering and leaving, having paid their respects. I noticed a guestbook and a police cap overflowing with cash on a table next to the door. I opened my purse and pulled out a couple of twenties, dropping them in the hat.

"Thank you," a woman murmured from close to my left.

I turned to look at her. "I'm sorry, who are you?" I asked as Angel, too, dropped money in the hat.

"Sandra's mother. Gloria Fredericks." She held out her hand. "Carter left her with nothing but debts."

"I'm sorry to hear that." I shook her hand. "Do you know what her plans are?" I asked, trying not to be nosy, but I was also curious.

"We're going to put the house on the market and she and Isabelle are going to move in with us until she gets settled. I'm hoping to eventually talk her into going back to school." Her gaze tracked her daughter. "If he wasn't dead already, I'd kill him," she muttered.

"Um... what?"

"Sandra saw that video." Her eyes blazed.

My heart broke for her. "I'm so sorry she saw that. We tried to get it taken down as quickly as possible, but it was difficult."

Gloria nodded. "I know. Her so-called friends haven't been very kind. I'm really worried about her."

"I can imagine." I reached a hand out to her and rubbed her arm in comfort. "She may need therapy to deal with it. Especially after seeing that video and hearing everything Carter did."

"You're probably right. Still, getting her out of here and back to Pasadena will be good for her."

"Yes, a change of scenery will probably help."

"If you will excuse me, I've got to thank a few more people."

"Of course," I assured her.

"Damn, I feel bad for her," Angel said, his eyes on Sandra and the tiny baby girl in her arms.

"Me too. She didn't deserve to find out that way." My gaze traveled around the room. I was still looking for George, but hadn't seen him.

"I'm going to grab a drink. Want one?"

"I'm good, thanks," I murmured, my gaze catching on Frank and Daniel. They seemed to be in a heated discussion, both of them looking slightly agitated. "I'm going to wander."

"Okay, I'll catch up to you in a few." Angel headed for the kitchen.

I moved toward Frank, keeping my eyes on the surrounding faces, trying to see if I picked up on anything odd. Funnily enough, the oddest thing was that just as I was about to reach Frank and his brother, Daniel looked up, saw me, and then turned and left.

"Was it something I said?" I asked as I reached Frank's side.

"What?" Frank frowned, his gaze still on Daniel's retreating back. "Oh. No. I was just arguing with Daniel because he showed up drunk."

I looked at Frank and noticed his gaze seemed a little glassy, and I wondered if he had had a few drinks himself prior to getting here. "You okay?"

He gave me a sharp nod. "I'm good. This..." He looked around the room and sighed. "This hits hard. I knew Nilsson. Never would have thought he'd be involved in that sort of thing. He was an affable guy and easy to get along with."

"You worked with him a lot?"

Frank shrugged. "Not really. I mean, he was often the patrol officer who showed up at scenes. He did his job well, seemed like a good guy. He was friends with Daniel. They knew each other back in high school."

"Did they?" I wondered if them running in the same circles in high school led to them both being part of the Circle of Justice. I didn't ask though. This wasn't really the right venue for that.

"Yeah. Nilsson was one of those guys who always had a girl on his arm, sometimes more than one. I'd thought he'd settled down finally when he married Sandra."

"Doesn't look like it," I murmured. "I just spoke to her mom. She said Sandra saw that video of Nilsson. I wouldn't wish that on anyone, let alone his wife."

"Yeah. I hate that he's left her with nothing. She won't even get his pension."

"I know. I donated what I could."

"Me too. Hopefully, she'll have more help."

I looked around the room again, trying to see if George had shown up.

"You looking for Reyes? I think I saw him go into the kitchen."

"No, I'm actually looking for George Peck. I thought he might show up here."

"Is he one of your suspects?" Frank asked, a look of concern on his face.

"No, not exactly, though I suppose he could be our killer. I just came across some information and I needed to speak to him about it, but he's missing. I'm afraid the killer already got to him."

"Oh, well, he didn't. George is in hospital."

I glanced up at him, frowning. "How do you know that?"

"He was trying to get a hold of Daniel, but dialed me instead. He was ranting and off his head, honestly. I went to go see him and try to help him because he was slurring really bad over the phone. I know he's got nobody. When I got to his place, he was unconscious and lying next to a pool of vomit. I took him to the ER, and they admitted him for alcohol poisoning."

Of all the places I'd looked for George, the hospital hadn't been one of them. "You've got to be kidding me."

"Nope. They said they were going to keep him until his vitals looked better. He was still there this morning when I went by there."

I shook my head and sighed. "Thanks. I guess I should have asked you sooner." I smiled up at him.

His lips twitched. "You had no reason to think I would know."

I relaxed a little now, knowing I wasn't going to be

confronting George any time soon. "Maybe not, but you've seemed to come through with important information just when I need it. You're like my very own magic eight-ball." I winked at him.

He chuckled softly and then cleared his throat as glances were tossed our way. "I suppose there are worse things I could be to you."

I suppressed a grin as Angel joined us. "Frank just told me where we can find George."

"Oh? Where, and how do you know?" He looked at Frank with suspicion.

I quickly explained and Angel relaxed. "So I guess we can give up the search for now."

"Yeah. At least we know he hasn't been killed by our vigilante."

"Not yet, anyway. I'd like to keep it that way."

"So you still working after this?" Frank asked.

I shrugged and looked at Angel. "I think we're off for the rest of the day, right?"

He nodded, looking between me and Frank. "That's right." He glanced at his watch and then back up to me. "I think I'm going to head out, see if I can catch Callie before she makes dinner plans."

I glanced at him, my brow furrowed. "You rode with me, remember?"

"Oh. Right." He scratched his head and looked a little uncomfortable. "Then do you wanna go?"

I turned my gaze to Frank, whose expression fell, but he quickly hid it. "Wanna go for a ride?" I asked, looking at him.

"Sure. Daniel was my ride, and I was going to call an Uber, but I don't mind taking a ride if it means spending more time with you." He smiled.

The three of us said our goodbyes to Sandra and offered more condolences and then we climbed into my car with Angel insisting he'd ride in the back.

As I pulled away from the curb, I noticed Glen Jefferies sneaking around the side of the Nilsson home. I had to wonder what he was doing there and why he was acting so suspiciously. "Did you see that?" I asked, putting my foot on the brake.

27

FRIENDS WITH BENEFITS OR SOMETHING MORE?

MARCY

After reparking, the three of us went looking for Jefferies, but we couldn't find him anywhere. I'd checked with Sandra, and she did mention him stopping in to give his condolences, but she didn't know where he went. I wondered if maybe I'd misread the situation and was seeing suspicious behavior where there wasn't any just because he was on that list.

"Sorry, I thought maybe he was after one of the others..." I said with a sigh as we got in the car again.

"No problem. I'd have thought the same if I knew what you did," Frank replied.

Angel snorted and climbed in the back again.

I had to look over my shoulder at him to see if he was actually pissed off at me. "You good?"

"Fine," he answered and looked out the window.

Thirty minutes later, I pulled up in front of Angel's house and it was as though he couldn't get out of the car fast enough. "See you tomorrow morning," I called out of my window as he jogged up his front walk.

Angel waved, but didn't look back at us as he let himself into his house.

"So... you and Angel ever...?" Frank asked, one dark eyebrow raised toward me.

I shook my head, a small smile on my lips. "Let's just say I learned my lesson with Jordan. I don't play where I work."

He nodded. "Got it. So no transferring over to LAPD for me," he teased.

I laughed. "Definitely not. My original rule was no more dating cops... I think I'm about to break that one, but at least you're SMPD, not in Los Angeles." I pulled out of the driveway and back onto the street. "Wanna grab dinner?"

"I'd love it."

"Anything in particular you want?"

"I'm open to whatever, as long as it means spending more time with you." His voice was husky as he tucked a strand of hair behind my ear and caressed my cheek.

I felt my face heat. The man was dead sexy and made all my lady parts come alive. I swear a swarm of butterflies had launched into a frenzy in my stomach at his touch. I tried to think of where to go that wouldn't be too expensive but also wasn't fast food or a bar. If we weren't in our dress blues, I would have suggested barbeque, but it was too messy to eat in our good clothes. I glanced over at Frank. "Ever been to Engine Company No. 28?"

"Is that a restaurant?" he asked, sounding skeptical.

I grinned and headed there. "Absolutely. It was a fire-house back in the day, built in the early 1900s, I think. Anyway, it closed down in the sixties, but sometime in the eighties it was restored and turned into a restaurant. They have an amazing meatloaf and fantastic sandwiches."

"Sounds great," he agreed. "So how long were you and Brasswell married?" he asked, sounding hesitant.

"About ten years. I shouldn't have stayed married to him, but I actually took my vows seriously and I guess I just thought I needed to make the best of it. Well, until I found out about his cheating." I rolled my eyes.

"Gotta say, I never really liked the guy. He's a bit of a douche-canoe."

I snorted out a laugh and then covered my mouth as I glanced at him. "That's a good description."

"He give you a hard time now that he's your lieutenant?"

I slid my gaze over to him and decided to speak my mind. "He does, but I'd rather talk about anything other than my ex-husband, you know?"

He shrugged. "Yeah, I get that. I never married, but I was with a woman for a few years. Things didn't work out. I guess I wouldn't want to talk about her much either."

I pulled into the restaurant parking area and found a spot to park. "So have you dated a lot since her?" I asked as we walked into the restaurant. I'd always loved the ambience and decided I needed to eat here more often.

Frank shook his head. "Not really. A few dates here and there, but nothing that stuck."

"How many?" a host asked as we reached their podium.

"Two," I answered, and they led us to a booth near the brass fire pole.

The restaurant was busy, but not overly so. The host left us with menus, and I watched Frank's eyes light up as he looked around.

"This place is great. I can't believe I've never been here before." He gestured to the pole. "Does it work?"

I arched a brow at him. "Yes. I mean it's a pole."

He laughed. "I guess what I mean is can people actually use it?"

"Pretty sure it's just for decoration now." I smiled.

"Well, damn. I would have loved to try it." He picked up the menu. "So you don't usually date cops, you said, but have you dated much since your divorce?"

Henry flittered through my brain, and I swallowed hard. "Not really. I was seeing a guy a few months ago. I really liked him, but he was killed." I couldn't bring myself to look up from my menu.

"Killed? What, like in a car accident?"

My eyes began to water, and my throat clenched. "No."

Frank sat quietly for a moment, and I could feel his eyes on me, watching me, probably wondering why I was getting all worked up. I decided I needed to bite the bullet and tell him about Henry, at least a little bit. I laid the menu down and folded my hands on top of it.

Taking a deep breath, I said, "Henry was a consultant on the Face Flayer copycat case. He had written numerous books on serial killers, including on Lemuel St. Martin. We got to know each other, but Nick was obsessed with me and found out about me and Henry and killed him."

"Wait, are you talking about Professor Henry Strauss?" Frank asked, reaching a hand out to cover mine on the table.

"Yes."

"I heard about his death. I'm so sorry, Marcy." He squeezed my hand. "You know it's not your fault, right?"

I raised my eyes to his and gave him a watery smile. "That's what my therapist keeps telling me." I shook my head. "I know the only person to blame is Nicholas Pound, and I pretty much agree with that, but every now and then a little bit of guilt creeps in, you know?"

Frank nodded. "I do. The job we do is hard. It can really get in your head sometimes."

I sighed. "It can, yes."

The waiter chose that moment to appear, and Frank drew his hand back and picked up his menu again. We placed our orders and within a few minutes we had our drinks as well as a plate of truffle portobello fries.

I decided to broach a different subject, one a little more pressing. "So... have you had any luck getting Daniel to turn himself in to IA?"

Sighing, Frank lifted his glass of Guinness and sipped it. "No. He only told me some of what he got involved in and he's been pretty closed mouthed about the rest. He wanted the women found though, so I did take that to IA for him. He figured the others in the Circle wouldn't, and he felt guilty for taking part in what they were doing. Not that he even shared what he did." He sounded disappointed in his brother. "I just can't believe he got involved in the first place."

I glanced around the room and then leaned forward. "When I went to see Selene, she gave me the list of cops she knew were involved and what they did. Daniel was one of the men who administered the drugs to them," I said, meeting his gaze to see if it was new information to him.

Frank's eyes widened and he looked shocked. "What?" His brow furrowed and his mouth opened and closed a few times. "I don't even know what to say."

"You didn't do it; you don't have to answer for it. Your brother does."

He dragged a hand through his hair, his gaze meeting mine. "I should have known what he was up to. I should have stopped him."

"You aren't your brother's keeper, Frank. This isn't on you."

His jaw locked and he gave a single nod. "I know. Just—" He grunted and lifted his glass to take a gulp of his beer. He set it back down on the table a little harder than necessary. "I'm so angry with him. He's out of control. Drinking a lot, ranting... I know it's the guilt of what he's done that's eating at him, but he won't do anything about it. He won't get in front of it no matter what I tell him."

"All you can do is be there for him when he falls, because he's going to. IA has his name. They're going to go after him. I'm sure they're already building their case. They have Grant in custody. I know they were working on bringing Sam Finlay in before he was murdered. I'm not sure where they are on the list I gave them, but you have to know how meticulous they are."

"I do." He blew out an exhaustive breath and looked weary again.

"And I hate to bring it up, but with Finlay and Nilsson dead... you need to let Daniel know he's in danger. This killer... he's going after Circle members."

He didn't get a chance to answer as the waiter returned with our meals and new drinks. Everything smelled absolutely divine. I had ordered the classic meatloaf, mashed potatoes, and asparagus, while Frank had the ribeye with baby potatoes, asparagus and onion. We ate in silence for a few moments, enjoying the food.

"Want to try a bite of the meatloaf?" I offered.

"It does look great," he replied.

I cut off a piece and set it on his plate. "It really is good."

"The steak is perfect; do you want some?"

I shook my head. "I'm not going to be able to eat all of this as it is."

He smiled. "You are a tiny little thing. I don't understand how you face down so many serial killers the way you do. It's impressive." His eyes sparkled as he looked at me.

I laughed. "I'm not that tiny. I'm five foot six; that's average height for a woman."

"That's tiny. Itty-bitty," he teased.

I loved the way his eyes brightened and the way a dimple poked out as he teased me. "Only because you are a giant. How tall are you anyway? Six-three?"

"Six-four and half." His grin widened.

"Oh, can't forget the half." I took another bite of potatoes.

"Absolutely not." He chuckled as he raised his glass to ask for another from our passing waiter.

The waiter nodded and murmured he'd be back momentarily with a new round of drinks. I was only drinking soda since I was driving though.

"So, since you're a giant, did you play basketball in high school? College?" I asked.

"Nope; no coordination for it. I played soccer and ran track." He grinned. "I'm pretty good on my feet."

"So you've got some fancy footwork, do you?"

"Yup. I still run pretty often. How about you? Did you play any sports?"

"No, not really. I do run when I can. It keeps me in shape, and it really helps on the job, you know?"

"I bet it does." His gaze slid over me, or what he could see of me across the table from him.

The waiter returned with our drinks. "Would either of you care to order dessert?"

"The chocolate ganache cake sounded good; why don't we try that?" Frank replied, looking at me.

I was surprised he'd even looked at the desserts when we'd had our menus. "Okay, sure, but let's split a piece."

"You heard the lady," Frank said, turning his gaze to the waiter.

"One slice of chocolate ganache cake, and two forks, coming right up." He smiled and returned to the kitchen.

"I'm really enjoying this. I almost hate to end it," Frank murmured, looking across the table at me.

"Who says it has to end?" I raised a brow.

"Would you be interested in coming in and watching a movie when we get back to my place?" he asked.

I smiled. "Sounds good."

We ate our dessert and then Frank insisted on paying the whole bill before we headed to his place. He turned on a movie and got us beers as I slipped out of my jacket and laid it across the back of chair and took off my heels. I was still wearing my dress blues, and I did my best to get as comfortable as I could. I rolled up my blouse sleeves to my elbows and undid the tie, taking it off and setting it with my jacket.

I took a seat on the couch, and we continued to talk as we watched the show and snuggled together. Halfway through, we'd had a few beers, and I was getting buzzed. Frank started nuzzling my neck, sending fire racing over my skin. He planted kisses on my neck, behind my ear, along my jaw, and captured my lips in a searing kiss that had me climbing into his lap as I tried to get closer to him. My skirt rode up to my hips so I could wrap my legs around his waist. The movie was forgotten as his hands roamed over me.

He tugged on my blouse, pulling it from my skirt, and a

moment later his large hands were cupping my breasts and my head fell back as he planted kisses on my collar bone.

I was on fire. I knew I should probably stop this, but I didn't want to. I liked Frank. A lot. I wanted to be with him. I drew in a breath and brought my gaze to his. "Bedroom?"

Without any hesitation, Frank stood up with me in his arms. I wrapped my legs around his waist as his hands cupped my ass and his lips landed on mine. He moved us through the house, down a hall and into a bedroom. He laid me on the bed, and moved to the nightstand, opening the drawer and pulling out a box that he dropped next to my head. I realized it was an unopened box of condoms.

After getting me out of my uniform, he joined me on the bed and made love to me multiple times throughout the night. I fell asleep in his arms. At least I remembered falling asleep in his arms, but that wasn't how I woke up. I startled awake, sitting up with a silent scream on my lips as I looked around trying to figure out where I was and what I was doing. It took me a few minutes to recall the previous night and to realize it was Frank next to me. He was on his side, softly snoring.

My heart was racing from the nightmare I'd had, but I couldn't recall the extent of it. It was vague, but it had involved Nick and St. Martin. Something about it had me frightened for Frank and I knew I had to get out of there. It was completely irrational, but I was suddenly terrified that Nick would learn that I had been with someone new and come after him. It didn't make any sense because Nick was locked up and couldn't even contact me anymore. There was no way for him to know about Frank.

Still, I climbed from the bed, grabbed my clothes, and

quickly got dressed in my underthings, skirt, and blouse. I hurried to the living room, grabbed my jacket, tie, shoes, and purse and left the house.

28

MAKING HEADWAY ON THE CASE

MARCY

As I got in my car, I noticed the sun wasn't even up yet. I was still in a fog from the nightmare and probably shouldn't be driving, but I needed to go home, clear my head, and get my act together before I headed into work.

I glanced up at Frank's house and felt a slight smile cross my lips, but then I shook it off, started the car and pulled out of his driveway. It took me forty-five minutes to make it home. It was still early, so I put on my running clothes. I added my holster and gun because I didn't go anywhere without my gun these days, but it was under my clothes so unless someone grabbed me, they wouldn't even know I had it on me. I grabbed my keys and phone and left my apartment.

Outside, I did a few minor stretches to warm up and then took off at a jog. After the first few blocks, I picked up my pace. I'd run about six miles by the time I returned to my apartment building. I walked up the stairs to cool down, then let myself into my place. Stripping, I got in the shower and let the hot water sluice over me.

The nightmare was a distant memory but had left an uneasy feeling in my mind. The idea that Nick might somehow get to Frank and hurt him lingered, even though I knew it was absurd. I decided to log in and message my therapist, just to get some reassurance that my thoughts were crazy and shouldn't be given credence. Once that was done, I felt somewhat better. Even though I hadn't gotten a reply, it felt good to just vent about what I was feeling.

I dressed for work, putting on my usual dress slacks, a nice blouse, blazer, and my sneakers. Heels made it hard to chase down suspects, so I didn't wear them unless I was heading to court or had to wear my dress blues. I made sure I had everything I needed for the day, and then left.

Angel and I had no plans to ride together, but I headed for the coffee shop and grabbed our usual anyway, then sent him a text.

> Hey, grabbed your coffee. See you at the station.

I put my phone away without waiting for an answer. It didn't take me long to reach the parking lot. I parked in my usual spot —not that it was reserved for me, but it was generally open by the time I arrived, so I called it mine. I didn't see Angel's car, so when I got in, I set his coffee on his desk and sat down at my own.

I'd been thinking about what we needed to do today. First on my list was speaking to George, even if he was in hospital. It would probably be better to speak to him there; at least we'd be able to find him. Then we needed to head over to Shipwrecked and talk to the bartender who saw

Nilsson and get an idea of what his last hours were like before he was taken.

Angel walked in a moment later, carrying a box. "Morning," he said. "How was your night?" He was wearing a strained smile that didn't quite reach his eyes.

"Good morning to you too. It was good." I studied him, my brow furrowed. "What's wrong?"

He sat down and turned away from me. "Nothing's wrong. Why?"

"Don't give me that shit, Angel. Something's bothering you. Now spill it."

His fist clenched and unclenched. He sighed and his shoulders dropped. "Really, it's fine. I'm just frustrated."

I waited for him to elaborate, but he didn't. "Something happen with Callie?"

"No. And that's the problem," he muttered as he flipped the lid of the box open and pulled out a crème-filled donut with chocolate icing. He passed the box to me. "Want one?"

I picked out one of the donuts and pulled a napkin from my drawer to set it down on. "What's going on? Did you not see Callie last night?"

"No. She went out with some friends." His gaze drifted over me and I'm not sure what he saw, or noticed, but his features tightened a little. "You had a good night though. What did you do after you dropped me off?"

"Frank and I went out to dinner, ate at Engine Company No. 28, then went back to his place and watched a movie."

"You stay over there?" His gaze traveled over me as though looking to see if I was properly dressed, which I knew I was.

I could tell he was holding something back, and I had to

wonder if he had a problem with Frank. "Angel, is there something about Frank I should know?"

That seemed to take him by surprise. "What? No. I mean, yeah. I mean— I don't know what I mean." He sighed and pressed his finger and thumb on the bridge of his nose. "Sorry, I'm out of sorts. Frank is a good man. I've never had a problem with him. Never heard anything bad relating to him."

"Okay, good. Because I really like him."

He gave me a genuine smile. "I'm glad. Just didn't think you wanted to date a cop after Jordan, so maybe I'm a little protective."

I smiled back. "You're not wrong. I didn't want to date another cop after Jordan. But he's not LAPD, we have our own precincts, and he's not in my pocket. You know what I mean?"

Nodding, Angel said, "Plus he understands the job, unlike a civilian would."

"Exactly."

"At least he's not holding the job against you." His lips twisted and pursed.

"Callie?"

He nodded. "She's getting a lot of pressure to break up with me."

"I'm sorry. I know you really like her."

"I do. That's what sucks."

"I—"

"Kendrick! Reyes!" Jordan yelled down the hall from his office doorway. "My office! Now!"

Rolling my eyes, I got up and grabbed my coffee, taking a gulp before setting it back down again. "We better go see what his majesty wants."

Angel snickered as we walked down the hall. "You bellowed?" he said as we entered the room.

It took all my willpower not to snort and to keep my expression blank. I swallowed my laugh and looked around the room, which was still in a bit of a shambles. Then I looked—really looked—at Jordan. He had dark circles under his eyes. His suit was hanging from his frame as though it was a size too big, like he'd lost weight. He had stubble on his cheeks, which was unusual; he was always clean shaven. A very small part of me, the part that used to love him, felt concerned and wanted to rush over and take care of him, but I squashed that feeling the moment it bubbled up.

Jordan's gaze flicked to me, and he looked almost angry as he said, "Thank you for your assistance the other day. I wasn't feeling well."

"Sure." I pursed my lips, waiting for him to continue.

"Where are we on the case? Have you pulled that witch in for questioning again?"

"If by 'that witch' you mean Ms. Webb, then no. I have spoken to her. I've researched every possible connection she might have had to former members of the Serpents, and to the Sidewinders, but there just isn't anything. We have nothing to bring her in on. She's not involved in our case, except for the fact she's the victim of our victims." I kept from him the fact that I still had the names of three women to check.

"This is bullshit. She has to be involved!" Jordan insisted, his face reddening.

"Look, we've got other leads, Jordan," Angel said.

"What leads?" he demanded to know.

"We've found the bar that Nilsson was at prior to his abduction, and we have a possible suspect from IA. They informed me that George Peck has been threatening Ms. Webb—"

"Detective Peck isn't in any position to be threatening anyone," Jordan blustered. "He's in the hospital with alcohol poisoning, so there is no possible way for him to be the one behind the threats."

I gritted my teeth. "We'd like to speak to him—"

"Absolutely not. You won't disturb that man while he's recovering in the hospital. Do I make myself clear?" Jordan slammed his hands down on his desk, his face as red as a cherry as he stood up and stared at us.

It bothered me that he was being so overly protective of George Peck. It made me even more suspicious of him. I narrowed my eyes at him. "You realize, with him being part of the IA's investigation, he could be on the killer's hit list?"

Jordan's face suddenly lost all its color as he sank back down in his chair. "I have calls to make. Get out."

"What about us going to see George?" I asked, pushing it.

His gaze flashed to mine and hardened. "I said no."

Without another word, Angel and I left his office and returned to our desks.

I was so mad I wanted to throw something. "I don't know what's going on with him but the longer this continues, the more involved I think he is."

"I agree. If you'd asked me a year ago if Jordan was corrupt like that, I'd have said there was no way, but... for the last year he's been off."

I snorted. "It's been longer than a year, but since this story of corruption dropped it's like he's on the fast track to hell. I don't get it." Sighing, I sat thinking about what we needed to do since seeing George was out. "It's too early to go to Shipwrecked, isn't it?"

"They open at ten."

"Okay," I began, thinking about our options, "let's head into the incident room and go back over the video footage from the murders, as well as the security footage from Elixir. Maybe we can identify the killer that way?"

"That's as good of a plan as any."

We grabbed our coffees and donuts, which had sat half-eaten on our desks while we spoke to Jordan, and got to work.

Three hours later, I had a migraine from studying every aspect of the killer that we could see. I couldn't even tell how tall the guy was because he seemed to be half-bent over, and I couldn't be sure exactly where he had the camera. It seemed to be on his forehead, but that was a guess. And the only time his body was exposed at all was in that one clip where Frank had noticed his arm hair and watch.

"Well, best we can do is rule out blonds and redheads," Angel said in frustration.

"What about the watch? Anything we can get from it?" I asked.

"It's just a regular watch you can pick up at any retail shop like Target. It's definitely a man's watch, and the wrist is thick, like a man's, so pretty sure our killer is a man."

"Right, but who? Do you think this guy is a cop?" I asked. "One of the Circle trying to cover stuff up before more comes out?"

"Either that or someone who's acting as a vigilante because they are watching Selene give her story to that reporter on the news." He frowned. "Have we looked at him?"

"Who? The reporter?" I paused. "We haven't. Think he's worth a look?"

"Yeah, maybe."

I glanced at the clock. "Okay, let's go over to Shipwrecked, and when we get back, we can dig into Bill Meeks' life. And I still have those women to look at too."

We shut things down in the incident room and I grabbed my purse on the way out of the precinct. Shipwrecked was in Santa Monica. It was almost beachfront and there was a really nice view, even though the ocean was a bit in the distance, that almost had a calming effect as I breathed in the sea air.

My phone buzzed in my pocket, and I pulled it out before reaching the bar's door.

It was Frank.

Missed seeing you this morning. You okay?

Yeah, I'm good. Working. You?

Also working. We good?

I had to think about that for a moment. On one hand, I was in the middle of a case and didn't have time to start a new relationship, if that was what this was. On the other, I really liked Frank and last night had been amazing right up until I'd had that nightmare. It was that nightmare that gave me pause.

I think so. Need to go. Talk later?

Sounds good.

I pocketed my phone and joined Angel at the door. "Sorry."

"Everything okay?"

"Yeah, it's nothing."

He gave me a suspicious look, but then nodded and opened the door. We headed into the dimly lit bar and walked up to the repurposed wooden bar top that looked like driftwood and flashed our badges. "Are you the bartender I spoke to the other day? Larry?"

"That's me. You wanted to know about Carter?" he asked as he wiped down the bar top.

"Yeah. What can you tell us about that night?" Angel asked.

I looked around the bar, which was decorated with memorabilia from various shipwrecks. There were the big wheels they used for steering, fishing nets, a ton of mounted fish and sea life, and pieces from ships on the walls. As I scanned the room, I couldn't help noticing there were cameras by the entrance, above the bar, and in a couple corners of the room. I nudged Angel and tilted my head toward them.

He nodded.

"He came in around eight, had a few drinks with a buddy, another cop I think, but he's not a regular that I know, so I don't know for sure. Anyway, the other guy left around ten. Carter stuck around, played pool, and then I noticed him chatting up a redhead around eleven thirty. They had a few drinks and left here together around midnight. Figured he was gonna hit that hot piece of ass." Larry's gaze flashed to me. "Sorry."

I shrugged. I'd heard worse.

"Can we see your security tapes?" Angel asked.

He raised his arm and waved us back toward the office. "It's gonna be a bit cramped, but you're welcome to take a look." He sat down at the desk and tapped at the computer, pulled up the right date, and fast-forwarded to Carter walking in the door. "This camera is probably the best angle, but there you could probably watch number three as well. You want it on double speed or four times speed?"

"Four. We'll slow it down when we need to. You don't have to stay."

Larry fixed it, hit pause, and then moved out of the way. "I'll leave you to it then."

Angel took his place at the desk and hit play.

We watched as Carter drank with a man I didn't recognize. "Get a screen shot of him and send it to me," I said. "I want to question him."

Angel nodded, hit a button to capture the man's image, and then started the video back up. In all it took about twenty minutes to get to the end. "Should I go back and try to get a still of the woman?"

"Yeah, there's something familiar about her."

"I think so too," Angel agreed, rewinding the video and then pausing on a shot of the woman.

"Can you send the whole video to me? I want to have a copy for us, so we don't have to come back here. Actually, get copies of all the camera feeds. We might need them too."

Angel spent a few minutes making copies of the videos and then emailed them all to me. "I think it's the same woman who was with Finlay. Just in a different wig," he said a few minutes later.

"Yeah, that's it. She moves the same and she's ordered the same drink, I think. The eye color is different, but I'd swear it's her."

"We need to find her," Angel said, staring at the still image of the woman.

29

DEAD ENDS, PIZZA, AND SEX
MARCY

Angel and I left the office and returned to the main part of the bar. I showed Larry the image of the woman and asked, "So has she ever been in before? Do you know her?"

Larry took the grainy computer-printed photo from my hand and looked at it. "It's kind of hard to tell."

I sighed. I'd had a feeling that the printed image might not be the best, so I pulled up the video on my phone and fast-forwarded to where we had taken the still from and showed him. "How about now?"

Larry held my phone and brought it close to his face. His nose scrunched up as he studied it. "No, I don't think I've ever seen her before. You might want to stick around and ask Dawn, and maybe a few of the patrons who are here daily. They may recognize her."

"You wouldn't mind us doing that?" I asked.

Larry shrugged. "No skin off my nose."

"What time does Dawn come in?"

He glanced over his shoulder at the clock above the bar. "In about two hours."

"Okay, we'll come back."

Angel looked at me with confusion but didn't say anything. As we walked out of Shipwrecked, he finally asked, "What are we going to do for the next two hours?" He pulled open the passenger door and got in. "I can't imagine we're driving back to the station."

I sat down in the driver's seat. "No. Figured we could find somewhere and eat."

I got back on Ocean Ave and headed north toward the Santa Monica Pier area. "Oh, let's try Big Dean's," I said, seeing it as we got closer.

"Sounds good."

We spent the next two and a half hours eating and enjoying the weather. The sun was warm and the breeze from the ocean carried the saltiness of its waters. I needed to make a point to get out here more often. It was relaxing and I needed more relaxing things in my life.

After we finished, we headed back to Shipwrecked, which was now busy, and the parking area was quite full. For a Monday afternoon I was a bit surprised. Didn't any of these people have to work? I wondered.

"Maybe they're tourists," Angel said when I muttered my thought out loud.

The idea hadn't occurred to me, but I supposed it probably should have. Santa Monica was definitely a tourist destination with the pier and the beach right there. LA was too, for that matter, but for entirely different reasons. So many people from all over the world were drawn to what they thought of as the glitz and glamour of Hollywood and

LA. You couldn't go a block without running into someone on vacation.

"Probably right. That doesn't bode well for our questions though, does it?" I sighed.

Angel opened the door, and we were assaulted by Jimmy Buffett belting out "Margaritaville". If this were my district, I might be inclined to issue a noise ordinance citation, but it probably wouldn't stick. It wasn't that I didn't enjoy Jimmy Buffett, just not at such a high volume. We headed to the bar and caught Larry's eye.

He waved, finished up the drink order he was working on and then joined us. "You're back," he shouted over the music.

I nodded. "Any chance of turning the volume down a little?"

He shrugged, looked around the room and then nodded. He held up a finger, moved toward the stereo system and rolled the dial back a bit, lowering the sound to a more reasonable level to my ears.

"Thanks," I said when he returned. "How do you hear your customers with it that loud?"

"Oh, it doesn't stay that volume, only when Jimmy's on. Our patrons like to sing along, well, usually, but this group seems a bit more subdued. Of course, that could be because it's early on a Monday. Give it a few hours and they will all be singing at the top of their lungs."

I didn't know about Angel, but I was secretly glad we would not be here for that. "Has Dawn shown up?"

"Yeah, she's in the office going over the books. Let me get her." Larry turned and went toward the small office we'd been in earlier.

A moment later he came back, followed by a pretty

younger woman with long blonde hair, blue eyes, and a bright smile. She was wearing a red crop top and jean shorts, and had a flower in her hair, which was tucked behind her ear and secured with a bobby pin.

"Hi, I'm Dawn Hassenback. You had some questions for me?" Her voice was cheerful and bubbly.

"Hi, Dawn. Yes, we wondered if you recognized either of these two people," Angel said, pulling out his phone to show her the image of the man Nilsson had been drinking with, while I showed her the picture of the woman on mine.

She took Angel's phone. "Oh yeah, that's Jesse Kemp. He's a patrol officer. Comes in occasionally with—" she paused, her eyes getting a little watery, "Carter."

"Thank you. What about her? Ever seen her before?"

She looked at my phone, tilted her head. "No, I don't think so. And I'd probably remember someone with long red hair like that."

"We're pretty sure it's a wig. Maybe just look at her face?" I asked, urging her to take a second look.

She focused on the woman's face, studying it a bit more. "She kind of looks like... that actress from that show... *Friends*? The one who played Rachel?"

"Jennifer Aniston," I murmured.

"Yeah, her, but toward the end of the series, not as she is now."

I nodded. She wasn't wrong. The woman in the photo did have a similar face, but I knew it wasn't actually Jennifer Aniston. "Okay, well, thank you. Mind if we ask some of your patrons if they recognize her?"

"Sure, go ahead, but most of these people aren't from around here. Try the two at the bar down there by the window—they're here pretty often—and the one over by the shark teeth, at the single table. That's Mike; he might recognize her."

"Thanks."

After speaking to the men Dawn pointed out, we were still in the dark about who the woman was. The two men at the bar, who were probably in their sixties, said she reminded them of a young Rita Wilson, while the other just grunted and said no, he'd never seen her before.

"Well, that was a bust," I muttered as we left.

"Not totally. We did get the name of the guy drinking with Nilsson. Jesse Kemp. We should go talk to him."

I nodded. "Good idea. I'll head to the SMPD headquarters."

It didn't take us long to get there. We went in and asked about Officer Jesse Kemp, only to be directed to the station on the Santa Monica Pier. So, five minutes later, we were back in the car, driving to the other station.

"You should text Frank. He might know Kemp," Angel suggested.

We pulled into the parking area near the SMPD station on the Pier. We had to walk to the station from there. I pulled my phone out and sent Frank a text.

> Hey, do you know an SMPD patrol officer named Jesse Kemp?

It didn't take long for Frank to text me back.

> Sure, I know him. Why are you asking? Is he involved? You don't think he killed Nilsson and Finlay, do you?

> I can't talk about the case, you know that. But we do need to talk to him. Know where we can find him? Headquarters sent us to the Pier.

> I know, sorry. Just surprised me. He's a good guy, or I've always thought so at least. But then I would have said Daniel was too, so what the hell do I know?

I frowned and was about to text him again, when he sent another.

> If he's not at Pier, he's on patrol, but they can call him back there. Ask the desk sergeant, Glenn. He'll get him for you.

> Thanks, Frank.

> No problem. Text you after work?

> I'd like that.

I put my phone away. "Frank says if he's not here to ask the DS, Glenn, to get him back here."

Angel nodded. "I know Glenn."

We went in and Angel talked to Glenn, who was a heavyset man with gray hair and brown eyes. He said that Kemp was on patrol, but it wouldn't take long to get him back to the station, and that we could wait in the breakroom and he'd let us know when Kemp returned.

He wasn't wrong. Kemp was back at the station within fifteen minutes.

"You were asking for me?" The young officer looked haunted and a little confused. He had light brown hair and eyes the color of coffee. He looked exactly like the still image from the bar.

"We were, Officer Kemp. I'm Detective Kendrick. This is Detective Reyes. We're working the Finlay and Nilsson murders. It's our understanding that you saw Officer Nilsson the night of his murder?"

"Oh. Yeah. I met him at Shipwrecked for a few drinks, but I left around ten. He was still there when I left—alive, I swear."

"Yes, we know, we've seen the video. We just wanted to ask you a few questions about that night. If you wouldn't mind?"

"Yeah, sure." He nodded, looking a little more comfortable.

"Did Carter seem like himself?"

Kemp seemed to consider my question before answering. "Yeah, he seemed like himself. He was a bit of a player, you know? He liked to talk about women, and he was always checking out all the women who were around him. He only married Sandra because she was pregnant. Probably the one decent thing he did giving the baby his name. He treated her like crap otherwise."

"Did he seem worried about anything?"

"No, he was just looking for a good time. He did get a little pissed off when Sandra texted him a couple of times. Said she wouldn't leave him alone when she knew he was out with his buddies. That's what he told her, that it was 'guy's night', but it was just the two of us, and as I said, I left by ten. I'm not even sure I was there more than two hours total."

"So was there trouble between him and Sandra?"

Kemp's shoulders lifted and fell, and he gave me a bewildered look. "I don't know for sure. Carter hated being tied down, so they did fight a lot, but they always did, so it wasn't unusual for them to argue. It was always about him going out drinking, and I'm pretty sure she knew he was with other women."

Angel said, "Did you see anyone watching Carter? Did you notice anything odd in the bar?"

"No. It all seemed pretty normal. Nobody paid any attention to us except the cocktail waitress who brought us drinks."

"What about outside? Did you notice anything odd? People who were hanging around but didn't belong?"

"This is Santa Monica; people are always hanging around, but nobody that seemed to be doing anything hinky."

"Okay, thanks," Angel replied, sounding worn down.

"If you think of anything, would you give us a call?" I offered him my card.

"Sure." He pocketed my card. "Can I go? I need to get back on patrol with my partner."

"Yeah. Be safe."

Nodding, he turned and headed back out to the front of the station.

Angel and I followed, waving to the desk sergeant before heading back to our car.

"Think this has anything to do with Nilsson's marriage being rocky?"

Angel shook his head. "Doubt it."

"I didn't think so either," I muttered, getting in the car and turning it on. "I am starting to believe we're one hundred percent dealing with a cop."

"I've been thinking that for a while now too. Everything's

been planned, and though with Sam's death it was hesitant, it was still meticulously cleaned up. Like they knew everything we'd look for. The videos have been carefully edited, not showing us anything they don't want us to see. The one slip was that tiny bit of forearm, which was only on screen for a second and really didn't tell us much."

"I bet that Bill Meeks has some videography experience. I suppose being an investigative journalist, he might have an awareness of police procedures," I suggested, thinking about what we needed to do next.

"That's a good possibility. You did want to dig into him. We've got a couple hours left before shift ends. Let's go see what we can find."

Three hours later, we were still at our desks turning over every rock in Bill Meeks' life. All his socials, every story he'd investigated, every person he'd been involved with. We left nothing untouched. And we were at a dead end.

"I'm finding nothing that ties him to these murders. Nothing that puts him at any of the scenes, no connection to our murdered cops. The only thing even close is that he's writing Selene Webb's story," I commented at five minutes to five.

"Same. Want to call it a day?" Angel asked, logging out of his computer.

"Yeah." I rubbed my forehead. I hated that we were getting nowhere fast. I also hated that we still weren't allowed to talk to George Peck. "I don't care what Jordan says, we're talking to Peck tomorrow."

"Is he out of the hospital yet?" Angel asked.

"I don't know. Let me call over there and see what I can find out." I picked up the phone and called the hospital. Ten minutes later, I had an answer. "He's being released this evening, but they're waiting on paperwork."

"Good, then let's head over there first thing in the morning."

I nodded. "And before Jordan can tell us no. His reasoning before was George was in the hospital. He won't be tomorrow, so there's nothing to say we disobeyed a direct order, right?"

"Exactly." Angel smiled. "I'm heading out. See ya in the morning, Marce."

"Bye."

I took an extra few minutes to close things down, grab my purse and head out to my car. As I got in, my phone buzzed. I pulled it out of my pocket and smiled. It was Frank.

Dinner? I've got pizza on its way here.

Give me an hour. Want to go home and change first.

I'll keep the pie warm for you.

I drove to my apartment, hurried in, and took a quick shower before changing into a pair of jeans and a cute blue top with capped sleeves. I started to leave and then recalled the night before. Tonight might be a repeat of that and I figured it would be better to be prepared than to have to rush home before work tomorrow, so I tossed a few things in a duffle bag and then jumped back in my car to head to Frank's place.

I wasn't mistaken. Frank met me at the door with an intense kiss that tasted like he'd already had a few beers' head start on me. We ate the pizza, drank a twelve-pack of beer, and ended up in bed together by nine thirty.

Sweaty and satiated, I was enjoying the sensation of being cuddled and cared for in his arms. I was relaxed, even though I probably shouldn't be. Guilt that I was here having a nice, relaxing, sexual encounter—okay, mind-blowing encounter—with one of the hottest guys I'd ever had the pleasure of knowing, while our killer was running loose made me tense up a little in his arms.

"What's the matter, tiny tornado?" Frank asked, kissing my temple.

I smiled. I liked the endearment. "Just thinking about the case. Feeling guilty for being here, having a good time."

"Are you?"

"Am I what?"

"Having a good time."

I turned in his arms and pushed up on his massive chest so I could look him in the face. "Yes. But that's not the point."

"What's the point?" He arched a dark brow at me but seemed intent to listen to what I had to say.

"The point is I don't know what this is between us and even though I'm enjoying it, I'm not sure I should be here. I know you aren't involved, but there is a someone out there who is hunting down cops and killing them. I need to find him. I need to catch him."

"And you will. You always do from what I can tell. You're very good at your job, babe. I've seen how intense you get when you're working a case."

My brow furrowed. How had he seen it?

He grinned. "You don't think I looked up every single thing I could find about you when I met you? I don't just call you my tiny tornado for how you are between the sheets."

He chuckled. "You stir things up, you whirl around chasing down every single serial killer with such intensity that you're like an F5 tornado. Small, but mighty."

I felt my cheeks heat. "It doesn't bother you?"

"Nope. You're competent and skilled. Even under pressure, when the serial killer is targeting you. It might take you a minute to get there, but you will. You have drive." He put his hand on my chest, over my heart. "You have heart, something in here that pushes you to give everything to everything you do, but especially in catching killers. It's impressive."

I leaned in and kissed him. I'd thought maybe what was between us was just really good sex, but if he kept talking like that, I was going to catch feelings, if I hadn't already. I folded my hands on his chest and rested my chin on top of them. "I like you."

He chuckled. "I like you too."

"How's Daniel doing?" I asked, knowing that he was worried about his brother. I wanted to show that I understood that.

His grin melted away and his gaze grew worried. "I honestly don't know. He's not answering my calls, or our parents' calls. He's stopped coming in to work. I'm really worried about him."

"I'm sorry," I murmured.

"I'm scared that the killer might go after Daniel next." He wrapped his arms around me tighter, holding me as though I was his life line.

I shifted and put my arms around him too. "I'm sure he'll be okay. I'm going to catch this guy. I promise."

I really hoped I wasn't lying.

30

EASIER SAID THAN DONE

I'd had to change my plans. I didn't like when things didn't go as I had planned, and it left me frustrated. Getting to George Peck was easier said than done, considering the man had drunk himself into such a stupor that he nearly killed himself with alcohol poisoning before I could get my hands on him.

It would have been too kind of a death, so I was glad he was recovering, but it put my plans for him on hold. Which was why I was sitting in my van with Carrie outside the hospital in the parking lot waiting for George to be released on Monday evening.

"How much longer do we have to wait?" she asked impatiently as she adjusted the jet-black, pixie-cut wig she was wearing. It didn't really suit her face. She looked much better as a blonde. She turned her currently violet eyes toward me, a look of irritation on her face.

"As long as it takes." If anything, I had an abundance of patience now that my plan was able to go forward. I couldn't afford to make a mistake. "You need to relax. There are people around and we don't want to be noticed."

She sighed. "Fine." She pulled out her phone and began watching videos.

Fifteen minutes later, George was wheeled out as a car pulled up to the entrance.

"Here we go," I said. "You remember the plan?"

"Yeah. I know what I'm supposed to do." She put her phone away.

As soon as the Uber driver pulled away with George, I followed at a distance. I was wearing gloves, so I wasn't worried about leaving prints on the steering wheel or anywhere else. My mask was waiting in my lap, and I'd be pulling it on as soon as we reached our destination. I had a feeling I knew where we were headed, but I wasn't taking any chances.

I followed the Uber to George's neighborhood and smiled. He'd gone home, exactly as I'd thought he would. I parked the van on the side of the road about a block away, where George wouldn't be aware of us until I was ready. I moved to the back of the van with my mask. "You remember what to do?" I checked once again as Carrie climbed into the driver's seat.

"Go, would you? I want to get this over with."

"Wait ten minutes, and then pull up and park. I'll meet you at the van when I've got him," I reminded her before I climbed out of the back, shut the doors quietly, and dashed across the street.

None of the houses had fences and the yards were quite large, which made it easy for me to move through them. Even if the people who lived in these homes were to look outside, it would be doubtful that they'd see me, dressed as I was in all black, with the sundown. There were no street-lights or yard lights out this far toward the back of their properties. I reached George's yard and headed up toward the house, staying low so that I wasn't taller than the bushes that marked his property line. Finally, at the back door, I used my lockpicks to open it as quietly as I could.

I heard George talking to Carrie at the front door as I entered the kitchen. "May I help you?" he asked, his voice raspier than normal.

"Hi. I'm so sorry to bother you, but my van got a flat and I don't have a jack to lift it up so I can change the tire. Do you think you can help me?" Carrie simpered.

I could picture her biting her enticing lips and giving him puppy dog eyes. There was a reason men loved paying her for her services. She could play the innocent with the best of them.

"I'm too sick to help you, but I've got a jack you can use. Give me a minute."

"Oh, that would be great," she said, sounding bubbly and full of sunshine.

As I heard George coming my direction, I moved to the far side of the refrigerator so he wouldn't see me as he pulled open the door I knew led to the garage. I'd been in his home often over the last few years. I wished I had never even met him. The man was vile.

I followed behind him, planning to take him out.

Unfortunately, things did not go as planned.

31

BEST LAID PLANS THWARTED

MARCY

I woke up wrapped in a pair of muscular arms to the sound of my phone playing "Mean" by Taylor Swift. I grabbed it from Frank's nightstand and sat up in the bed, the sheet falling to my waist. It felt wrong to talk to Jordan with my breasts hanging out, so I pulled the sheet back up to cover me.

"What?" I said, not even caring that I probably sounded rude. He was the one calling me at six in the morning.

"Marce?" His voice sounded off, shaky and as though he was upset.

"Yeah, Jordan. What do you want?"

Frank sat up and kissed my shoulder. "Coffee?" he murmured softly.

I nodded and watched as he climbed from the bed, padding across the room to grab a pair of boxers before going out the door.

"George Peck has been murdered," Jordan whispered into the phone.

"What?" I nearly dropped my phone.

Frank popped his head back into the room, a concerned look on his face. "What's wrong?"

I waved a hand at him as I spoke to Jordan. "When and where?"

"Sometime last night. A neighbor found him on his lawn about twenty minutes ago when they were out for a morning run. I'm headed over there. Can you and Angel meet me there? Patrol is on their way to secure the scene."

"It's going to take me a while to get there. I'm not at home."

"Where the fuck are you?" he demanded.

"That's none of your damn business, Jordan. I'll be there in about forty minutes." That would be a miracle, if I actually made it in forty, but I'd do my damnedest to be there by then. I hung up before he could say anything else.

"What's happened?" Frank asked again.

"George Peck was murdered sometime last night at his house," I said as I got out of his bed and reached for my duffle to get dressed.

"Coffee is brewing. I guess you'll be taking yours to go," he said with a sigh.

I paused and looked up at him. "I'm sorry. It's the job."

He smiled. "I know, tiny tornado. You get dressed. I'll hand you your coffee on your way out the door."

I quickly slid into my dress slacks, blouse, holster and weapon, and my socks, then ran into the bathroom and brushed my hair. I tossed everything into the duffle, put on my sneakers, and rushed toward the living room. Frank was waiting there with a tumbler of coffee for me. He pulled me into him and kissed the ever-loving-shit out of me and then opened the door.

"Drive safely and try not to break any land-speed records, okay?" He smiled.

I laughed. "I'll make no promises on the last part, but I'm always safe." I winked and jogged to my car. I tossed the siren onto the dash, and turned it on as I backed out of his driveway. I could see him waving to me as I sped down the road.

I called Angel on the way, and told him I was coming from Santa Monica and that I was thirty minutes out. He said he'd meet me there, though he did offer to get coffee on the way, but I told him not to bother with one for me because I already had one.

I made it to the scene in forty-three minutes. Better than I expected, honestly. The siren helped, even though there were idiots on the road who refused to get out of my way and I'd had to go around them. If I could have, I'd have pulled them over and written them tickets. Not that traffic violations were within my purview.

I had turned off my siren as I entered the neighborhood; no sense disturbing the neighbors, though they were probably already disturbed. George's front lawn was surrounded by yellow crime scene tape and there was a massive white tent on the lawn. A crowd of people had gathered at the edge of the tape, as well as several news reporters, their camera people taking in the scene.

I flashed my badge at Officers Kim and Desmond, who were manning the tape and making sure nobody who wasn't supposed to cross did. I could see Jordan and Angel standing just outside the tent and I headed over to them.

"What happened?" I asked.

"It's about damn time you got here! I should report you for incompetence—" Jordan blustered.

Gritting my teeth, I shook my head. "I was off duty and not on call, and what I do on my own time is my business, not yours. I got here as soon as I could. Now, what do we have?"

"Looks like whoever attacked George attempted to knock him out, but George fought back. There is a mess and a lot of blood in the house that leads out the front door to here," Angel said, directing my attention to the tent.

"Don't ignore me," Jordan shouted at me, his face turning red. "I'm your superior officer. I demand—"

I whirled around and got in his face, keeping my voice calm and quiet because nobody needed to know my business. "You are my lieutenant. However, you have no right to demand anything from me about my whereabouts when I am not on duty. I will be taking this up the chain and if you don't stop harassing me, I will make sure IA gets involved."

Jordan's face was almost purple with anger, but he didn't say another word.

I turned back to Angel. "So how did he die?"

"Believe it or not, he was shot in the head. I think because he overpowered our killer at some point at the beginning of the encounter. I'd say he was lucky, but considering he still ended up dead, I guess not."

"How do we know this was our guy?"

"Come take a look. Damien's in there now. Lindsey and her team are in the house."

I followed him into the tent. I could see immediately how Angel knew it was our killer. George's body was naked and bound, there were multiple stab wounds to the body, and he also had numerous taser marks. What didn't make sense was that Angel had said he'd been shot in the head.

"So, did the killer do all of this damage and somehow George got away and that's when he was shot?" I asked.

"No, he was shot first." Damien turned the body and pointed to a spot on the back of the head. "See this? I believe the killer tried to hit him first, but the blow wasn't strong enough to knock George out. So there was a struggle. You can see the bruising on the arms where they probably grappled." He pointed to the purpling skin.

"Okay, so what then? They grappled, George got away, made it out here and the killer shot him, then did all of... this?" I waved my hand over the body.

"Pretty sure he was shot just inside the hallway, but with all the adrenaline in George's body, he made it out here and collapsed. He probably died before he hit the ground though. All these stab wounds are more jagged than they were in the previous kills. As though the killer was angrier, and the thrusts are deeper than the ones on the previous bodies. I'll know more when I get him back to my autopsy table."

"Okay. Thanks, Damien." I headed back out of the tent. "I want to see the scene."

Angel and I walked toward the house with Jordan following hot on our heels. He didn't say anything, but I could feel his fury wafting off him in waves. Whether that fury was directed toward me or the killer was a question for a different day. Like, when pigs learned to fly, because I really didn't care about the answer.

As I stepped into the hallway, I could see smears of blood on the walls and on the floor. Furniture was overturned, knickknacks were shattered on the floor, and picture frames were hanging cockeyed on their hooks. "Do we know if all this blood is George's?" I asked.

"Not sure yet, but we're taking samples of all of it back to the lab," Lindsey said, joining us in the front hall. "There's a lot to process here, but I can tell you that the altercation looks to have started in the garage." She led the way to the door leading to the garage.

"So, what? The killer was waiting in the garage for him?"

Lindsey hesitated. "I don't think so. The back door was unlocked, but I could see scratch marks on the lock itself, like it was picked. My guess would be the killer was in the house, George went to the garage for something and was attacked from behind. So the killer was here as George started into the garage." She indicated the area that led to the kitchen.

"What makes you believe that?"

"Well, there's nowhere for the killer to have been hiding to have been able to hit George from behind. George would have seen him. Plus, you can see that the fight doesn't make it past this step. There's no blood or anything leading into the garage, but there is leading into the house itself."

I nodded and followed the path Lindsey led us through. The struggle went from the garage, down the hallway, into the living room, then back to the hall by the front door and then outside. "Send me your results and report as soon as you've got them ready."

"Will do."

I headed outside with Angel, Jordan still tagging along like a lost puppy now. As though he had no idea what he was supposed to do. He looked whipped. Almost afraid. I looked at the news vans and the people crowded around trying to catch a glimpse of what was going on, and as I scanned the faces, one stood out.

I narrowed my eyes and tried to get a better look without

drawing attention to what I was doing. The woman held her phone out as though filming the events taking place. Her phone panned in our direction, and I took a step forward, my eyes still on her.

"What are you looking at?" Angel asked.

"A woman, to the left of Desmond, jet-black hair in a pixie cut. Wearing jeans and a T-shirt," I murmured.

"Got her," Angel murmured as we both started toward her.

"Where are you going?" Jordan asked loudly.

The woman's gaze flicked up from her phone screen to me. She backed up quickly and then turned and took off down the street.

"Angel—" I started as I ran after her.

"I see her. She's headed for a car. We need to follow her!"

I changed my trajectory and headed for my car, pulling my keys out as I ran. "Don't take your eyes off her."

"Where are you going?" Jordan shouted after us, about ten steps behind.

If he thought I was going to wait for him, he had another think coming. I yanked open the door and slammed my key into the ignition. Angel slid into the passenger seat, and I threw the car into gear and stepped on the gas. We were both still trying to get our seat belts on as the car jolted forward. I could see Jordan shouting as he stood in the middle of the road.

We raced after the blue Honda that was taking off down the street with the woman I knew was part of all of this.

I watched the Honda, which I now recognized as a Civic hatchback, race out of the neighborhood. The woman pulled into the intersection, in front of several cars, nearly causing a collision, and then made a hard left.

"Siren," I muttered, knowing what I was about to do was dangerous.

Angel hit the button for the siren, and I kept my eyes on the cars in the intersection. There were a few oncoming cars, but upon hearing the siren they slammed on their brakes, thankfully, and we sailed into the intersection. I yanked the wheel to make the same left turn our suspect had.

"She's gaining speed," Angel said, "and she just turned right."

"Got it. Put out an APB on her," I replied.

Angel picked up the radio and called it in. Dispatch asked for a plate number, but we hadn't gotten close enough to see it. "Don't have it. It's a blue Honda Civic hatchback, probably 2010-2015, with a female driver. She's got short black hair."

"I'll put it out over the radio. We'll have patrol looking for her."

"She's turning left," Angel said to me.

"I see her. Can you make out the plate yet?" I pressed on the gas trying to gain on her, but she wasn't slowing down.

"No—" he started, but then suddenly he shouted, "Watch out!"

Everything had come to a standstill and I had to slam on my brakes. I stopped the car about six cars behind the woman we were chasing. The good news was, she was also stuck in the traffic jam. There was no escape.

I shifted the car into park and got out.

"Marcy, wait—" Angel called, but I was already out of the car.

I started toward the woman in the Honda, but she must have seen me get out of my car because she was climbing from hers as well. She glanced at me and then took off running. "Stop! LAPD!" I shouted after her.

Angel was a couple feet behind me as we wove through the stopped traffic. I watched the woman head into an older building that had plastic covering several broken windows. It stood about twelve stories high and was made of brick, but it seemed to be ready to come down at any moment.

I followed the woman through the front of the building, but it was dark. I pulled my weapon, and heard footsteps on the stairs. I couldn't tell if they were going up or down though.

"Marcy!" Angel called from outside of the building.

"Come on! She's in here," I replied.

"We need to wait for backup!"

I knew he'd called them, but I didn't want to give up the chase. I started toward the stairs. The alcove they were in was dark and it was hard to see. I stood at the top of one staircase that led downward, but next to one that went up. I tried to listen to see which direction she had gone, but I couldn't be sure.

The next thing I knew, I was shoved from behind.

As I tumbled down the stone stairs, I covered my head, trying to protect myself. Thankfully, the staircase was only six steps total before it hit a landing. I lay there for a moment assessing my body, trying to figure out if I'd broken anything.

A light flashed in my face and then illuminated the area.

A person wearing a dark ski-mask covering their face stood over me, holding a phone with the flashlight on. In their other hand was a gun. And it was pointed right at me.

32

A CLOSE ENCOUNTER

MARCY

I was suddenly terrified that I was about to die. My gun had flown from my hand when I fell, and I wasn't sure where it had ended up. I could tell from the clothes the person was wearing that I was dealing with the same woman I'd been chasing.

"Damn it. You aren't the cop I'm after. Stop chasing me or I'll have to stop you," she said, her words harsh despite the melodic tone of her voice.

"Who are you after?" I asked, trying to think of whom she could have expected to chase her.

"Not you and not your partner, but someone who could—"

"Marcy!" Angel called from somewhere behind the woman.

"Time for me to go," she muttered as she clicked her flashlight off, sending us into darkness again.

I had no idea where she went. I heard her feet on the stairs, moving upward, which had to be right, considering to go downward she'd have had to step over me, but I wasn't sure where she went after that. I knew I wasn't going to be able to get up on my own though, since I was pretty sure I'd twisted or maybe even sprained my ankle.

"Angel? I'm down here," I called.

Angel rushed down the stairs. At least I hoped it was him, but he was just a black mass moving in the darkness. "Marcy, are you okay?" His voice was anxious as he reached me.

"Yeah, but I think I sprained my ankle. Can you put your phone's flashlight on? My gun is here somewhere, and I'd rather not leave it."

"Shit, yeah, hang on."

A moment later the staircase lit up. I saw my gun about a foot away toward the edge of the landing heading to the next set of stairs. I scooted over and grabbed it, checking it before sliding it into my holster.

"Where'd she go?" Angel asked. "Did she go upstairs or down?"

"Pretty sure she went up, but where she is now, I don't know. If you didn't pass her on your way into the alcove, then she probably went up another floor. I doubt she's still in the building though. She most likely went out via one of the fire escapes." I sighed.

"How did you end up at the bottom of the stairs? Did you not see the steps?"

"Of course I saw them. She pushed me. I thought she was going to kill me. I'm honestly not sure why she didn't."

"Did she say anything?" Angel asked as he helped me to my feet.

"She said we weren't the ones she was after and if I didn't stop following her, she would stop me." I snorted. "I don't think I could have followed her if I wanted to. Pretty sure my ankle is the size of a baseball right now."

"Good to know we aren't on her hit list. Let's get you up these stairs and outside. Backup should be here by now. Maybe they'll see her coming out of the building."

I wasn't going to hold my breath. The woman seemed to be able to escape everything. I had to wonder whom exactly it was she actually was after. There had been any number of cops roaming around the scene. Maybe she thought one of them would give her away? I wished she'd elaborated and told me whom she'd been after and why.

Outside the building, several patrol cars were parked along the road. The officers had their weapons drawn as they surrounded the building. I hobbled out with Angel's arm wrapped around my waist, keeping me upright. My ankle hurt like a bitch, and I was cussing under my breath, the woman forgotten for the moment.

"Looks like I'm driving you to the hospital."

"No, just take me back to the scene. If anything, Damien can look at it. It's not broken, just swollen, and probably sprained really bad."

"Marce, you're bleeding," he practically growled.

"I'm fine. Take me back to Peck's house. We still have a scene to finish processing."

My car had been moved to the side of the road and a patrol officer was standing near it. He handed Angel the keys and then he helped me into the passenger seat. It was my left ankle that had been damaged, so I probably still could have driven, but I really didn't want to because I was in more pain than I was letting on. I hoped Angel didn't realize how much pain I was actually in. If he did, he'd ignore my request and take me to the hospital anyway.

Fifteen minutes later we were back at the scene, and I relaxed a little bit. "Thank you," I said, opening the car door.

"Don't you dare move. I'll get Damien." Angel hurried from the car and toward the tent.

I noticed that the crowd had thinned and the news vans were gone. I wondered if we'd been gone longer than I'd thought. Maybe Damien wasn't even here anymore. I shouldn't have doubted it though, because I saw him with Angel and Jordan a minute later walking toward me.

"Angel said you fell down some stairs?" Damien dropped to a squat in front of me.

"I didn't fall, I was pushed, but yeah. I think it's sprained."

Damien unlaced my shoe, slid it off my foot and pulled off my sock. He sucked in a breath as he took in the swelling. "Oh yeah, pretty bad one by the looks of it. You need to get it wrapped and some ice on it. Then elevate it for a few hours. Ibuprofen for the pain."

"I figured." I nodded as he pressed gently on my ankle. I wanted to scream but I wouldn't.

"I'll take her home," Angel said.

"Wait, no, I don't want to go home. Anything more you can tell me about the body?"

"Not right now, Marcy. You need to go home. I'll have more for you soon." Damien stood up.

"Look, I swear I will do everything you asked, but I'm not going home. I'll go back to the station."

Damien shook his head. "You are so stubborn," he said as he moved from the car.

"What the hell did you think you were doing going after that woman?" Jordan was seething as he switched places with Damien.

I felt like I was at a disadvantage seated in the car seat while he stood blocking my only exit. "I am not in the mood, Jordan. I recognized that woman from the security footage from both bars. And she pretty much confirmed she's in on this when she held me at gunpoint after shoving me down the stairs, so get the hell out of the way and let me get my ankle taken care of." I turned to sit fully in my seat.

"This isn't over, Kendrick. You disobeyed orders," he said, backing up and slamming the car door.

Luckily, I had already moved my legs back into the car, because he'd have incapacitated me further if I hadn't. "Asshole," I muttered.

Angel got back in and turned the car on. "Let's get you fixed up, yeah?"

"Yeah." I sighed. "This is not how I thought my day would go."

Angel tossed me a wry look as he turned the car around. "What, didn't have near-death experience on your bingo card for today?"

I laughed. "Nope. Not today. I was saving that for Friday."

33

IT'S NICE TO HAVE PEOPLE WHO CARE

MARCY

I hobbled into the station with Angel's help. My sneaker wouldn't lace anymore, and my foot was about three times its normal size. I didn't even know how I'd gotten the shoe back on my foot. I was pretty sure I needed to remove it, but I was going to wait until I was inside where I could get it bandaged up.

I made it to my chair in time to see Jordan storm in and head to the captain's office. I figured he was going to give Robinson the rundown of George's death as well as tattle on me. Of course, I had been doing my job so there really wasn't anything he could do about it.

"I'll grab an Ace bandage and an ice pack for you," Angel said. "Stay off your foot."

"Yes, Doctor," I replied, rolling my eyes, but then added, "Could you grab me some Ibuprofen too?"

Angel laughed. "Yes."

While I waited, I sent Frank a text.

Hey, last night was great.

Enjoyed that, did you? :)

I laughed, even though my foot and ankle were throbbing. I took a deep breath and did my best to distract myself as I typed out another text.

I really did. Hoping it wasn't a one-off. Okay, two-off.

I hope not too. I was hoping for a repeat performance tonight.

That might be a problem. :(

Why? You working late or… wait, did you catch the killer?

No, and no. Unfortunately. Nearly caught part of the act, but she got away.

But you're close?

Not really. Had a close call though. Almost didn't live to tell about it.

I bit my lip as I waited for him to text back. Only he didn't. My phone rang in my hand. It was a generic ringtone because I'd yet to assign him one. I was waiting to see if we stuck.

"Hey," I answered.

"What the hell do you mean you almost didn't live to tell about it? What happened?"

I explained about recognizing the woman in the crowd of crime scene junkies and following her. "I chased her into a building, and she managed to get behind me, then pushed me down the stairs."

"Are you okay?" he asked, his voice strained.

"Yes. I wasn't worried until she pulled a gun on me, but apparently, I wasn't who she was after. Or so she said." I sighed.

"She talked to you?"

"Just for a second, and then she was gone, leaving me with a severely sprained ankle."

"My tiny tornado has a sprained ankle? How are you going to chase down the killer now?"

Was it wrong of me that I liked how he was feeling the same way I was? He already knew me well. I smiled, but winced as Angel returned and pulled my shoe off. "Ow!"

"What happened?" Frank asked, his voice full of concern.

"Doctor Angel just pulled my shoe off like he was yanking on a pull tab," I grunted, flashing Angel a disgruntled look.

"Reyes is taking care of you?" he asked, a twinge of something in his voice that I couldn't quite place.

"Yeah. He got me a bandage, an ice pack, and some painkillers. We're at the station."

"Why didn't he take you home? You should be off your foot," he started.

I smiled. "I told him no."

"Of course you did." He laughed. "You're a workaholic, you know that, right?"

"Well, if these killers would take a day off, maybe I'd get one too."

He chuckled. "Can I text you later?"

"You'd better."

"Stay off your foot, okay? You can't chase down the bad guys with a sprained ankle, at least not for long."

"I will. Bye." I hung up and glanced at Angel.

"That Frank?" He was nearly finished wrapping my foot.

"Yeah." I watched him, waiting for him to say something more, but he only nodded.

"Let me get you a chair to elevate it on." He went into the incident room, grabbed a chair, and brought it back over to me.

I put my foot on it, and he wrapped the ice pack around it. It was one of those large square ones, but it would do for now. "This might not be high enough. Isn't it supposed to be higher than my heart?"

Angel shrugged. "Probably, but unless you want to go home…" He let his words trail off.

"Point taken." I didn't have a choice, because I wasn't going home.

I motioned toward Robinson's office. I could hear the captain and Jordan shouting at each other, but I couldn't make out the words. They were still a bit muffled because the door was closed. "What's that about, do you think?"

Angel shook his head. "No idea. He's supposed to be briefing Robinson on Peck's death."

I was about to comment, but my phone rang. "Kendrick," I answered.

"Detective, this is Lieutenant Hartley."

"Good afternoon, Lieutenant. What can I do for you?"

"We've heard about Peck. This killer of yours is making a mess of our case."

"I'm sorry to hear that. I'm trying to catch him, but as you can imagine, he's a bit slippery," I said, a little bewildered that they were calling me to complain about my not catching the guy yet. "Things changed with this murder. It's possible he was injured this time and we'll be able to get a lead on him."

"That's good to hear, but it's not why I'm calling."

"So, what can I do for you?" I asked again.

"In your investigation, have you interviewed any of the men on the list that Selene Webb gave you?"

"Well, no, actually. George Peck was on our list to speak to, but then Nilsson was killed, and it got pushed to the side, then George was admitted to the hospital and my boss refused to allow us to speak to him while he was recovering. The plan was to see him today, but the killer got there first."

He sighed. "That's too bad. Would have been nice to have that interview on record. Have you dug into any of the other men on the list? Specifically, Daniel Maldon?"

I felt my heartbeat pick up at the name. "No, why? Do you think he should be moved higher up on my suspect list?"

"No, not that I'm aware of. I was hoping you'd spoken to him, or at least had an active number to reach him at. We've tried his number on file, and we are rerouted to a full voice-mail box. We've tried his home address, and it appears he's not been there for some time."

I swallowed hard. Had the killer gotten to Daniel? Frank would be devastated. "I don't have anything more for him than the cell number, but I do know Frank Maldon. I can see if Frank has heard from him, or if he has another number for his brother."

"That would be great. Actually, we'd like to speak to him again too. I may give him a call myself. Thanks for the idea, Kendrick. If I do track Daniel down, I'll give you a heads-up. I'm sure you may want to speak to him for your case as well."

"Thanks, yeah." I hung up and stared at my desk phone. Had I just thrown Frank under the bus? I shook my head. No. Frank wasn't involved. There was no reason he shouldn't talk to IA. Right?

"What's wrong?" Angel asked, probably because he noticed the expression on my face.

"That was Hartley, from IA. He was asking about Frank's brother."

"Oh?"

I nodded. "I guess they're wanting to speak to him, but can't reach him. Frank said something about not being able to reach Daniel the other day." I raised my gaze to Angel's. "What if the killer has already taken him out and we just haven't found the body yet?"

"That seems unlikely. He's been pretty meticulous about making sure those bodies are posed and found exactly as he wanted them to be found."

"True," I replied, taking comfort in that. So if Daniel wasn't dead, where the hell was he? I wondered. I picked up my phone and sent Frank another text.

> Hey, just had a call from IA.

> Just got off the phone with them, too. They want me to come in.

I hesitated, trying to figure out how to say what I knew I needed to say without pissing him off. We might know each other biblically, but I was still learning what triggered him and what didn't.

You haven't done anything wrong. There's no reason not to go talk to them. I've been called into IA so many times. It's really not that big of a deal.

I know. I'm just worried about Daniel. I haven't been able to get a hold of him and he's not been home. He's not showing up to work. I'm really afraid something's happened to him.

Angel and I were just talking about that possibility. I think he's okay, maybe hiding out to avoid the killer.

You think so?

This killer likes his kills found. If Daniel were a victim, we'd know about it by now. So that means he's probably in hiding, right?

I really hope you're right. I'm supposed to go talk to IA tomorrow.

Just tell them the truth. You've got nothing to hide.

I sent the text and then immediately felt nervous about it. I thought I knew Frank fairly well, but what if I didn't? What if he was snowing me along this whole time?

As I sat there waiting for him to reply, I noticed the icon saying I had mail was flashing at the top of my phone. I clicked on it to open it and realized it was a response from my therapist to the message I'd sent yesterday.

Marcy,

It's good to hear from you. I'm glad you're getting back into circulation, and it's natural to have those feelings. You need to remember that Nick is no longer able to get to you. He is locked up and will be for a very long time. He has no access to you or your life.

You are free to live it as you see fit. We should schedule a session soon.

Have a good rest of your day,

Dr. Fellows

I had forgotten about the message almost as soon as I'd sent it. Writing it had been almost as freeing as actually speaking to Dr. Fellows, but having an answer was nice too. I smiled as I clicked on his work calendar and scheduled a session for late next week. I really hoped we'd have this case wrapped up by then.

As I confirmed the appointment, my phone pinged with an incoming text from Frank.

> Sorry, didn't mean to take so long to answer. Working still. Was watching a drug house, and a dealer we've been after showed up.

> Then what are you doing texting with me?

> LOL We're watching, not busting. Not yet. That will happen later when the bigger fish shows his face.

> Okay, be careful.

> Always. Anyway, I wanted you to know, even though I'm nervous about IA, I will always speak the truth.

His words were a welcomed relief. I was about to text back when he added another.

> Always to you especially.

And wouldn't you know it. I caught feelings. Big, messy, undeniable feelings.

> I'm glad. Gotta get back to work. Text later?

> You got it, TT.

Definitely had caught feelings.

34

A CHANGE OF COMMAND
MARCY

"I'm gonna go out and get some coffee. You want one?" Angel asked, standing up from his desk.

I'd been sitting completely spaced out for the last ten minutes as I contemplated how I'd managed to fall ass over teakettle for Frank. I glanced over at Angel, who stood waiting for me to reply. "Oh, yeah, that would be great, thanks."

"Anything to go with it? We missed lunch."

I reached for my purse and pulled out my wallet, then handed him my card. "Sure, just get whatever. I'll buy."

"Then the sky's the limit, so I'll be back with lobster and steak," he replied gleefully.

"Funny man. Don't you dare." I laughed but choked to a stop as a twinge of pain raced up my leg. I'd accidentally rolled my foot on the chair, hitting the damaged part of it.

"You okay?" he asked, his face full of concern.

"Yeah, I'm good, just hit a tender spot. As long as I don't move, it's not too bad."

"Then don't move. You're not a cyborg; you feel pain." He winked. "I'll be back."

"Sure, Arnold." I grinned and rolled my eyes at his *Terminator* references.

He left and I continued to sit at my desk trying to be more like a cyborg and not feel pain. It wasn't working and my ass was getting numb. I shifted in my seat, trying to get more comfortable. It didn't really help. I pulled my desk phone closer to the edge so I could reach it better and dialed the office in the lab.

"Lindsey Stone's office," a voice answered.

"Is Lindsey available?" I asked.

"May I ask who's calling?"

"Detective Kendrick."

"Oh, right. One second." The line clicked and went silent as they put me on hold.

I sighed and drummed my fingers on the desk as I waited. I scanned the room as other detectives came and went, going out on calls that Jason was directing them to go on. He'd gotten pretty good at managing that particular area of the job lately, even though it was probably well above his paygrade. I knew he was only doing it to help the captain out. He was Robinson's right arm most days.

"Marcy?" Lindsey came on the line.

"Hey, I just wanted to see if you'd discovered anything yet."

"Unfortunately, yes. We got the results on all the blood spatter. It was all Peck's. Not one drop of the killer's."

"Well, damn." I sighed. "I'd hoped we would catch a break."

"We're still going over all the fingerprint analysis, but so far no hits."

"Probably wore gloves. He was in all the video footage, so it would stand to reason that he did at Peck's place too."

"Right. This killer doesn't leave much behind that doesn't belong to the victim."

"I really need to catch this guy, Linds." I was starting to feel the pressure.

"We'll get there. We always do. I don't have anything else for you right now, but I'll get my report to you asap, okay?"

"Sounds good."

"Oh, and Marce?"

"Yeah?" I frowned, putting the phone back to my ear.

"We should do lunch soon. A little birdie told me you've got tea to spill," she said with a laugh.

"Tea to sp—" I stopped, and my cheeks heated. "Okay, yeah, maybe I do." I laughed. "Tomorrow?"

"Sure. See you."

I hung up just as Jordan slammed open Robinson's office door. It was so hard it bounced off the inside wall and made a loud boom. He didn't even look back. Robinson appeared in the doorway looking almost defeated as he closed the door. I was suddenly very worried.

Jordan seemed irritated as he started toward the hallway, but then turned back around and marched back over to me. "Robinson's leaving."

I blinked. "What?"

"He's taking a leave of absence and he's going to call in Brass from Santa Monica to cover us," he seethed.

"Okay, that sounds reasonable. He's been through a lot with this divorce and—" I started.

"I'm the next highest ranking officer," Jordan interrupted. "He should trust me to cover the station in his absence!"

Everyone turned to watch us as Jordan lost his shit. I

couldn't believe what an ass he was being. There was no way on earth Robinson would leave Jordan in charge with the way he'd been acting lately. He was too volatile. He was all over the place emotionally, not to mention his anger issues, which he still hadn't gotten a handle on, despite having to go to anger management classes.

"I'm sure Robinson has his reasons," I murmured.

"And you!" His eyes blazed. "You disobeyed an order at the scene and Robinson couldn't give two hot damns about it."

"Because he's not an unreasonable asshat?" I suggested, keeping my voice soft so others couldn't overhear me.

"What did you just say to me?" He looked like a puss-filled pimple ready to pop.

I arched a brow at him. "I'm sure you heard me and I'm not going to repeat myself. Was there something else you needed to discuss with me? Because I have work to do."

He stood there glaring at me.

A thought occurred to me, and I decided to push him even further. "By the way, what was it that George dragged you into exactly? You were saying something about that the other day when I drove your drunk ass home."

His mouth opened and closed a few times as his eyes shot daggers at me. If we weren't in a police station, I might have feared for my safety because he looked about ready to kill me. "None of your fucking business," he finally said, and he spun on his heel and marched back toward his office.

I was still damn curious about what George had supposedly dragged him into, and I knew I would find out eventually. I had my gaze on Jordan's retreating back when a box was set in front of me, steam billowing from the slits in the sides. I drew in a breath and smiled. "You got tacos." I glanced up at Angel.

"And coffee." He set the cup down next to the box.

"You're a godsend." I grinned up at him.

"So what was that about?" he asked, his gaze traveling down the hall after Jordan.

"Jordan avoiding the painful truth, but I'm going to get it out of him, one way or another. You can count on it."

35

A DARING PROPOSAL

MARCY

I couldn't go down to the medical examiner's rooms when Damien called, so Angel went and FaceTimed me in. It wasn't the most ideal situation, but with my ankle swollen, I needed to stay off it.

"How's the ankle?" Damien asked as soon as the screen lit up.

"Still hurts some, but not as bad as when I fell. I've got it raised and an ice pack on it and Angel wrapped it for me."

"You might still visit Urgent Care after work. With it so swollen, I can't be sure you didn't tear something in there."

I sighed. "Yeah, okay. If Angel can drive me after this, I'll go. It's not like I can do much here. I'm still waiting on Lindsey's full report."

Damien nodded.

"I'll drive you," Angel replied. I couldn't see him on the screen, only hear him.

"So what can you tell us?" I asked.

"George was definitely shot prior to being stabbed and tased," Damien answered. "The wounds didn't bleed like they would if he'd been alive when he was stabbed. Also, as I mentioned, the wounds are deeper, angrier. There's more of a ripping motion, as though the killer was in a hurry as he pulled the knife out. And the wounds aren't strategically placed, as they were in the previous two kills. These are in clusters all over the body. Even the tasing was done in random spots, as though the killer had to do it but didn't care where the taser landed, which is different than the others." He pointed out various areas of the body and I noticed some deep bruising on the side.

"What is that bruising from?" I asked. "There on the side. It's pretty large."

"Ah, that would be from a couple of kicks to the body, probably right after he fell, when the body was still warm. My guess would be that shooting George had not been his plan and he got angry to have his plans thwarted."

I nodded. "That sounds about right. He didn't get the confession he was after. Since George had the door open, I bet he was going to escape, and our killer couldn't have that, so he shot him."

"That would be my take as well," Damien agreed.

"Anything else we need to know?" Angel asked. "Do we know the time of death?"

"I'd put it within an hour of his leaving the hospital, which was around six last night. It was dark out. Nobody noticed what was going on at George's house. The yards are a couple of acres wide, and the houses are even further apart, meaning that while they might have heard the gunfire, they probably didn't know where it came from, and with there being little light, they wouldn't have seen anything."

"That's a good point; someone might have called it in. I'll

check with dispatch. Maybe we can get an idea about the exact time," Angel replied.

"I can also tell you his last meal was a piece of chicken, small potatoes, and corn, probably from the hospital. There was no alcohol in his stomach, but he had severe liver disease from all of his drinking. If he hadn't died, I probably would have given him about six months to live anyway."

"He wouldn't have been able to reverse it?" I asked, curious.

Damien shook his head. "No. Even if he had lived and stopped drinking altogether, I doubt it. He maybe could have gotten on a transplant list, but given the deterioration of the liver, I don't think he'd have lasted long enough to find a donor match."

"Think he knew it?" I wondered.

"I spoke to his physician. Yes, he was aware, had been for a while," Damien answered.

"If he knew he was dying anyway, I wonder why he fought so hard to survive the killer's attack," I voiced my thoughts.

Angel answered, "Because at that point he was in fight or flight mode. The liver disease was a slow death; he couldn't physically fight it. The killer he could. It was instinct to fight back and then try to flee."

"Angel's right. Imminent danger will trigger those primal instincts to fight for survival. I see it all the time in those who've come across my table."

Since we didn't have anything else to discuss, Angel ended the call and we decided to call it a day so he could drive me to the after-hours clinic.

He even stayed with me while I waited to be seen, which didn't take too long, thankfully. And, luckily, I was right; it was just a really bad sprain. The doctor removed the bandage and put a splint around my ankle, then rewrapped it, giving me orders to stay off it for a few days, keep it elevated, and ice it every few hours. He also suggested crutches for me to get around and keep me off the foot. Angel offered me his from when he'd broken his leg several months ago.

"Thanks. That would help." I smiled as he helped me into his car.

"Sure. Let's swing by my place, then I'll take you home," he offered.

"Do you have plans tonight?" I asked as he drove to his place.

"No. You?"

"Not that I know of," I replied. I'd texted Frank, telling him what the doctor had said, but he hadn't replied yet.

"Wanna grab dinner?"

"Sure, sounds good. We could get it to go and eat at my place."

An hour later, we were seated on my sofa, my leg propped up on the coffee table on top of a stack of throw pillows, eating pizza. I turned on the TV and we watched the latest Marvel movie on Netflix.

Halfway in, my phone buzzed with a text from Frank.

> Wish I could see you tonight, TT. I'm sorry about your foot. Anything I can do?

> Me too, and not really. It's just got to rest and heal.

> You going to work tomorrow?

> Yup. Angel's lending me his crutches. Luckily, I won't have to chase anyone tomorrow. At least I hope not! :D

> Me too! You get some sleep and I'll text you tomorrow. :)

> You too and I'll look forward to it.

I put my phone away with a smile. I glanced over at Angel to see him watching me, an unreadable expression on his face. "What?"

His brow rose. "Frank?"

I nodded.

He stood. "I think I'm going to go. It's getting late and you should probably get some sleep."

"Okay. Thanks, Angel. I don't know what I'd do without you. You're seriously my best friend." I smiled up at him.

He leaned down and hugged me, then kissed my cheek. "I'll pick you up in the morning."

"See you," I whispered back. Moments like this had me almost regretting my resolve to not date my partner. I really liked Frank, but Angel and I had a connection that was really strong. I knew neither of us wanted to act on it though, so I shoved those feelings into a box in the back of my mind as I said, "Drive safe."

He winked. "Always."

A moment later, he was gone. I clicked off the TV, then used the crutches to stand and head to my room. It took longer than usual to get ready for bed. The crutches made it hard to change clothes, but I eventually got it. I set my alarm for an hour earlier than normal, so I'd have time to get ready for work before Angel picked me up. I slept with my foot propped up on a couple of pillows, but by the time I woke up, they were all over the bed and my foot was flat on the mattress.

Sitting up, I poked at it and realized it didn't hurt even half as bad as it had the day before. It was a little tender, but not nearly as swollen as it had been. I was relieved. I figured if I babied it for a day or two, I'd be as good as new.

I got dressed, wearing a skirt today, even though I hated to, but it was easier with the splint. Skirts weren't really conducive to chasing down suspects, but I wouldn't be chasing anyone today. I also chose a pair of flats... well, not a pair, since I didn't put a shoe on my injured foot, but wearing the flat shoe looked better with the skirt than my sneaker.

I was already downstairs, waiting outside on the curb when Angel arrived. He got out and helped me into the passenger seat. "Good morning," I said as he came around the car.

"Hey. You know I would have come in and helped you out of the building."

"I know, but I'm feeling pretty good. It doesn't hurt really."

"You heard the doctor, though. You need to stay off it for a few days."

"I know and I am. I'm just saying it feels better today and the swelling has gone down a lot."

"Good." He went around the car and got in on the driver's side. "Coffee?"

I nodded. As he drove, I said, "So, I've been thinking about the case."

"Okay?"

"From the list of names, only one of the major players is

left, Grant Weaver, and then there are the couple of mid-level members: Daniel Maldon, Glen Jefferies, and Byron Steiner. The others on the list partook in the use of the women, and took drugs with them, but Selene didn't list them as active in the functioning of the group. They didn't drive them from one location to another, or administer the drugs."

"So they're small fish. You don't think the killer is going to go after them?"

I shook my head. "If he does, it will be after he kills Weaver. That makes the most sense, right?"

"It does, but Grant's in jail. I'm not sure how he's going to get to him."

"True, so that leaves Glen, Byron, and Daniel—and he's missing. IA can't find him, and Frank said that he hasn't been able to reach him either. He's not shown up for work, and he's not been home."

"Okay. What about Glen and Byron? Should we go talk to them?" Angel asked.

I paused as I thought about what I wanted. An idea popped into my head, and I smiled at Angel.

He looked at me and arched a brow. "I know that grin. You've had an idea, so what do you want to do?"

Angel knew me so well. "I want to get permission for Grant to be released into our custody to attend George's funeral."

"What?" Angel sounded incredulous. "You want to use Grant as bait?"

"Yup."

"He's never going to agree."

"Probably not, at least not at first. Grant is a narcissist. He'll eventually agree because he'll think he can outsmart the killer, and maybe even use the opportunity to work a deal with IA."

Angel was quiet for a minute, but then nodded. "It could work. We'll have to run it by the captain."

"Robinson's taking a leave of absence. He's bringing in Brass from Santa Monica and Jordan is pissed off that he's not going to be in charge."

"Was that what had him all riled up yesterday?" he asked as he pulled into the coffee shop.

"Yup. That and I asked him about George and what secrets he was hiding about him. He wasn't pleased and got all pissy at me."

"I'll try and run interference between you two today. I wish he was the one taking a leave of absence."

"Me too. He needs to. I don't know why he's behaving so irrational these days. It has to be something to do with the case. I just don't know how he's involved."

"Secrets like that don't stay secret for long, so it'll eventually come out." Angel opened the car door. "I'll be right back with our coffees."

As I waited in the car, I felt my phone buzz in my pocket. Pulling it out, I saw Frank had texted and I couldn't help but smile.

> How's my little tiny tornado this morning?

>> Doing better. Swelling is down and it doesn't hurt as much. How are you?

> Would have been better to wake up with you in my arms, but I'm okay. We're busting that drug ring at some point today, so I may be incommunicado until tonight.

Okay, be safe.

I will. You too, TT.

I slid my phone back in my pocket as Angel left the café. He opened the driver's door and handed me both coffees. I put his in his cup holder and held onto mine, taking a sip. "So good," I murmured.

Angel dropped a bag in my lap as he got in. "Figured we could use a few donuts too." He turned the car on. "I got one for Robinson to butter him up."

I laughed. "Well, it couldn't hurt."

Angel had to carry my coffee into the precinct as we went in, since I was on crutches. We didn't get the chance to go to Robinson first, because Jordan was at our desks awaiting our arrival. I sighed, wishing I didn't have to deal with him first thing in the morning, but if wishes were horses, beggars would ride, as the saying went. Then my mind went off on a tangent wondering why beggars would wish for horses when they could just wish themselves money so they wouldn't have to beg anymore.

"Kendrick, I asked you what you're doing to find this killer. You've already gotten two good men killed because you haven't caught him," Jordan blustered.

"It's too early for this, Jordan, and your definition of 'good' must differ from mine." I glared at him. "Also, their deaths are no one's fault except the killer's and maybe their own. They did the actions that drew this vigilante's attention."

He glowered at me. "What are you doing about it?"

I glanced at Angel, and he nodded.

"Look, from what IA has told Marcy, there is one major

player that we know of from the Circle that is alive. Grant Weaver. There's a mid-level member, Daniel Maldon, who is currently in the wind—"

"What makes you think he's still alive? This killer of yours is taking them out like he's Rambo," Jordan seethed.

"Stop calling him my killer. He doesn't belong to me. And think about it, Jordan. If Daniel were dead, the killer would have left him on display like he's done with every other victim."

"Okay, you have a point," he said, seeming to calm down a little. "What about the others who were part of the Circle? Have you found them?" His voice had a nervous tick to it, and I had to wonder once again if he was involved somehow.

"No," I said, drawing the word out slowly as I noticed Lindsey's crime scene report on my desk, "not yet. There are two other mid-level members besides Daniel, and then several who are small players. My guess is that the killer is taking out as many of the top members as he can, so he'll go after these mid-level members if he can't get to Grant, but I'm guessing that Grant is top of his list. These deaths have all been pretty meticulously planned. Well, except George's didn't go as planned, but he still left us nothing to track him on."

"So what are you thinking?"

"I'm thinking that we're dealing with a cop. Someone who knows how we work."

Jordan sucked in a breath and had a sour look on his face, but he nodded. "Makes sense. The Circle was mostly cops." His eyes widened as though he'd just heard what he said, and he added, "From what I've heard."

"Right." I didn't want to antagonize him, so I tried to keep my suspicions from my voice. "Anyway, I think we need to try and get permission to use Grant as bait."

"How is that going to work?"

I explained my thoughts and then Angel said, "We need to take it to Robinson. He's the only one who can put in that kind of request."

"I could do it," Jordan suggested petulantly.

My lips tightened. "It might be better coming from the captain."

"Fine. Let's go talk to him."

I glanced at Angel, and we followed Jordan to the captain's office.

Twenty-five minutes later, we'd finally gotten Robinson on board with my idea. He looked weary and worn down when we came in, and now he just seemed defeated, but behind all of it was a determination to support us and make sure we had everything we needed. His office was even more in a disarray than it had been before with half his things boxed up, though it didn't look as though he'd been sleeping here anymore. I figured he must have found a place to stay.

"I want extra guards on Weaver," Robinson said. "Not just the two of you, especially you, Kendrick, with your foot out of commission."

"My foot should be fine by the time we get this all set up, sir. George's funeral hasn't even been announced yet, and Damien still has his body."

"I still want extra security. I know there will be a lot of cops around, but if as you suspect this perp is a cop too, and you have no suspects, I don't have a lot of confidence in keeping Weaver alive without the extra help and I'm not willing to put your lives on the line to protect his, do you understand?"

"Yes, sir."

"You've already had one close call with one of the suspects, which was too close for my liking, Kendrick. I don't want to lose you."

"I appreciate that, sir." I did. It was nice knowing he cared.

"I have calls to make to get things in motion. I'll let you know if he agrees. You can go." He nodded toward the door.

"Sir?" I said hesitantly as I waited for the others to leave.

"What is it, Kendrick?"

"I just wanted to say, I hope you'll be back. We're going to miss you."

He smiled and it even reached his eyes. "Thank you, and I think I will. I just need some time to figure some things out. And don't worry, I won't be leaving Brasswell in charge. I've got Captain Stanford coming up from Santa Monica. He's got a competent lieutenant to take over daily affairs there, and he'll be available for consultation with them if they need it. He's also aware of the issues between you and Brasswell. He'll keep an eye on him."

I was grateful that even when his life was a shambles, he was thinking of not only the department, but me as well. "Thank you, sir." I swung myself out of his office on my borrowed crutches.

"All good?" Angel asked when I reached my desk.

"Yeah, just letting Robinson know he'll be missed."

"Absolutely."

The day passed slowly since all I could really do was go over the reports and various paperwork from the case. I'd had a vague text from my brother telling me he had found Rick and would be out of town for a while, but he didn't say where. I wasn't too worried about him because I was so focused on the case. I still had no clue who this vigilante Broken Badge Killer could be. Lindsey had noted in the report that George's badge had been shattered as well, but was found under a throw pillow in the living room, so it hadn't been seen immediately.

I was ninety-nine percent sure we were dealing with a cop. The problem was I had no idea which cop had apparently had a mental break and decided the best way to deal with all of this was to become judge, jury, and executioner. And who was the woman helping him?

An idea struck me about that. Could it be possible that one of the women Selene had mentioned was helping this killer? I needed to find them, sooner rather than later.

36

THE PLAN COMES TOGETHER
MARCY

I spent the afternoon tracking down the three women. Holly, Pepper, and Taffy. It had taken some digging to find their surnames, but once I'd done that it had been fairly easy to find them.

Unfortunately, all three were accounted for. Two of them, Holly Springfield and Talia, aka Taffy, Mercer had been arrested for prostitution a couple of times over the past few years. I got their addresses from their arrest records and from there found they were both deceased from drug overdoses. The two were found with fentanyl and heroin in their systems about a year ago in their shared apartment.

Pepper Kline had returned to Iowa after being arrested for prostitution, but the charges against her were dismissed. Instead of sticking around LA, she'd moved to a small town in Iowa and was now a waitress at a diner. So that had been a dead end. It still left me wondering who this woman helping the killer was.

When I got home Tuesday night, I put my foot up and iced it. It wasn't feeling too bad, but I didn't want to chance it.

George's funeral was finally set for Friday, and the Police Commissioner had agreed to our plan to use Grant Weaver as bait. It had taken a little more convincing to get Grant to agree, but by the time our shift ended on Tuesday, we had all the key people in place for my plan.

Now we just had to wait.

That was the hard part.

My mind was racing, going over every scrap of evidence trying to figure out connections, but so far, I was coming up empty.

I was about to give up and go to bed when my phone buzzed with a text from Frank.

How's my tiny tornado?

I couldn't help the grin that spread across my face. This man made me almost giddy. It was getting dangerous. I was falling hard and fast for him, and I still didn't know if it was the smart thing to do. Both our jobs were dangerous and high adrenaline. Though I had to admit I did love the fact that he was actually supportive of me doing the job and never treated me like I couldn't do it.

Good but sleepy. Long boring day of planning.

A moment later my phone rang. It was Frank.

"You've got a plan to catch your killer?" were the first words out of his mouth. It made me smile that he sounded excited by that. It was like he got it, got me.

"Yup. We're going to use Weaver to draw the killer out at Peck's funeral."

He paused for a moment and then said, "That could

work, but might be dangerous. Especially since you're still recovering. Want me to help keep an eye?"

My chest filled with a warmth at his offer. "That would be great. It's on Friday. We've got a team set up, but extra eyes would be helpful. Heard from your brother yet?"

"No. I'm really worried about him. Mom and Dad are too. It's like he's dropped off the planet. I've even tried to trace his phone, found it at his place."

I could hear the anguish in his voice, and it hurt my heart. "I'm sorry. Maybe he's gone to ground trying to keep out of the killer's crosshairs."

"I hope that's the case. I just don't know what to think. I didn't tell you that I went in and talked to IA again. Told them everything I knew. They already knew all of it though, from what I could tell. Still, they assured me they rescued the other women. They have them in protective custody along with Steiner and Jefferies."

"You got more out of IA than I did. I'm glad you spoke to them. And I guess that rules out me questioning those two." I frowned. Still, it was probably better that IA had them and could charge them for what they did.

Frank chuckled. "I think they only told me because I was the one who brought it to them. They want Daniel in custody too. I'm afraid that's why he's hiding. Not from the killer, but from facing what he's done." He sighed.

"We'll find him," I assured him. "He can't hide forever."

"I know what he did was wrong. Hell, he knows what he did was wrong. He was really angry at himself for being caught up in everything that happened. My biggest fear is he's going to or already has offed himself." His voice was stressed, and I could hear the pain he was in over that thought.

"Do you think he'd do that?" I asked softly.

It took a moment for him to answer. "I wouldn't have thought so, but he was pretty messed up over everything and was drinking heavily. I just don't know."

"I can make it a priority to try to find him, if you want?"

"Thanks, TT. If anyone could find him, I know you would, but let's hold off. Maybe I'm worrying for nothing, and he'll show up."

"Of course. You want me to start looking, let me know." I yawned. "I should probably head to bed now. Can we talk more tomorrow?"

"Of course. Sweet dreams."

Over the next couple of days, my ankle fully healed, and I was able to lose the crutches and put weight on my foot. I felt good when I woke on Friday morning. Angel and I were going to the detention center before the funeral to meet with the team and Weaver, so I was up early and dressed in my blues. I'd had them dry cleaned since the last funeral, so they were a little stiff, but wrinkle-free.

Angel picked me up and we drove to the Metropolitan Detention Center where Weaver was being held. He had a six-guard detail, and though they'd allowed him to wear a suit, it wasn't his dress blues. He was much more subdued than he'd been the last time we spoke to him. I supposed knowing two more of his buddies had been murdered was weighing on him.

"You ready for this, Weaver?" Angel asked.

Grant nodded. His hands were handcuffed in front of him, but his feet were free. The guards led him out, keeping him in the center of them as they watched for snipers and any other incoming attacks. They managed to get him into a police van that I knew had bulletproof glass for windows.

Angel and I returned to his car and followed behind the van. "Frank's going to help keep an eye out too," I murmured. "He's already at the church." I'd gotten a text from him while the guards were loading Weaver into the van.

"You've been talking with him a lot lately." His expression was blank, so I couldn't decide what he meant by that.

"Yeah, I guess we're kind of dating? We haven't exactly defined anything, but I really like him. How are things with Callie?"

"Better. We've made plans to go to Lake Tahoe next weekend. I'm hoping this case will be wrapped by then."

I smiled. "We'll make that happen. Even if it's not, you should still go. You deserve a break after the last several months."

He chuckled. "You do too."

I shrugged. "Maybe."

At the church, we positioned ourselves close to Weaver and the team of guards, but not right on top of them. I scanned the mourners' faces to see if anyone was taking special notice of Weaver, but for the first hour, the only one I noticed paying any actual mind to him was Frank, and he'd caught my eye several times to let me know he was watching too.

It wasn't until almost the end of the service that I saw something unexpected.

Someone came in the door on the side of the church, and I could have sworn it was Daniel Maldon, but as I attempted to track him, he disappeared, and I couldn't be sure I'd actually seen him.

If he was supposed to be in hiding, why show up to Peck's funeral?

37

A HEART-WRENCHING EPIPHANY
MARCY

George's repast was being held at his brother Jeff's home. It was a bit of a security risk, as he'd arranged to have the gathering in the backyard with the caterers serving the food in a picnic-style atmosphere. Jeff had claimed that George always enjoyed a good backyard get-together, so it was a nice way to celebrate his life. I didn't know George well enough to know if that was true or not.

Angel and I had driven by yesterday to assess the area. Jeff lived in a small house in a rundown neighborhood. Several of the houses had been abandoned and were boarded up. Jeff's front yard was no more than a postage stamp in size. The backyard wasn't much bigger, and it was surrounded by a chain-link fence that had seen better days.

When we pulled up to the house after the funeral, Jordan was standing at the front door, and I got a really bad feeling. He looked like he'd had a few drinks already, and I didn't want to deal with him being belligerent at me. The van with Weaver and his six-man team of guards pulled up to the curb as we reached the step and Jordan.

Jordan glanced behind us as the team got Weaver out of the van. "I just spoke to Jeff. He'd rather only a couple of the team stick with Weaver, and the others stand guard out front."

I frowned. Since when did civilians get a say in police procedures? "Captain Robinson—"

"I've already cleared it with him," Jordan said, cutting me off. "It's not like Weaver's going to try and escape, and we're all cops; we'll stop anyone who tries to get to him. He'll be fine."

I narrowed my eyes at him. "You spoke to Robinson about this?" I asked as Weaver and his team joined us.

"Yes. Now do what I said," he demanded, but he looked off to me. Like he was stressed and anxious. "Two of the guards can go with Weaver, the other four can spread out and watch for anything suspicious. This whole plan is stupid anyway. Never should have listened to you." He spun on his heel and went inside.

"Ma'am?" Officer Carroll, who was the team leader, questioned. "I'm not sure this was what was agreed to. I'm going to need to call it in."

I nodded. I knew I'd be more comfortable if they had approval from their superiors. "Go ahead. We'll all wait right here."

"What is he thinking?" Angel muttered. "And for Robinson to approve it?"

"I know. I'm not feeling great about this," I replied as Frank's truck came down the street. My stomach did a little flip upon seeing it. "I guess if we have to do it this way, at least you, and me, and Frank will be on guard along with the two guards who will stay with Weaver, assuming Carroll's supervisor approves the modifications to the detail."

"I guess so," Angel said. "Did you see anyone suspicious?"

"I don't know if I would call it suspicious, but I thought I saw Frank's brother at the service."

"Maybe he felt he needed to pay his respects."

Officer Carroll turned to me. "Ma'am, we've got approval seeing as the property is not very big. We'll post someone here at the door, one inside, one on either side of the house, and then we'll have two guards stay with Weaver. I'll be one of them."

"Don't I get a say in this?" Weaver huffed. "You're making me a bigger target by taking out my guards."

"You'll still be surrounded by cops, Weaver."

"If I get killed, I'm going to come back and haunt you all," Weaver muttered.

I snorted. "Do you think the devil will let you come back?"

He glowered at me but didn't say anything.

"Let's go," Officer Carroll said, directing Weaver into the house.

While we'd been talking, he distributed his men where he wanted them, and Frank joined us. We walked through the house to the backyard. There were probably fifty people sitting at picnic tables and gathered in groups around the yard with drinks in their hands. Caterers manned a buffet-style table filled with all kinds of foods.

The three of us stood off to the side while Officer Carroll allowed Grant to pay his respects to Jeff and his family. Once they were done, they allowed Grant to decide where to go in the yard. Angel, Frank, and I gave Jeff our condolences and then moved to follow Carroll, Grant, and his other guard whose name I wasn't sure of.

Frank raised his right arm and waved to someone, and I noticed he was wearing a watch. Something about it triggered something in my mind. The killer had worn a watch too, but on their left wrist. It had been just a glimpse, but I knew the man in the video had dark hair. Not only did Frank have dark hair, but Daniel did too, and he had been part of the Circle of Justice. Frank had said Daniel was very angry and irrational. Was it possible that he wasn't hiding because he was afraid, but because he was the killer?

I was terribly afraid that might be the case, but I didn't want to voice my suspicion in front of Frank. What if I was wrong? I glanced at him and gave him a tight smile. There was no way I could crush him like that. He was going to be devastated as it was if it turned out to be true. I just decided I needed to be extra vigilant as I watched the people who came and went.

Thirty minutes later, my heart began to race when I thought I saw Daniel on the other side of the yard. I stiffened and moved, trying to catch a glimpse of the person, but they were gone. I looked over at Angel. "You know that bad feeling I was having?"

Angel's eyes widened. "It's back?"

"It's intensified."

Frank frowned. "What's up? You see something?"

"Not sure. Just keep your eyes open."

We were standing a few feet in front of Grant and his two guards, who were in a group near the fence line toward the back part of the property. I glanced at them, but didn't notice anything out of the ordinary. The problem was everything in me was screaming that something was about to go down. I rested my hand on my service weapon, ready to pull it the moment I saw something off.

It was then that I heard a yelp, and I spun around to see Carroll and Weaver's other guard go down. I screamed, "Down!" and ran toward them as I pulled my gun.

Angel and Frank turned but there were too many people around and all of them seemed to be in shock.

Daniel tossed a rope around Grant's neck as he yanked on him, attempting to drag him toward the gate of the chain-link fence. Carroll and the other guard were on the ground. I wasn't sure what had happened to them, but they were moving, so I didn't think they were down for good.

"Daniel Maldon, you are under arrest!" I called as I pointed my gun toward him.

"No! He has to pay! We both do!" Daniel was strong and he'd already gotten Weaver through the fence and out into the driveway before I could reach him.

There were mourners everywhere, many of them cops, but not all. Most hesitated, unsure of what to do.

"Get out of the way!" I called, trying to get them to act and get the civilians to move and find cover in case we ended up in a shooting situation.

By the time Angel and I got through the crowd, Daniel had dragged Weaver down the drive and across the street to one of the abandoned properties. I could see that Weaver was struggling, dragging his feet, and trying to make it difficult for him, but with his hands cuffed, he was at a bit of a disadvantage.

I wondered what happened to the other guards who were supposed to be surrounding the property, but then realized I couldn't worry about them at the moment. Hopefully, they were merely incapacitated and not killed.

"Daniel, stop!" I shouted as he entered the house on the other side of the street.

He continued into the building, dragging Weaver right along with him. I had no idea what he was planning. A public hanging maybe? He had the rope already around Weaver's neck.

"Angel, we need backup; can you radio it in? And Frank? Where's Frank?" I asked, not seeing him in my peripheral vision.

"I'm here," Frank answered, somewhat gruffly.

He still sounded shocked that his brother was behind it all, and I couldn't blame him. He was doing his job because that was what he was trained to do, and it was more automatic than conscious, I was sure.

"You need to try and talk him down," I said. "And get him to surrender. That's the best scenario."

"Right, I'll try," Frank said from behind me as we entered the property.

"Angel, where are we on backup?"

"On the way. There were a number of patrol at the house. They're coming, and I've got them spreading out and surrounding the property. He's not going anywhere."

"E-T-A?"

"Two minutes to have everyone in place," he said hesitantly.

"I'm going in."

"Marce, maybe we should wait?"

"Weaver could already be dead. We don't have eyes on him or Daniel."

"I've got your back," Frank said.

"She's my partner; I've got her back. You focus on talking

your psychotic brother down before he shoots us," Angel barked.

I cleared my throat, and growled, "Knock it off. We need to get in there."

"Go," Angel answered.

The three of us entered the house and cleared it. It was only four rooms, and when we reached the gutted kitchen, the back door was hanging open. I caught a glimpse of Daniel with Weaver in the back yard. He was penned in. The yard was surrounded by another chain-link fence, but on the other side of the fence to the back was a tall brick wall that went the length of the yard and extended past the two yards to either side of this property. The sides had the fence as well, but the yard to the left was full of debris and the yard to the right had a large Rottweiler mix, who was barking angrily at us.

"Frank, talk to him," I said, trying to keep my voice calm as we stepped through the back door to the flat cement patio.

"Daniel, you don't want to do this... Please," Frank attempted to reason with him. "You're better than this. Let Weaver go to prison. We'll get you help—"

"No! He'll only get a slap on the wrist. He'll twist things and make it so those girls disappear and there will be no one to testify against him! He needs to pay for what he's done. We both do." Daniel seemed completely panicked.

"Please, think of Mom and Dad. You're going to break their hearts," Frank tried again. "Brother, you can make this right. We'll get you help. Please don't do this."

"Stay back!" Daniel shouted, holding the rope tight with his left hand while he pulled his service weapon from his holster. "He's going to pay!" Daniel loosened his hold on Weaver and raised the gun, firing a shot at him.

Weaver screamed and fell to the ground.

Then chaos broke out as Daniel aimed the gun toward me, Frank, and Angel. I could see it all happening in slow motion. He wanted to die. I could see it in his eyes. I threw my arm out to try and stop what was happening. "No! Don't shoot!"

But suddenly there was shouting and a volley of shots.

Daniel collapsed under the barrage of gunfire. His last word was, "Sorry," gasped out as he fell to the ground.

"No!" Frank rushed toward his brother.

I was pissed. This wasn't how this was supposed to go down. Backup wasn't supposed to open fire on the suspect without a signal from the lead detective. I was livid. Who the hell gave the signal to fire, I wondered as I turned around to take in the scene behind me.

I narrowed my eyes as they landed on the last person that I expected to see standing in the doorway of the house. My ex-husband. Jordan Brasswell.

38

AFTERMATH

MARCY

For a few moments, the back yard of the abandoned property was complete chaos. There were minor arguments breaking out between several of the officers about whether they should have opened fire or not, but I heard several of them say they'd heard the lieutenant say it was the Broken Badge Killer and to fire, so they had.

I couldn't believe that Jordan had interfered. I was in charge of the scene, not him. He shouldn't have been anywhere near here. I marched up to him, my heart pounding with anger. "What did you think you were doing?" I demanded to know.

"What you wouldn't," Jordan said smugly. His eyes were bloodshot, and he smelled of too much whiskey and stale cigars.

"You're drunk?" I stared at him, incredulous. "You came to a scene, interfered in it, and you're drunk."

"I had a few drinks. It's not a big deal. We were at a repast, celebrating a friend's passing," he tried to defend himself.

I shut my mouth and looked over toward a couple of the officers standing near the fence. "Kim, Desmond? Got a sobriety kit on you?"

"What?" Jordan blustered. "I'm not taking a sobriety test!"

"You damn well will if you want to prove that you were sober enough to make the call to kill my suspect."

Jordan crossed his arms and looked mulish. "No."

"Your choice, but given the outcome of this," I waved my arm around the scene, "and how many witnesses there are, you might want to reconsider, because I will be taking this to IA." I glanced at Kim, who had returned with the breathalyzer. "What's it going to be?"

He huffed. "Fine. But it doesn't mean anything. I didn't shoot anyone."

"Right, you just gave a bunch of rookie patrol officers the order to."

It was as though it suddenly dawned on him exactly how much trouble he was going to be in.

I watched as Officer Kim administered the test. He read the test and his eyes widened. He looked over at me, then walked over and showed me the reading.

"Unbelievable. How much did you drink, Jordan?"

"I don't know. Why? What did it read at?" He looked petulant.

"It's .21 over the limit. That's the equivalent to nearly nine drinks for a man your size." I was trying to remain calm, but I wanted to slug him. I looked at Kim and said, "Put him in the back of your car and take him home. But get his statement before you leave and give it to Dr. Stone when she gets here."

"Yes, ma'am."

"Wait, you can't—" Jordan started.

"I just did." I turned and walked away as Kim and Desmond took care of Jordan.

Paramedics had arrived and were working on Weaver, whom I hadn't even bothered to check on in the chaos. I wasn't concerned if he lived or not, but I supposed I probably should be somewhat interested considering I was responsible for him. Well, I and the guards who had been taken out.

I joined Frank and Angel, who were sitting on the ground near Daniel's body. "Frank."

He turned his gaze to me, but he seemed shell-shocked. His eyes were watery, but I could tell he was trying not to cry. "I don't know how I didn't see it. How I didn't recognize how far out of his head he was. It's my fault. I should have been paying attention, but—"

"Nope. This isn't on you." I got on my knees in front of him and looked him full in the face. "Everything your brother did was on him. From getting involved in the Circle in the first place, to his decision to murder the other members of the group. Not one bit of this is your fault. You are not your brother's keeper. He was a grown man who made multiple bad decisions and when he thought you might figure it out, he went to ground and hid from you. You couldn't have stopped him, Frank. Not at that point. He'd already killed Sam and he wasn't in his right mind anymore."

Frank nodded. "I know you're right, but everything here," he patted his chest, "says I could have fixed him. I could have saved him."

I sighed. "I know that feeling. You need time to process

everything, and you'll see it wasn't your fault and you couldn't have saved him, but I get it. I've been there."

He leaned his forehead to mine. "I am going to need time, tiny. I need to get my head together before we can... before *I* can be what you need." His voice was barely a whisper. He gripped the back of my head and kissed me hard, then let me go. "I'll give Dr. Stone my statement, and then I'm going to go away for a while. Don't try to call me, okay?"

I sniffled. I understood he was saying goodbye. Maybe not forever, but for a while. "Yeah. Okay." I sank back on my heels, my chin resting on my chest as he got up and walked away from me.

A heartbeat later, Angel asked, "You gonna be okay?"

I looked up, took a deep breath, and nodded. "Yup. We've got a scene to process." I stood up and ran my hands over my hair, smoothing it, then marched over to Damien to find out what he could tell me.

I didn't think anyone except Angel noticed that my heart was shattered. At least I hoped not.

39

CONSEQUENCES
MARCY

Three months and five days had passed since that fateful day in the abandoned back yard where Daniel Maldon had attempted to murder Grant Weaver, but had succeeded in committing suicide by cop. By a group of them actually. I'd also had my heart broken when Frank walked away from me in the aftermath. He hadn't so much as breathed in my direction since leaving me on my knees in that yard with my lips swollen from his final kiss.

Angel had been a godsend, keeping me sane during the repercussions of everyone's actions on that day. I'd had to report Jordan to Captain Stanford, and he had immediately put Jordan on administrative leave until a full IA investigation could happen. It was currently still ongoing, and I'd had to give numerous statements to Lieutenant Hartley, not only about that day, but about everything else that had been going on. Every time they came across a report of Jordan's misconduct, I was the first one they called in to give a statement. I was pretty sure he wouldn't be coming back to work, but maybe that was just wishful thinking.

Speaking of wishes, I really wished Frank would message me. In the short time we'd gotten to know each other, I'd grown used to his texts wishing me a good day and calling me his tiny tornado. I missed it. I missed him.

I had picked up my therapy sessions again, going a little more often than I had been because of everything that happened. Dr. Fellows had assured me that giving Frank space while he sorted things out was the best thing I could do. It was hard though.

The only thing that continued to bother me about the Broken Badge Killer case was Daniel's missing helper. We hadn't been able to find her. She was on the loose somewhere, living it up with all that he'd paid her. From looking at his bank withdrawals, he'd given her sixty thousand dollars. She could be anywhere by now, but that didn't stop me from continuing to look for her. That part of the case was ongoing.

Today I was headed to court for the beginning of Grant Weaver's trial. The other two, Jefferies and Steiner, had cut a deal and would be turning state's evidence against Weaver in exchange for lighter sentences. The DA had said I might be called to testify, so I had to be there. I would have gone anyway. Not for Weaver, but for Frank. Even though he wouldn't let me comfort him or be there for him at all physically, I wanted him to know I was there to support him, even if only from a distance.

It was heartbreaking listening to Selene and the other women give testimony about what Grant and the others of the Circle had put them through. Frank was seated directly behind the DA, but he didn't turn around to look at me. He kept his gaze forward and occasionally on Weaver, who was now short one ear, it having been shot off by Daniel.

Weaver seemed to have a dead look on his face. Defiant almost, but definitely not remorseful. I really hoped he got the maximum penalty. He was a vile human being and he needed to be locked up for as many years as the law allowed.

Day two of the trial was even worse. That was when Frank was called to the stand. He spoke about Daniel. Explaining how he'd been pulled into the group by Peck, taken under Weaver's wing and given an important position in the group, or so he'd thought. I wondered how Frank knew all of this, and luckily, the DA asked.

"I found his journal when we were cleaning out his house. He went into detail about everything. Not just what he did, but what they all were doing," Frank answered, staring at Weaver. "In the journal Daniel said he'd been recruited by Peck to help maintain the women. To administer the drugs, provide them with apparel and food, and for that he could..." Frank's composure shattered, and he had to take a moment before he could continue. "He was given permission to be with the women whenever he wanted without paying the fee Weaver was charging others."

"Your honor, we'd like to enter this journal into evidence," the DA spoke, holding up a leatherbound book.

"Objection," Weaver's lawyer called out.

"Denied," the judge answered.

The trial went on with Frank giving lengthy testimony and then a few others took the stand in the state's case against Weaver. On the fourth day, Weaver took the stand and blamed everyone who was dead for all the things that happened.

On the sixth day, the state rested their case. The jury took a little more than twenty-four hours to deliberate. Weaver was found guilty on all charges and sentenced to a hundred and seventy-five years for human trafficking, with an additional twenty-seven years for drug running. All without the chance for parole. He would have to serve his time until he died.

I walked out of the courthouse feeling relieved. Frank had seemed better upon hearing the verdict and the sentencing, but he'd ducked out before I could speak to him. Not that I was going to approach him. He'd asked me to leave him alone and I'd honored that.

My phone buzzed as I walked down the stone steps, and I pulled it from my clutch purse.

It was a message from Stephen.

> Hey, court finished? Wanna grab lunch?

I looked up at the sky. It was a bright, clear day, the sun was shining, Grant Weaver was locked away and wouldn't be getting out at all, and I had nothing better to do.

> Sure. The usual place in thirty minutes?

> See you there.

I met him at our usual table at our favorite Mexican restaurant. He was doing so much better, and I was proud of him for getting his life back together. He was still in therapy and from what I could tell, it was going well. He seemed to be thriving.

"Hey, how's Yazmine?" I asked, knowing he'd been seeing the woman for about a month now.

"She's good." Stephen smiled as he bit into a chip. "I'm taking her to dinner tonight."

"Oh yeah? When am I going to get to meet her?"

"Uh... not yet. Maybe give it a little longer?" he asked, looking shy for the moment.

I could understand him wanting to keep her to himself for a bit. I hadn't exactly been forthcoming about Frank until he'd broken my heart by walking away.

We ordered our food and chatted for a bit about the trial and Weaver's sentence. Then I decided to change the subject. "So, you never said what happened with Rick."

His smile brightened. "That's right, with everything you had going on, we haven't gotten a chance to talk about it. After Mom made him leave, he was pretty broken. He decided to head up to Alaska and got hired on as a deckhand on one of the fishing boats up there."

"Wow, that's not an easy job. Is he still doing that?"

"No, he worked it for a few years, made enough to buy a semi, and he started an independent trucking company. He's living in Washington now and doing really well. He's got a wife and a couple of kids. Marcy, he named his daughter after you."

That took me by surprise. "Why?" I asked softly as the waitress brought our food.

Stephen waited until she was gone before saying, "He said you were the sweetest, kindest little girl he'd ever met, and he missed getting to watch you grow up. He's followed your career and is impressed by how you've turned out. He wants his daughter to have a role model to look up to."

"Wow, I'm flattered. I wish I could remember him more. I've recalled a few things since you started talking about him. He was a kind man, always bringing us food, and I think I remember him getting me a stuffed dog once."

"You called her Muffy," Stephen replied.

I giggled. "That's right. I wonder what happened to it."

"Probably got tossed after we moved from that apartment. Mom didn't let us take much."

I frowned. I was probably four when that happened, and my memories were pretty vague about that time in my life.

We ate in silence for a little bit, and then he asked, "So did you see Frank?"

"I saw him, but he didn't speak to me. I wish he would. Hell, I wish he'd let me comfort him. I know I can't exactly know how he's feeling with his brother turning into a cop-killing serial killer, but I can empathize with him. I can be there for him. I just don't understand why he's still avoiding me."

"Marce, you know that everyone heals in their own time, and he's got a lot of healing to do. You need to give him the space he's asked for. He may never be ready to connect with you again because he may associate you with what happened, and you'll have to find a way to be okay with that if that's the case."

I stopped eating, my fork midway to my mouth. "Did you suddenly get your therapist license without me hearing about it?"

He laughed. "I've been to so much therapy I think I could probably do it, but yeah, no thanks. I've got enough trauma of my own to deal with. I don't need anyone else's."

We finished eating, said our goodbyes, and I headed back to my place with his words ringing in my ears. Frank might never want to be with me, and if so, I'd have to move on.

I really didn't want to, but I knew if he didn't contact me soon, I'd have to believe that was the case.

Please contact me, Frank, I sent out into the universe, hoping he would hear me but knowing that wasn't the way the world worked.

40

LIFE GOES ON
MARCY

When Angel picked me up this morning, which happened to be a Friday, I was in a good mood. It had been a month since the trial and things were finally starting to calm down around the precinct and in the public. There had been a little bit of a kerfuffle when a civil suit was brought against Frank by the women who'd been held captive, but it was quickly dropped because he hadn't been involved and had gone straight to IA when he'd been told about those women. I had been glad to hear about it being dropped, but disappointed that he still hadn't contacted me.

Today was a really good day though because I had two things to celebrate. First, Captain Robinson was finally returning, and we were going to have a party to welcome him back. Second, IA's investigation into Jordan had concluded and after giving their report to the police commissioner and mayor, he had been fired.

They'd found him negligent in his duties, but the fact that he'd given the order to shoot while he was heavily intoxicated had been the final pin in the pin cushion of his career. Did I regret bringing that to IA's attention? Absolutely not. Jordan brought all of this on himself, not only in the way he'd treated me since getting his promotion, but also by sending us on a wild goose chase while he covered for his good buddy George, and I didn't have one ounce of regret about it.

Angel and I reached the station early to get ready for the party. We were having BBQ brought in and I'd ordered a cake to be delivered just before Robinson was due back. Captain Stanford was still here, and wouldn't leave until the commissioner arrived with Robinson.

"Everything looks good," I said once the food had been delivered and we'd gotten it all set up in the break room.

"Smells good too," Angel replied. "How long do we have?"

I glanced at the clock. "Should be here any moment."

"We should get out there."

We'd hung a large banner across the detective pool from the ceiling tiles that read, *Welcome back, Captain Robinson!*, and we'd tied balloons to all the desks. All in all it looked pretty festive.

Captain Stanford came out of the office and announced, "They just got on the elevator."

We all stood up in anticipation. As soon as Robinson and the commissioner appeared, we all called out, "Welcome back, sir!"

Robinson smiled and thanked us. He looked as though he'd lost about twenty pounds, and his hair had thinned more. He still looked tired, but he seemed happy. He chatted, and ate, and acted as though he was glad to be back.

I started over to talk to him, and caught the tail end of his conversation with Captain Stanford.

"... so you won't have to deal with that anymore. He's been let go. Lucky he's not facing any criminal charges. We could have pressed charges against him."

"I'm sorry you had to deal with that mess, Will. It was never my intention to leave it in your lap."

"I'm just glad you're doing better." Stanford clapped a hand on his shoulder. "You've got good people here. They've missed you."

Robinson smiled. "I do. I missed them too."

As their conversation came to a close, I moved forward. "Sir, welcome back."

"Thank you, Kendrick. I hear things have been relatively quiet for a bit?"

"Unusually so, sir. Just the everyday nonsense. Been pretty relaxing."

He chuckled. "Well, you know that never lasts, so enjoy it while you can."

"Yes, sir." I smiled.

After work, Angel drove me home, and I was looking forward to a nice relaxing weekend. "You got plans with Callie?" I asked.

Things between them had gotten better after they'd taken that trip to Lake Tahoe, and they'd been nearly insepa-rable most evenings and weekends. I'd even joined them for dinner twice. I liked her. She was really nice and, in my opin-ion, good for him.

"We're going to Venice Beach," he replied, smiling at me as he pulled into the parking lot of my apartment building. "Um, looks like you might have plans too." He nodded toward the entrance of my building.

I looked over and my heart began to beat wildly in my chest.

"Go on, go talk to him." He grinned.

"See you Monday," I murmured, getting out and closing the door. I stood on the sidewalk staring at Frank, hoping he wasn't an illusion. Of course, Angel had seen him, so he probably was really here, but I just couldn't believe it.

"You gonna say hello, tiny tornado? I don't think I've ever seen you so still." He grinned.

I slowly walked toward him as though I might spook him if I ran at him and jumped into his arms. "You're here."

"I'm here," he said, his face growing somber. "I'm sorry it took me so long to figure things out. Am I too late?"

"Nope. Just on time." I smiled. "Wanna come up?"

"I thought you'd never ask, but first..." He wrapped his large hands around my waist and pulled me toward him. "I missed you," he whispered.

"I missed you too," I murmured just as his lips descended to mine.

And just like that, my world felt perfect. Maybe it would last for a minute, or maybe it would last forever, but I was going to enjoy every single second of it.

THANK YOU FOR READING

Did you enjoy reading *Dark Duty*? Please consider leaving a review on Amazon. Your review will help other readers to discover the novel.

ABOUT THE AUTHOR

Theo Baxter has followed in the footsteps of his brother, best-selling suspense author Cole Baxter. He enjoys the twists and turns that readers encounter in his stories.

ALSO BY THEO BAXTER

Psychological Thrillers

The Widow's Secret

The Stepfather

Vanished

It's Your Turn Now

The Scorned Wife

Not My Mother

The Lake House

The Honey Trap

If Only You Knew

The Dream Home

Lie to Me

Theo Baxter Psychological Thriller Box Set

The Detective Marcy Kendrick Thriller Series

Skin Deep - Book #1

Blood Line - Book #2

Dark Duty - Book #3

Kill Count - Book #4

Pay Back - Book #5

Lost Souls - Book #6

Made in United States
North Haven, CT
22 April 2025